THE TARGET

NOLON KING
JOHNNY B. TRUANT

STERLING & STONE

THE TARGET

ONE

Fucked From The Start

YOU KNOW your life is over when the Venn diagrams for drugs and weapons start to overlap.

I'm thinking this as the bestubbled man wearing the Bachman-Turner Overdrive shirt picks up a knife without dropping his jug of shake-and-bake. He's probably forgotten he has it. Probably too far gone. Now he's double-fisted, unaware that he might be this scene's reluctant hero.

The thing in his right hand is a bona fide moonshine jug, brown glass with a handle and all but a series of X's on the side. He might be using it for a quickie infusion because he thought it'd be sturdy or because someone told him the acetone inside might leach polymers from a plastic bottle, whereas glass would be safe. You know: *Safe*. But as far as I'm concerned, that brown jug is just shrapnel that doesn't know it yet. An army of silicate soldiers who don't realize they've enlisted but could be deployed in a blitzkrieg of shards at any moment.

You can't snort a silenced Colt, but the low-brow hobby of everyone in this room could literally blow the skin off all our bones. They'd find us in a ring, blown out from the central cistern like the laziest game of Ring Around the Rosie. I have no idea what's in the cistern. To the Crewtown Posse, it's already meth. I know better. You have to extract the pseudoephedrine using a hydrocarbon solvent. Other items in the methamphetamine cookbook include anhydrous ammonia, which helped bring down a sizable building in Oklahoma City, acetone strong enough to strip paint, hydrochloric acid, and lye, all of which will eat off your hands and only one of which will trigger pain to let you know, phosphorous with its white-hot flashpoint, and toluene, which you might know as the final "T" in "TNT."

A lot of people want to stop the spread of meth, but in my opinion, we should let them go. If you manage to make the stuff without blowing your face off, my philosophy is you earned it.

"Let's all just ..." I don't think Emil thought he'd get too far into his sentence. If he has something in mind for everyone to *just*, we'll all be waiting to see what it is. Stymied, he tries again the way you'd kick a truck from the mud with a running heave: "Let's all just be cool."

The guy with the BTO shirt is either excited, agitated or has some sort of a seizure disorder. Everyone's attention is on Emil, thanks to all those guns. Everyone but Mr. BTO has at least one weapon, and more than half are aimed at Emil. A few are pointed peer-to-peer. Several of the rednecks are targeting their fellows rather than us, either because what's happened here is a combining of two Florida factions that don't know each other or because these people have so many cousins, they forget who's who until the time comes to cornhole each other. Only three of the guns in the room are aimed at me — and if we're being technical, it's possible those three are covering the door behind me. I'm not too insulted.

"Robert," Emil tells me without lowering either of his weapons. His pistols are pointed full-arm out to opposite sides like he's trying to impress John Woo. "Get the car."

"The fuck you say?" The guy with the snubnose .38 is about four hundred pounds with a good complexion and perfect teeth. It's like nobody told him this meth job had a dress code. The others in the tarpaper shack got the memo: add the molars, incisors, and bicuspids of the other six men in the room together, and maybe you'd get a full set of choppers. Maybe if you put those six guys back-to-back and bundled them with rope, they'd be as big around as one normal person. They've all got sores on their skin. Sunken, red-lined eyes. I'll bet I could pretend to throw a tennis ball right now, and half of them would be confused enough to go for it. *That's* what meth heads are supposed to be, and Fats here is way out of line with all his coherence and composure.

"Robert," Emil repeats evenly. "The car."

The fat man laughs. The guy with the jug, Mr. BTO, manages a little chuckle that spends half its time in my general direction. It's like he's following his boss's lead, unsure of his own laughter. The knife shakes in his hand. The jug sloshes. I want to ask why he couldn't wait. Shake-and-bake meth is fast and easy but not exactly pure. Or clean. I guess he couldn't wait for the big batch. Had a jonesing he needed to handle. When nature calls, the tweaked must answer.

I'm sure the seven armed meth heads will stop me, but not a single gun twitches as I move toward the door. I look at Emil once there.

He nods encouragement. "Go on."

"And where exactly are you going?" Fat Man's eyes tick to the two dead men on the floor.

Anyone who showed up now would think we're doing okay; we got two of nine and don't have a scratch on us. In truth, Emil killed them before the others arrived. There'd been four; Fat Man had been checking the cistern when I broke the window, and BTO had been shaking his bottle. Even the two by the door — now face-down in their own blood and bile — were surprised. We'd have been in and out if they'd stayed that way. We couldn't have cared less about their little cook lab.

But then the taller of the two had gone for a pistol tucked into the back of his belt, and worse, once it was out, its muzzle had strayed in my direction. That had been the beginning of a three-second end. I keep telling Emil I can handle myself, but he's never listened. I guess I'll have a protector forever, no matter where I go.

Now, I think the meth heads actually care whether we leave peacefully. They keep looking at the dead men, unconvinced it's water under the bridge.

"We got no quarrel with you," Emil tells them.

"Oh. *You* don't, do you?"

"Lower your weapons. My brother is already out the door."

Fat Man laughs, so Emil continues.

"He can go for the cops, or he can ride off with me. Maybe we say nothing about what we found here. We can end this right now — no harm, no foul."

Fat Man looks down. "What about Jimmy and Ron?"

Emil looks down too, but he manages not to laugh as I see him wanting to. Death is nothing new to us, and the fallen rednecks landed in some hilarious poses. The tallest one looks like he might be doing his impression of a little teapot. "Well. No *more* harm or foul, anyway."

I'm halfway out the door now, surer than ever that the shooting's about to resume. After Jimmy and Ron, the only ones left with guns high were me and Emil. That's when the pickup truck showed, bearing five men with shotguns. I still don't know where they came from, what tipped them off, or if their arrival right after our little skirmish was a coincidence.

It doesn't matter. We have to be crack shots to do what we do, but with two already dead, something tells me these raccoon-fuckers won't be caught off guard. Emil can clip one, maybe two. If I'm fast, I can plug a third. But by my math, that's still not enough. Four swamp degenerates minus two plus five reinforcements still equals seven men standing. The fat man grabbed a pistol, and Mr. BTO only has a knife, but to get out of this by brute force alone, we'd still have to dodge some point-blank buckshot no matter how you slice it.

"You're in a dangerous line of work," Emil answers. "Shit happens, even to Jimmy and Ron."

"Jimmy was my cousin," says a kid of about nineteen. No teeth on this one, either.

"He must be so proud."

The kid racks his shotgun, but it's only for show. There's a shell in the chamber already. Dumbshit. He's made his point, though, and makes it finer by raising the barrel to center on Emil's chin. "You wouldn't be so funny without a goddamn mouth."

It's a terrible comeback. No wonder these guys have to cook meth this far off-grid. No respectable criminals would have them.

"Robert," Emil says, looking right at me.

Other heads turn, but I don't give them time to center those guns in my orbit or fire. Instead, I'm out and running into Emil's car, pulling the keys from atop the center console and shoving them into the ignition.

I turn, but nothing happens. The car is dead. It doesn't so much as crank. Like I'm a goddamn ghost. Like the engine doesn't have enough respect to even try or acknowledge my presence.

I shake my head. I bang my fist on the wheel after a few more attempts. I don't really care about dying. Emil and I ride every day with death riding shotgun; that's part of the job. I care about what's coming my way from Emil once he finds out.

Can't even start the car? You're worthless, little brother.

I'll show him who's worthless.

Emil carries guns like most people carry a spare tire. Literally. In the trunk, under the deck, beside a tire iron with blood and hair clotted on the end, plus a jack that's never been used in the conventional way. The spare well is full of firearms like a party grab bag, all of them loaded. I keep waiting for one to go off and shoot us through all that thin aluminum and plastic whenever we hit a bump. Emil says I'm being paranoid. Tells me I'm being a pussy.

I select a nice little MAC-10. I've used it before at the range, which is what Emil calls the rising slope behind the log cabin he found six years ago before turning it into his most rustic squat. Hold the MAC's trigger too long, and you're suddenly out of bullets.

I'm at the window ten seconds later. It's the one Emil kicked in, but nobody sees me. They're all focused on my brother, with his double guns. Scenes like this, they're not actually about might or firepower. They're about balls. The two of us have walked into situations more unexpected and hairier than this one holding only our nuts and somehow walked out tall with all the marbles and our enemies pissing their pants.

You can get away with just about anything if you do it with confidence. Walk into a sporting goods store and walk out with a canoe. Walk right into a mall Santa display and pull all the plugs, turning Winter Wonderland into something dark and soulless. That's the secret right there, Emil says: *Never ask permission. Just do, and see if anyone stops you. They won't,* he says. *Because people obey. When it comes right down to it, people are sheep.*

"Tell you what I'm going to do," Emil says, and here I see him look toward the window, at me and through me and past me, the only one now who's still curious as to my whereabouts. "I'm going to walk out that door and leave you alone. You're going to let me go because none of us want trouble."

"You already made trouble, friend," says a voice I recognize as the fat man.

"*More* trouble," Emil clarifies.

With that, his brow creases just a little, and he manages to shoot me a covert glance, and I know Emil's wondering why I haven't yet gunned the engine. But really, that's not the biggest of my concerns. If he doesn't know the engine died (cables cut by the newly arrived rednecks, perhaps; they're good with greasy things), anything short of clearing the board inside will leave us with problems. There are two other vehicles out there, but I've already peeked inside, and neither left their keys on the dash or seats. Chances are, those keys are in the pockets of people who are still armed and very much alive.

I'm supposed to be our strategist. The brains behind the brawn. With all our data, I calculate our probability of getting out of here intact at fifty percent. I give our chances of getting away clean, without cops on our tail, at twenty right now — and easily below ten if we kill more than the two who are already napping. Ironically, leaving a few of them alive helps us. If they're all dead, neighbors will find the scene and fink on us. If some live, at least they'll try to cover the crime.

But I've been at this for our entire adult lives, and as much as I'd like to believe in happy endings, I know this scene won't have one. I see the slight twitching of muscles in Emil's forearms. I see a prominent vein on his forehead. I can smell adrenaline and sweat even from the window, knowing that these hicks aren't as cool, calm, and collected as my brother and me. One feathered gunshot, and we'll be up shit creek. If not dead, unemployed. We'll miss our window and the senator. Nothing will change. Not for the world or for us.

I've almost got Emil convinced: We make our one big dent, then walk away. I've even found an island where we can hide. We can drink mai tais all day. Little umbrellas in every one.

Emil moves for the door. I raise my MAC-10 when everyone flexes to stop him, but nobody loses their cool. I could take a few of them out ahead of time (so nobody *ever* loses their cool), but something tells me to keep waiting. It seems like Emil always gets the kills, ends our targets every time. Something tells me he'd be pissed if I sniped them now, and he's already going to kick my ass thanks to our truck not starting. If he opens fire and runs out to find we have no way to escape? I'll never hear the end of it.

So I stay low, hating my obedience. I've always nodded along with Emil's bit about being like sheep, knowing he meant everyone but us. Yet here I am, with three or four perfect shots, and nobody's even looking my way except for Emil. It would be easy, and yet I hold my peace. Wait until he needs me. Emil always has something up his sleeve.

He's still moving. Now around them, guns out, delicately holstering one so he can use the freed hand to take the knob.

"I'm going to go," Emil tells them as I look over my shoulder, as I think of that car with its dead battery. "I'm going to go now, and you're going to *let* me."

"Stop," says the kid whose cousin was killed by Emil. "Stop, or I'll blow your fuckin' head off."

I peek back in. I figure he's just being another dumb kid with more dick than brains, but a glimpse at the scene by the door convinces me otherwise. Now the kid has the shotgun six inches from Emil's face, and Emil's gun hand is trained on one of the many other gunmen. His second weapon is in his belt, and his hand is stretched back to take the knob. The kid won't back down, and Emil is in exactly the wrong position to try and stop him.

My pattern recognition recognizes a new one. My algorithm discards all I was sure five minutes ago would happen and computes a brand new outcome.

Emil dead.

Me stranded, soon to be just as dead.

And Senator Bisset? Well, he'll be just fine.

Indecision frustrates me. My finger applies increasing pressure to the sensitive trigger. When I look down at that traitorous digit, I don't understand why it hasn't yet fired. I squeeze more, and more, and more, still pulling all my punches and hoping what needs to happen will happen by accident.

What's the poundage on this trigger, anyway? A million?

I sight on the kid with the shotgun. He's sidelong to Emil, and Emil is sidelong to me. If the kid would only refocus his eyes a quarter-inch downward, he'd see me in the window's corner, waiting to turn him to confetti.

I calculate, knowing how my brother will respond. He's

seen me; he's seen the gun. If I shoot, he has his next six moves planned already. Maybe we can get out of here. *Maybe*.

I give us fifty percent.

"Tell you what," says Emil.

But I don't get to hear what. The jug of shake-and-bake meth, agitated by the shaking BTO had been giving it before our arrival, suddenly blows like a bomb. It takes half of his face with it, pushing BTO's skin from his skull like a winter tarp from a boat at the beginning of summer. I see a brilliant flash, big like a movie explosion rather than the inelegant sledgehammer of a real-life detonation.

It's the acetone, I think. *Acetone, maybe butane, maybe hexane, maybe even gas.* Stupid hicks; I wouldn't put it past them to extract with gas.

A fireball fills the room, and it's lit for a full second. It jolts Emil, but not as much as the others. He's been watching me, knowing I might fire at any moment. This is different — a new strain of unexpected. But he keeps his cool enough to turn and fire: first at the kid with the shotgun, then back at his original target.

I've got my MAC up now, ready for real, but the fireball knocked them all to the deck. I stand fully, arms out and waiting, but seconds later, Emil sprints at my window and yells for me to duck, to get the fuck out of the way because I'm always right in the goddamned way, and I do as I'm told because despite my being the brains here, let's face it: Emil has always been the brains.

He thinks, I do. He says, I comply. It's like I'm nothing but a goddamn puppet.

Through the window, bullets flying behind. Emil hits the grass, and I reach to help him up, but he bats me away as if I'm responsible for all of this. He's up before I am, sprinting for the woods. It's swampy out there, and I keep thinking alligators.

Emil's arm is covered in blood. Same for his neck.

"You're hit."

He barely looks over. "I only told you to get the car."

"It won't start."

"Jesus fucking Christ, Robert. You can't start a car?"

"I can," I say with gritted teeth. "But it won't."

Shouts from inside the shack, which is now burning. I saw Emil plug two people before running out, and the blast took care of BTO for us. But there should still be two men left. Three, if any of Emil's shots weren't fatal.

"Goddammit, Robert."

"I can't start a car that won't start, Emil!"

"How exactly do you expect us to get out of here now? I told you before: *Just do as I say.* That means *no shooting.*"

"I didn't shoot, Emil."

"That fucking jug about blew my dick off. You think of that?"

"I … You think *I* made that thing blow up?"

Emil falls silent, watching two men emerge with their weapons.

"God *dammit*, Robert."

"This isn't my fault!"

"One thing I asked you to do. *One thing.*"

"Hey, fuck you!"

But now, there's a splash from behind us. From this ass basket backwater shitburg motherfucking swamp we wandered into, and goddammit if we're not even supposed to be here.

How far is Bisset from here? A state? A country? A planet?

I stop in the middle of being offended and look back to

see two enormous dark shapes in the shallow water behind us.

"Fuck," says Emil.

I aim my MAC-10 hand at the alligators but seem to have dropped the MAC-10 itself. I try to hide the motion once I realize I'm empty, but of course, Emil sees it and knows the contents of my head.

"Oh, fucking brilliant," he says.

"You've got a gun!"

Emil puts it to my head and pulls the trigger. His face is angry and frustrated — the way he used to look when I borrowed his Big Wheel. When I ran it into the mud, he forced me to clean it off. "Seven rounds. I told you I'd need more than seven rounds."

The slide locked open. As if this is my fault. As if I chose Emil's weapon, then forced him to use it and refused to let him take an extra magazine. He's the one who wanted big caliber. That tends to accompany small capacity. He could have gotten a nice little 9mm, but *no*, he wanted the .45. I don't even know how he managed to fire seven times. I wouldn't have been as sure as him. In Emil's shoes, I would have put a gun to my head and pulled the trigger only to learn I'd miscounted, and Little Brother is dead.

"How is that my fault?"

"You planned this trip."

"What, you can't take care of your own ammo? Do you want me to wipe your ass for you, too?"

The alligators move closer. Their mouths open slightly.

"I think you have to run in a zigzag," I tell him, but Emil only scowls.

"Two guys left. The building is on fire, and we've got two fucking lizards behind us. We can't drive off and don't have any ammo. How is this any closer to where we want to be, Robert?"

"Oh, and it's all on me?"

"Of course, it's all on you!"

There's a new sound, and all four heads turn as a new truck roars from a distance with its brights at full bore. We're about to be even more outgunned than we already are, and the best we can hope for is that the newcomers will shoot us outright instead of feeding us to the animals.

But then the truck swerves, and I see that it's puke green, and there's only one person in the world who'd own a piece of shit like that.

The truck barrels into the two remaining rednecks one at a time, starring the windshield with one and making mud pies of the other.

With the headlights back on us, a silhouette emerges.

"Get in," it says. And just in time, because now in the distance, here come even more redneck engines.

"Is that …?" Emil squints into the light at the truck and the driver's backlit silhouette.

Of course, it is.

I should have known.

This job? It was fucked from the start.

TWO

A Million Plus

WITH NOTHING TO FOCUS ON, your mind goes just about anywhere.

You're playing with coins on the table — a cash tip from the last diner the server never cleared, say — and suddenly you're thinking about that shirt you never returned even though it was two sizes too small, six months old and therefore forever one of the deep tracks in your wardrobe's extensive discography.

You think about the thyroid pill you took this morning, suddenly sure it was the wrong color and hence the wrong dosage, or possibly another medication entirely, even though there are no other meds (or other dosages) in the usual drawer.

You wonder if anyone ever inspects the underside of tables in restaurants or if the *Air Bud* movie franchise is done forever.

You start to think about high school chemistry, about that time Maddie Vickers set her hair on fire. Maddie was hot before that, then hot even after, when she returned with a shortened bob that was somehow even cuter than her long hair. You wonder what Maddie's doing now.

You wonder if the wrong pill you took this morning will have any adverse side effects. Like: Maybe you'll flip your thyroid from hyp*o* to hyp*er,* and suddenly it'll be too active. Maybe it'll swell, like a goiter. Good luck flying under the radar when everyone knows you as the team with great aim and a giant neck.

It's like someone else is in control of my brain, digging through a grab-bag of thoughts.

I wonder what the bathroom of this place is like.

I wonder if I should switch from canola to olive oil.

I remember this kid, in second grade, who a bunch of us convinced was living a dream. He bought it for about a half-hour, then told the after-school counselors we were messing with him.

I remember the shape of our father's hand.

I know that blood cells have to go through our smallest capillaries one at a time, so I picture a queue of big red donuts made of hemoglobin waiting patiently inside my ring finger, except that one of them is an asshole with a hipster fedora and a cigar, and *that* blood cell just takes his sweet time while the others wait, with an attitude like, *Oh, yeah? Well, what the fuck are you going to do about it, smart guy?*

Nobody would ever like that red blood cell. They'd probably all gang up on him in the spleen, forcing him to jump ship into pus or offal. Or they'd hold a molecular knife to his round red lack-of-a-neck and bully him into apoptosis — that programmed cell-death thing. My mind always imagines it as happening like hari-kari: cellular samurai falling onto microscopic swords in a ritual act of self-immolation.

Emil slides into the booth across from me. His food arrives at exactly the same time, with mine ten seconds later. He looks at my plate with disgust before noticing his own.

"It's like someone took a shit, then baked it."

I look up.

He adds, "You heard me."

I glance back down at my meatloaf. Ordering meatloaf in a restaurant is like playing slots. Every once in a while, you get lucky with all of those cherries lined in a row. More often, you pull nothing and end up with something that looks like it's been digested a few times already.

"We've been on the road too long," I tell my brother. "I need some decent food to counteract all the garbage."

Emil looks at the meatloaf.

"I had to try. It was this or the fifteen-dollar salad."

He rolls his eyes. He's got an enormous plate of beer-battered fish. The menu said the fish came with a side of fries, but in reality, the fish is served *entangled* with fries. There's no order on Emil's plate. There's fish; there's fries; there's even a small side of fruit that was probably some manager's idea of raising the bar. But it's all in a pile, like dry jambalaya. Like the waiter tripped on her way to our table and tossed it all in the air but managed to catch the plate before it hit the floor.

"You're going to Hell anyway," Emil says.

I fork off a piece of my gray-looking meatloaf. It tastes better than it looks, but that's barely saying anything.

"Uh-huh."

"You can *uh-huh* me all day. But it isn't me you need to convince."

I don't look over. Even if I couldn't see him in my peripheral vision, I know this routine by heart. He's pointing upward at the yellowed drop ceiling stained by asbestos-filtered water. I'm supposed to know he's pointing at God, but even if I was a believer, *up* wouldn't make sense. Earth rotates. So is God's home planet "up" at noon or midnight? It can't be both unless God orbits us in geosynchronous orbit, which definitely isn't what I'd do if I was all-powerful and could watch celebrities in the shower. And what about the Chinese? Whenever we're "below" God's 10-20, all those Asians on the other side of Earth had better know to point at the ground when getting pious.

I wonder what Mel Tormé would be doing right now if he was still alive.

I wonder if I actually lost one of my forks — or if it's in the disposal, waiting until I flip the switch for a deafening discovery.

"God doesn't care if I eat meatloaf."

"God cares *all day long* about your meatloaf. That's the problem with you, Robert. You don't believe what you read."

"Today? Yeah. I *don't* believe what I read. Kind of hard to believe *anything* you read in this day and age."

"Except that the Bible is God's diary, straight from His lips, and nothing to do with our day or age."

"I don't think God has lips."

"Of course he has lips! You ever seen a fresco?"

"You're thinking of Jesus."

"Fuck you, *I'm thinking of Jesus.* I know the difference between God and Jesus. There's that mural where he's like this." Emil points at me, but his arm is soft and flamboyant. "And he's like, '*YOU*, Adam. You da man.'"

"Are you talking about the ceiling of the Sistine Chapel?"

"Fuck you, *Sistine Chapel.* I'm talking about the mural where God and Adam are like, *All riiight.*'"

I think of the blender Emil wants to buy.

I wonder what happens if you die on a plane. Do they

keep you buckled in, and your seatmates simply have to deal? It's probably that or the bathroom, and bathrooms reek enough as it is.

I picture God and Adam starring in *Dazed and Confused*. He's Matthew McConaughey, saying to Adam, *Alright, alright, alright!*

"That mural is *not* God and Adam saying, *'All riiight.'*"

"It's—"

"And the Bible is not God's diary."

"You know what I'm talking about."

"Do *you?*"

"I think we were talking about how you're going to Hell."

"For eating meatloaf?"

"What day is it, Robert?"

"Friday."

"But not just any Friday."

We go through this every year. I always forget Lent. I only learn about it in retrospect, after Easter hits. Emil goes to St. Anthony's and gets ashes on his forehead every year, and I always point it out, thinking he accidentally got a smudge on himself somewhere.

I pluck a fry from Emil's plate, then dip it in some of the ketchup on mine. I hold it up like a freshly severed spine, still dripping on one end. "So what you're telling me is that Heaven has a really big problem with my eating meat on Fridays during Lent."

"You bet your ass."

"But not with us killing people."

"That's work."

"It's okay to kill people if it's for work," I say.

"Sure."

"Like how Amish people can use power tools so long as it's for work."

19

"Exactly."

"And drive to job sites."

"Gotta get to work somehow."

"So faith matters," I say, wanting to get this right, "but not as much as a steady paycheck."

"You know what I mean."

"Fish is meat, too, you know," I say, indicating Emil's plate.

"No, it's not. Fish is fish."

"It's the flesh of an animal. That's 'meat' by definition."

"Fish aren't animals."

"Fish are animals, Emil."

"Well, fish are fine."

"Why?"

"Because it's in the Bible."

"What about salmon? Can you eat *salmon* on Fridays?"

"Salmon are fish. So yeah, that's fine."

"Yeah, but everyone says it's so close to red meat."

"Except that it's not."

"What color is it, then?"

"Well … It's red. But—"

"What about portabella mushrooms?"

"What about them?"

"People say portabella mushrooms are like meat, too."

"Except that they're not."

"Mushrooms are connected by mycelium. A lot of people say they might possess a primitive kind of intelligence, like an underground brain that connects them all."

"Whatever."

"You know. Like in *Avatar*, where all the plants were connected."

"Just shut the fuck up, Robert."

I rarely get the upper hand with my brother, so I let

myself enjoy it for a few moments. Emil has something to tell me, but right now, he's too annoyed to do it.

"You know what I wonder?" I ask.

"I don't give a shit."

"I wonder what happens if you're in a car, and you're eating a burger, and the car's driving east at like ten minutes after midnight early Saturday morning."

"Look," he says in his most dismissive voice. "I got a message this morning from—"

"Because you might cross a time zone, is what I'm saying."

"Robert …"

"It's technically Saturday when you start, but then you cross the time zone, and it's Friday again. You've got a full burger in front of you. What do you do?"

"You stop eating until it's after midnight where you are."

"What if you've got a bite still in your mouth? Can you swallow it?"

"I don't fucking know. I guess you spit it out."

"What if you don't know you crossed into a new time zone?"

"Then it's okay."

"Kind of like how if you kill someone by accident, it's okay."

"That's different."

"Are you sure, Emil? We're talking about the fate of immortal souls."

"Hey! Just because you lost your—"

"Okay. Okay. I've got one."

"Shut up, Robert."

But I push on, ignoring his interruption, thoroughly on fire. "You got the fish, right? And I got the heathen's meatloaf. So you're okay, and I'm going to Hell. So far, so good."

"Robert ..."

"Let's say I'm really going to town on this meal. I'm *fucking this meatloaf up*. And in my frenzy, I accidentally fling a wad of meat your way. A piece of the loaf lands in your mouth, and you start choking on it."

"Okay. That's enough."

"You can't even hock it back up. Everyone's tried the Heimlich, and nothing's doing because it's not really in your trachea; it's right at the fork and keeps flapping back and forth between windpipe and esophagus. But! There is a way out, Emil. There's still a way to save yourself."

I take a dramatic pause, but my brother doesn't bite.

"Swallow the meat, and you'll live. Of course, you're then doomed to fire and brimstone just because your brother is sloppy, and you decided, in a moment of crisis, to save yourself. So, Emil, tell me you think *that's* fair."

Silence at our table. Emil has his hands on the edge, with the posture of a gopher about to climb out of his hole. Before I know what's happening, he pops upright in his seat like a Jack-in-the-box and jabs me in the face with his fist. An instant later, he sits right back where he was. It's over so fast, I might not even believe it happened if not for my bloody nose.

"You done?" he asks.

"I'm done."

Emil hands me a bright white handkerchief. I know for a fact that I've bled on one just like it before. How does he get them so clean? Does my blood just vanish as if it was never there, or does Emil have a dispenser full of them, plucked from a box like Kleenex?

I consider asking Emil if I'll go to Hell if I swallow any of this blood but decide to quit while I'm ahead instead.

I've been trying to be more assertive lately since I can rarely manage more than a few words with Emil, but my assertions wreak all sorts of havoc with his worldview. I represent everything Emil is comfortable not accepting, and I'm not even trying.

"Like I was saying," Emil's tone makes it clear that the last discussion didn't happen — and that if it did, he won, "I got a message this morning from Heinzie."

"About a job?" I dab at my bloody nose, pretending it's not happening. Same as everyone else in the diner. Several people looked over when Emil jumped to his feet but stopped caring after he hit me. Either no one's sympathetic, or everyone heard what I said to earn my beating.

Don't argue with big brother.

It was true when we were kids, and the object of debate was the family's single Big Wheel. It was true in George Orwell's novel, and it's true today.

Emil nods. "A toss-up job."

"No."

"Yes."

"I mean, no, we don't want to do a toss-up."

"So you're in charge now? You decide which jobs we take and which we let go?"

"I suppose it's up to you who's in charge." Pause. Then I add, "Do you want to take it?"

"It's 1.2 million Pentz."

That hits me like a miniature bomb. That many Pentz translates to … Shit, I don't even know. *A lot* of dollars. Enough that I understand why Emil didn't shut Heinzie down the second he made the offer. But a toss-up? We'd decided. Both of us, together.

"Who's the target?"

The booths behind each of us are empty, but we're still

in a public place. Emil calls up a photo on his phone and slides it in my direction.

"You're kidding," I say.

"I'm not kidding about a million-plus-Pentz job."

"If we *get* the million," I remind him. "Remember Fresno?"

How could he forget? The target of the Fresno job was a snaggletooth everyman named Gordon Roberts, CFO of a small company called Baker Financial. Heinzie said the client wanted him out of the way because Baker was poised for a several-billion-dollar buyout … *if* Roberts would stop blocking finance's approval.

The job was a toss-up. The client, through Heinzie, had hired three different assassins. We found him first with a substantial lead over both our competitors, then got starry-eyed dreaming of a quick end to an easy job. We tried to scare him first, knowing the fallback clause would deliver two-thirds payment so long as the deal went through, even if Roberts stayed alive.

When that didn't work, we showed up at his office on a Saturday. Problem was, our scare had raised his antennae. Roberts was a bleeding-heart social justice type, but he turned hardcore when pressed. Long story short, I managed to cut one of his arms mostly off and scramble his kidneys using an ornamental sword he'd had on his wall. The asshole ended up in a hospital two cities away, at which point Nisha Swartha walked in under an assumed visitor name and injected him with an anticoagulant. Roberts bled out, and the doctors couldn't stop it. Heinzie gave Nisha the bounty, even though she only exacerbated the wounds we'd already given him.

"It'll be different this time," Emil says, shoving breaded (and holy) fish into his face. "I reminded Heinzie about Fresno. He knows we got fucked and promises that if anything like that happens again, he'll go to bat for us with the client."

"So he says."

Emil shrugs. Heinzie is an impenetrable buffer but also a total and complete goat fucker. I'd have a problem with it, but it's not like there are a lot of assassin brokers in the market.

"You want to do it," I say.

"I want the payday. Maybe if we get it, you can finally have your way."

"*If* we get it."

"We'll get it."

I look down at the photo still visible on Emil's phone. It's Senator Simon Bisset, who I, of course, know on sight. He'll be the hardest job we've done, and the presence of competitors won't make it easier. Considering Bisset now, I sure hope we *do* get the bounty if we take the job. With a gig that high-profile, everyone involved will need to hit the dirt for a while. There will be a ton of cops. PI's. FBI. Hell, knowing Bisset? There might even be CIA and NSA … and that's not even counting the public shitstorm that, by nature of Bisset's business, will surely erupt the second he's hit.

I sigh. For months now, I've been on edge with every job. Something changed, and now it feels wrong in the air. I keep telling Emil that we need to get out. Quit while we're ahead. But he still steers this ship for both of us, and that means I've been losing. A score on this job would satisfy us both. I want out, and Emil wants us rich. Both happen if we can take down Bisset. We'll be ordering mai tais and rinsing the blood from our hands.

"How many in the toss-up?" I ask.

"Four."

"Four other contractors, or four including us?" We count as one person — long-established, no need to clarify.

Emil finishes chewing before replying. "Four others."

I shake my head, looking down.

"So you agree," Emil says.

This isn't really a question.

"Fine."

"We have a score to settle anyway."

It's one of many fights Emil has imagined for me, and which I'd never give another thought if left to my own devices. I try to see it as sweet: brother protecting brother. In practice, it's kind of annoying.

"Just promise me one thing," I tell Emil.

"Anything."

"If we kill him on Friday, don't eat him. I'm already going to Hell, but at least save yourself."

My brother doesn't respond.

THREE

No Rules

ONLY, there are seven instead of four other assassins in the toss-up.

If I know Heinzie, there were at least five when he told Emil there were four, and he'd planned to use administrative sleight of hand to make us all believe the competition was lighter than it was. He'd probably started to sweat logistics after hitting six ... and once the field reached seven, he'd had no choice but to call a fellowship to make sure we were all on the same page.

I can see him now, slinking around in the back of the bar, pretending dishes were in need of washing to steer clear of our glances. Emil and I aren't the only ones pissed off. His plan seems to be getting us all together without him to dilute our initial aggressions, then slip into the mix once we're calmer. Whether it's working or not is yet to be seen.

My mind starts to wander. To take it all in.

I think about my first-grade teacher, who told me I'd come to a bad end.

I wonder what the inside of Heinzie's skull looks like.

I wonder if anyone's ever played solitaire with a fully shuffled deck but found that the cards came out in perfect order by chance.

Emil says, "Pay attention. A professional uses his eyes and ears more than he uses his weapon. Ninety-nine percent of the job is observation. Anyone can pull a trigger."

I roll my eyes. Not only have we been through this ad nauseum in the past, and not only have I learned it repeatedly on more jobs than I can count, but Emil constantly reminds me.

I know it, Emil. I know it like you know it.

I settle for belligerence. "I *am* paying attention."

"No, you're not. You're counting bottlecaps or something."

"I am not counting bottlecaps."

"You know what I mean."

"There's not even anything to pay attention *to.*" I switch from denial to justification. We're talking in hard whispers — the kind where you add force to compensate for quiet. "Look around. He just wants us to shark-tank in here without him. Maybe thin the crowd before he has to jump in and explain the job to all these pissed-off people."

I scan the crowd. I know almost everyone, but curiously I had no idea that some of them were in the business. Len and Kerry, for instance. Like us, they're considered one player rather than two, but I don't know them as assassins. I know them as the husband-and-wife realtor team who negotiated Emil's lease, and from the signs bearing their faces in yards all over town — the signs where Len looks like a serial killer.

I watch them now from across the pitted mingling floor of Heinzie's pub, called The Rear End, without any irony, and I think: *I should have known.* What kind of realtors don't have last names? I assumed there just wasn't room on their signs, what with all the space required for Stepford grins and sensible housing in the background.

My eyes continue to scan.

If I believe enough in reincarnation, can I come back next time as a tortoise? Tortoises don't have to deal with shit like this. Almost never.

The woman everyone's calling Dahlia, I know as Rachel. A barista at our Starbucks for a while. My brother thought he had a shot at nailing her. Seeing her and the realtors here — three people we know, but not as killers — makes me wonder. Has someone been scoping us for a hit? It's possible, seeing as Heinzie once approached us about hitting Terry Bartow, who's also here. Paranoia begets paranoia. Taking out some insurance begets insurance against your insurance. Not a peaceful field of work, murdering people for money.

I glance at Heinzie. He's the only one who knows all of what's happening here. He has his client snowed, I'm sure of it, arguing that *more is better* for this seemingly important job and arguing (more importantly) for a commission on each black hat he brings to the party. He's invited eight singles or teams of killers, but not because he's being thorough. Heinzie is greedy.

If we all kill each other and the mission suffers, he won't care. Heinzie probably has side bets on all of us. One of us will inevitably kill this job's target, but along the way, he can also contract with Terry to eliminate us and contract with Len to kill Terry and contract with us to get rid of Len.

Once we get to know each other, new animosities will form. It's inevitable when enough of us bump elbows. We're like beta fish. Put one of us in a tank, and we'll do as we're meant to. Put two in a tank, and one will chase the other into corners, bullying all the way. Put eight of us (ten if you're counting individuals) into a tank, and it'll be a fucking bloodbath.

Heinzie is too smart to let all that opportunity go. He'll collect payment from the survivors, then keep the deceased's initial deposits. The target will end up a nice bonus.

"Emil ..." I whisper indistinct sounds and wave him toward a plant that's either naturally lacquer-sheen or made from green wax. "We need to excuse ourselves from this one. Just take the exit."

Emil looks only half surprised. "I told you. It'll be fine. We'll either get the collar or—"

"—end up dead?"

There's a moment of confusion, but then his eyes close and reopen. "Oh. I get it."

"There's too many people here. Blood in the water."

"What, you think there'll be a loose cannon?"

"I think we're in a room *full* of loose cannons. This field is *made* of loose cannons."

"So we'll stay out of their way. Whatever the most obvious start is, we'll head in a different direction."

It's how we tend to work anyway. If you're looking for a spot in a crowded parking lot, you can linger in the aisles behind other waiting cars and just accept that they'll take any spot before you can reach it, or you can drive all the way to the very back of the lot and park without the hassle.

Most professionals in a toss-up do something like the former, always tripping over each other's heels, hitting the same clue points, and relying on speed, stealth, and back-stabbing to reach the next waypoint first. But Emil and I have always been circuitous, looking for less obvious ins to our targets. Our way is harder and longer, but it avoids the infighting and crowd-pushing that ultimately costs more time and life than it saves.

That's been our method for a while, and so far, it's kept us alive and well-fed.

"I'm not worrying about the field being *crowded*. I'm worried about the field being *hostile*."

"What, like Heinzie's brought in so many professionals to thin us out?"

"It's happened before."

"When?"

"San Francisco."

"*Oh*, that was different." Emil's body relaxes as he decides I'm hysterical.

"Emil, I'm serious."

I'm always serious about these things, and I've made the mistake of saying so. Now I'm the boy who cried wolf — and a baby brother, and everyone knows what whiny little bitches *those* can be.

"I know you," says a voice.

Emil turns. There's a man behind him who's built like a fireplug: five-three at most, so musclebound he can't lower his arms. Mahogany skin, no fat beneath, and a shaved head. Stripped bare and oiled up, he probably looks like a walnut.

"Yeah?" There's a challenge in Emil's voice. Fireplug may know my brother, but I get the feeling Emil doesn't know Fireplug. I certainly don't. An imbalance of knowledge in these situations can be fatal, so everyone puffs their chests. It's measuring dicks, and even the ladies here swing a six-pound hog.

"Yeah. They say you're crazy."

"Who?"

"They."

"And who the fuck are you?"

31

"I'm Rock."

"Of course you are."

"Rock Harder."

"I'm sorry," I say. "I can't rock any harder than this."

Rock, *Fireplug*, doesn't even look my way. His attention is fixed on Emil, begging for a fight.

"Your name is *Rock Harder,*" Emil says.

Eyes still on Emil: "That's right."

"Is that your professional name or your porn name?"

"You think *I'm* funny? You should talk to The Duck."

"Donald or Daffy?"

Rock smirks. "Daffy *fucked* Donald."

Emil isn't sure what to do with this. "Okay."

"Not the other way around. Donald is definitely the bottom. I mean, he wears a fucking sailor suit."

I agree with this logic and note that Donald Duck never wore pants.

Rock says, "Fucked him right up the cloaca."

"What?"

"Because birds don't really have an asshole. It's just one big orifice for everything. They piss, they shit, they fuck. All from the same place."

"Okay …"

"It sounds efficient," Rock continues, "but can you imagine if humans had cloacas? I mean, how would that even work? Both sexes have the same thing. No dicks, no pussies. Would we just scissor everything, rubbing our cloacas together?"

Emil is trying to extricate himself. He's off to the bar, but Rock is following right behind him.

"Can you imagine? All sex is anal. Every time you want a shag, you end up getting pissed on. Brown hail with golden showers 24/7."

"Huh," says Emil, now full-on ignoring Rock with a bottle of Johnnie Walker Red.

"You're just looking for a bit of the ol' slip-and-slide … but then suddenly your dick is coated in shit. Only not really shit. It's all white paste. Or more accurately, uric acid."

"Are you a bird scientist or something?" I ask.

There's an electronic tap: the whomp of a Nerf bat magnified a thousand times. We all look up to see Heinzie on the small stage where bands perform, tapping the mic.

"Can you all hear me?"

"Take it off!" someone shouts.

Then someone else said: "Show us your tits!"

This may be some sort of first and last straw for the microphone because Heinzie drops it on the floor, probably trying for drama, and makes an ass out of himself instead. It's not like he's got a sound engineer running the board, so when the thing hits the ground, it's like someone punched a hundred cats. Even the most hardened killers are flinching.

Heinzie walks off the stage, repeats himself using only his voice, then realizes he's still being picked up by the stage mic and has to enter the booth beside the bar's liftgate to kill it. The transaction robs the moment of its drama, and Heinzie returns like a dumbfuck instead of a fearless leader. From Bosley to Maxwell Smart.

"Can you all hear me?"

"Get on with it," says a man leaning against the emergency exit's alarm bar. His face is so horizontally distended his driver's license must be the width of a dollar bill. I don't have to ask. He's shorter than Rock Harder and, in this light, looks sickly green. It must be The Duck. He and Rock probably got in here for half price, seeing as they're too little for the big-kid rides.

So Heinzie gets on with it and introduces us all to each other — not so we can be buddies, but so we can decide to team up if we dare. This is the biggest toss-up Emil and I have seen, but even the smaller ones end up playing like that old TV show *Survivor*. Alphas form alliances to bulldoze everyone in their way, and betas form them to backdoor the alphas.

Heinzie repeats the bounty (1.2 million Pentz, paid through two proxies and spendable anywhere the black market opens a franchise), then asks if we have any questions. What a motherfucker. Of course, we have questions. We knew the bounty coming in, and this room full of idiots is a distraction.

"No questions?" We've surrounded Heinzie on the big open floor. It's like we've formed a dance circle, and it's his turn to boogie. We'll cut him into little pieces if he doesn't. It's not the friendliest dance circle in the world, but this ain't the junior leagues, neither.

"Who's the target?" asks a voice.

Everyone looks, and we all see a man wearing a black sweatshirt, its hood raised like the Reaper's cowl. He's also wearing black pants, black socks, black shoes, black gloves, and either has black skin or some sort of veil. I know who it is without asking, though I've never seen him in person. I look at my brother to gauge his reaction, but Emil pretends that nothing's changed. We knew there were seven teams, but I'd only counted six. This had to be the seventh.

"Is that …?" I whisper.

Emil shushes me. Playing this game, you hold your cards face-out so everyone can see. The trick is to have a secret hand. To show one set of cards while betting on another. I know I've got a legend card showing. I know I'm waving my awe in the air the longer I stare at our hooded fellow, and I know it's doing none of us any good.

"The target is Senator Simon Bisset," Heinzie says.

Even in a room this stone-faced, there's a mumble and hush.

"First to bag him gets the bounty," Heinzie says. "Beyond that, there are no rules."

FOUR

Untouched By The Modern World

THERE'S a flier beside the bathroom sink showing all the things you shouldn't do at a dinner party.

You shouldn't exhale little red dots into another person's face.

You shouldn't make out with the host while surrounded by little red dots.

You shouldn't walk around the party, rubbing little red dots onto everything and everyone.

You shouldn't squeeze your abdomen and snot little red dots into everyone's food.

In reality, the laminated sheet tacked beside the mirror is a CDC flier with tips on how to spread the flu. It's probably supposed to be about how to *prevent* spreading the virus, but there's a lot more about what *not* to do. You'd think the opposite based on the illustrations and the absence of universal NO signs. I picture some rogue CDC designer putting this form together on the day she's finally fed up enough, daring her boss to find and fix her subversive infographic. But the fliers escaped discovery, and now there will be a pandemic. The hallways here are full of people operating on half their mental cylinders. They'll be spitting in each other's faces, blowing palmfuls of ground cayenne at their tablemates at dinner. Pandemonium and riots. The flu will win, and humanity will lose. *Good riddance to bad rubbish*, Emil would say.

I obey the only conventional tip on the flier, washing my hands while inspecting my face. I was never supposed to look this old.

I emerge to find Mabel Robertson at the door. This happens often. She thinks she's our grandmother.

"Were you up late last night?" she's asking Emil.

Mrs. Robertson might be nearly Emil's height, but age has bent her into the shape of a hangman's gallows. Some of the residents here need walkers to get around, but Mabel needs one to stay upright. She hovers above it, eyes down as she prowls the carpeted hallways as if searching for change.

"No, Mrs. Robertson," Emil says.

"Have you been getting enough to eat?"

"Yes, Mrs. Robertson."

"Will I see you at dinner?"

"Wouldn't miss it for the world."

"Be early. The Jews are *always* early."

"We will, Mrs. Robertson, thank you," Emil says and closes the door. There's a poster there, too, except that it's about preventing the spread of STDs. Apparently, they fuck like rabbits in here.

"Again with the Jews."

"When you're old, it's okay to be a bigot." Emil crosses behind me, then sits in the lift chair. He keeps it halfway up, says it's nice to save himself the effort of standing. "There were wars, you know, back when she was little."

"There are still wars."

"And video games. Now, if you want to kill people, you can do it from a thousand miles away."

"And we should talk?"

"Being a pro is one aspect of my life, Robert. Just one. I refuse to let my profession define me." Emil reaches for a magazine, probably to end this discussion. AARP monthly is in every room here, plus a *Time* and a *Quilter*. This must be why paper magazines still get printed.

"Are we going to talk about Bisset?" I ask.

"No."

"Are we backing out of the toss-up?"

"No way. You got me thinking. We nail this, we can stop."

"I thought you didn't want to stop."

"Everyone wants to stop, Robert. Everyone, everywhere. Rest is the natural state of things. Being alive is about fighting entropy."

I sit. There's a remote control on the little glass table between us, but it's like something from a cartoon. The buttons are the size of silver dollars, the entire works big enough to use as a dinner tray. Everything here is slightly different. The bed is high, so it's easy to rise from. The toilet is so tall, I feel like I'm at a barstool while crapping. There are railings everywhere and little lamp cords tied in bunches wherever a person is likely to fall. Mini shampoos in the shower have caps on them the size of spigot wheels. Everything is in large type, so big it feels like shouting. MIND YOUR TELEVISION VOLUME is on a folded card beside the TV, and WINDOW DOES NOT OPEN is on the wall behind Emil's head. I've neither turned on the TV nor tried to open the window, and yet every time I look around, I'm sure that I've done something wrong.

"I'm hungry."

"Dinner is in a half-hour," Emil tells me.

I look at the wall clock. "It's four o'clock."

"Dinner is in a half-hour," he repeats.

"You told Mabel we'd join her."

"We have to, or she'll have to sit with Jews."

Emil and I have met the Jews. I think there are sixteen out of four hundred residents. I got bored yesterday before the time came for Heinzie's little meet-and-greet and walked every hallway, noting the names on the door. I get that not all Jews are named Schwartz or Goldberg, but I don't think Mabel's discrimination radar is much more sophisticated than mine. We've seen the residents in many settings, and nobody's making matzo or spinning dreidels. I've yet to hear an *Oy vey* or *Shalom*. I've only ever seen Mabel look askance at Moishe and Shirley Silverman, who tend to eat a lot of rolls when they sit for dinner. It might be this offense that's so upsetting to her Christian heart. You're supposed to break bread, she's told us, not smuggle it into your purse for later when you think nobody's looking.

"So we're staying."

"We're staying."

I sit in an uncomfortable wooden chair with an uphol-stered oval on the seat and back ugly enough to look cross-stitched in anger. Those little signs grandmas make that say *Kiss the Cook* or *Bless This Mess*? If the pattern under-neath me now had words with it, it'd say *Fuck This Shit*. Someone must have done it as a grudge. No happy person could make something so hideous.

I look out the window, where a red hummingbird feeder full of pink sugar water hangs from the branch of a cherry tree. The facility changes the water regularly and keeps the feeders clean because the residents like looking at them far more than they enjoy sitting around wondering why no one ever comes to visit. A bird approaches, investigates, then flies off. Must not like the sugar water Shady Acres is putting down. What an elitist asshole.

"If we're doing the job, we should talk about the job," I say.

"What about it?"

"How the hell are we going to get at Bisset?"

"Why comes first. How comes later," Emil tells me.

"Okay. Then *why* are we going after Bisset?"

"For the money."

"That's a little obvious, don't you think?"

"Please. As if we need a reason to erase *that* stain from the planet."

I look to the wall beside the window. At first, I think what I see there is another CDC poster, but it's actually an excellent imitation of the same style. This one must be homemade because it's on Shady Acres stationery. Scanning, I see similar fliers everywhere. Whoever made them must have wanted to be an illustrator but ended up manning the phones at a retirement home instead. If I look at the drawings through that lens, they're much more interesting.

A pinch warning near the adjustable bed shows a man with his hand nearly sawed through. There's a choking notice on the wheeled meal tray, but the person behind him performing the Heimlich looks like he could just as easily be taking the choking party up the ass. It's as if every drawing has an edge. As if the illustrator tried to contain the rage she feels about her failed life, but her anger was all expressed in these little block-like bits of art.

There's a notice like this in the east wing that large-print-shouts CAREFUL, STEP, but the icon man with his walker drawn upon it is already tipping, about to kiss concrete.

The RETURN TRAYS HERE sign in the dining hall

seems innocent at a glance, but there's a figure off to one side wearing an apron, watching the icons as they queue up to return their trays. You think that aproned figure is only watching, but I'd swear there's something in his hand. A knife, perhaps, because the illustrated cafeteria lady didn't get the life she wanted, either.

At the salad bar, a notice asks users to COVER YOUR SNEEZE, but the illustration's sneeze is clearly penetrating the sneeze shield if one were to look closely. This could be a simple mistake, but with my lens in place, I see it another way. Either the illustrator is suggesting that residents keep themselves from sneezing at the salad bar until they manage to get some snot past the shield, or she's saying that the disgruntled workers (who, like illustrator and aproned figure, hate their lives, too) already have.

"We need phones," I say.

"Later."

I pick up the iPhone we've been using to stay in Heinzie's loop. He gave us the basic logistics on the Bisset job at the fellowship meeting — the what, when, where, and other whos involved — but there are running updates on Heinzie's server behind all of its firewalls.

Updates were once handled in mail drops, but about five years ago, Heinzie caved and went high-tech. Emil resisted with his usual obstinance until we missed a venue change posted online, got sniped, and lost fifty thousand Pentz that should have been ours. After that, he reluctantly tossed a few of his Luddite chips and gave in.

But Emil won't even get himself a burner.

They're always listening to you, he snarls whenever I bring it up. *They listen to you, they decide who you are, then they reverse engineer what to sell you. Forget machines taking over the world. They won't have to, as long as we keep giving it away.*

So this was the solution — Emil's way of playing

Heinzie's tech game without dirtying his hands with smart-phones, tablets, or social media. He says all phones are tracked, even the burners, even if you walk into Shitbox Cellular and pay the toothless criminal behind the desk in cash.

There are cameras everywhere. Even if you pay with cash, you leave fingerprints.

It's worst if I try to help.

You'll fuck it up, Robert. You'll fuck it up, and then we'll get pinched. And then where will you be? Fucking dead, that's where. And won't I be relieved.

After four years of practice, we have our scheme down.

You find out where the job is, then get out a map and draw a hundred-mile circle around that point. Just outside of that circle, you find a retirement home in a well-off area. You don't want a *rich* nursing home because those come with their own problems, like con artists trying to bilk old billionaires by getting into the wills before their time expires. We always look for upper middle class — enough wealth to be comfortable with money, but not so much as to be cavalier.

Eliminate all homes with exterior corridors. You want one that's all indoors, like an enormous hotel. Comings and goings, seen from the outside, are so much less obvious there.

Then you call the front desk and book a tour, saying you've got a relative near move-in age. On the tour, ask about visitation. You're looking for homes that keep a few guest rooms handy for overnight stays. Some places with guest rooms will make you pay to use them, so eliminate those. Credit cards leave a trail, and no legit home will allow you to pay in cash.

Also, use the tour to scope the place, noting, in particular, the fullness of hallways, how robust or feeble the resident population is, and the length of the location's corridors. It's easy to forget that last one, but places with just a few long, straight main hallways keep everyone walking through the complex on display, and a few corners go a long way to keeping your profile low.

As your tour winds down, ask if you can eat a meal in the dining room, citing concern over your aged relative's environment and eating habits. Sit with residents and strike up a conversation. With some poking, you'll inevitably find a resident who is A) mentally foggy enough to believe they know you or B) still sharp but lonely or bored enough to lie and say they do. The final step is to circle back, being careful to speak with staff who don't recognize you, and claim to be a relative of your senior partner-in-crime. Request a few overnights, and make yourself at home.

I sit. I breathe. The place has a stale camphor smell that could easily be alleviated by opening a window, but apparently, WINDOWS DO NOT OPEN. It's like the home is encouraging ageism. Like its corporate policy to incubate Old Person Smell that has no need to be there.

We've been here for over a week. Long enough that I'm slightly self-conscious, figuring we're overstaying our unpaid welcome. But there are three other guest rooms, and none are occupied, and Mabel has maybe let herself forget that Emil and I aren't really her grandchildren, and my brother, for all his rough edges, loves these people.

Old people are pure, he tends to say. *Untouched by the modern world.*

Although according to the STD flier on the back of the door, they're plenty touched by each other.

Once you've moved your day bag into a home's guest room, take some time to meet a few people (*just* a few) and to make yourself known (but only a little). Residents' clocks move faster than younger folks, and in our experience, if we're cool and polite and help where we can, they accept us in a matter of hours. You're free to snoop and explore after that.

This is where the ruse pays off. Residents usually don't trust banks. They cash their Social Security checks (or, in many cases, bountiful pensions) and stuff the money under their mattresses. Little old ladies have jewelry boxes stuffed with diamonds and gold. All of that makes lesser criminals rob them blind, but cell phones are the only thing Emil and I ever look for.

Stashed in the backs of drawers or the bottom of boxes. Behind acres of picture frames with their screens covered in dust. The phones we're looking for are almost always drained of power, disused so firmly they might as well not exist. Residents never realize they're missing. Some younger relative bought the thing for them, but it never got used. They have live service contracts under another person's name. *Those* phones, we can use to play Heinzie's electronic reindeer games without folks like the FBI ever being any the wiser.

I open the clock app on our current phone. Every time we power on an old device, I start the timer. This one has been running for twenty-six hours. I like to swap phones at least once a day for security, meaning that this one's run its course.

"We need a new phone," I tell Emil.

"No, we don't."

I show him the timer, and it's twenty-six hours. Emil shrugs.

"Time's up."

"We don't need to check-in," Emil says over the top of his magazine. One of the cover stories promises to explore *Menopause and You,* and I'm somehow sure that's what Emil is reading right now. "We're good until Tuesday."

"There may have been updates."

"No updates until Tuesday."

"See, this is what you get wrong, Emil. The whole point of having an online checkpoint is so that anyone can look in it at any time."

"Why would we check it if we're not expecting any changes?"

"How would Heinzie notify us of changes if we never check it?"

Emil mutters something about electronic handcuffs. About being trained like chimpanzees. I hear the shadow half of a tiny conversation between Emil and himself about the many infuriating ways the world has gone to shit. I wait for it to end, knowing the fire will spread if I toss kindling onto it. Soon, Emil's old-man rant dies on its own.

"Fine," he says. "Go steal another one."

I don't like the word *steal* in this context. Technically we're stealing, but these phones have been forgotten. We might as well be stealing the pen cap from the dusty bottom of a disused purse. We're gentlemen here. Even if it wasn't the best way to lay low, it's courteous. The way Emil is about old people, it's more than that. He probably wishes he could be ninety, having grown up without the internet, social media, or texting. He'd be one of those ancients who could only talk to someone after sidling up their front porch to sit a spell. An ideal life for Emil.

But then the phone does something strange. It vibrates as if with a new message. I glance up to see if my brother has noticed, but he's still reading about his changing uterus. I return my attention to the screen and see that the notification is from Heinzie's web app, pushed out the way

46

I'm sure all the other assassins in the toss-up are receiving their notes.

But why am I getting notifications? I didn't sign up for them, and we sure as hell would never tie one of our phones to Heinzie's little dance. I look up again at Emil. My mouth opens, but I close it without a word.

What, do I think *Emil* was the one who signed up? He'll barely touch the phones we steal.

"Shit," I say.

Now Emil looks up. Behind him, perfectly framed, a warning seems to show a man being cut in half between sill and sash. There's no reason for that one. The window can't be opened. It's as if the artist wants to rub their imprisonment in the residents' faces.

"Bisset's agenda has changed."

Emil drops his magazine.

"We should go," I say.

"Where?"

"Florida."

"Bisset is going to Florida?"

"Bisset is going to Los Angeles. And it says here—" I scroll down, ignoring my brother's expression. If you want to agitate Emil, you just need to start speaking or gesturing like someone familiar with modern tech. "—that there's also been a credible threat on Bisset's life."

"So he'll have bodyguards."

"If not Secret Service."

"Everyone will follow him. Everyone will go to LA."

"Which is why we're going to Florida."

Emil rises from his chair and starts packing our bags without a word.

"We need to toss the phone before we go." Sometimes even these fancy homes have incinerators, and when they do, it's like we have an evidence-eradicating jackpot. This is one of those, and the chute is just one floor down.

"That's not all," Emil says.

I look around, knowing he means wiping the room to erase our prints.

"Not that," he says, watching me.

"What, then?"

"Dinner," he says.

"But Bisset …"

"Dinner," he insists. "First Mabel, then the Silvermans."

"Two dinners," I deadpan. "Two dinners in an old folks' home, while the other six teams rush after our 1.2 million target."

He's holding the phone. Not the smart one, but rather the dumb one attached to the wall. "You're right. I'll call them both. We'll do them together."

"But they're enemies."

Emil smirks. "I met Moishe's brother the other day. Turns out, he married Mabel's sister."

Then I get it. Mabel doesn't dislike Jews. She dislikes in-laws. It's a prejudice everyone can get behind.

"Don't pack that," Emil says, putting his hand over the receiver in case someone picks up. I look at the thing in my hand, which I'm not supposed to pack. It's candy. A small bag of Werther's Originals from the store downstairs.

"Something for Mabel to remember us by," Emil explains.

Ah, yes. Classic Emil.

Burn the world, but treat the right ones kindly.

FIVE

Zero

THE CONSOLE between the front seats of Emil's car is full of smartphones. We've never seen such a bounty. Three are in one of the oversized cup holders, splayed like a bouquet. Four have been bundled with rubber bands, bound like bills from a bank. At least a dozen more inside the latched compartment, in cases ranging from practical to peculiar. More than half have been stuffed into blinged-out cases covered in sparkles and rhinestones. Grandma phones, set that way by middle-aged children who hoped their mothers would use the things but knew deep down they'd end up getting dusty in a drawer instead.

I'd have to go on a ridiculous safari to find them all, but I know we stole fifteen phones before leaving Shady Acres because I got a notice this morning that $1500 in cash had been withdrawn from our account. Emil must have sneaked out to get that money while I was sleeping. Every time we steal a phone, he puts a portrait of Benjamin Franklin in its place. $100 is light fare for an iPhone, but it always goes to people who've forgotten they own one. I've stopped arguing with my brother about it — about the low price he's paying, or conversely about the fact that he feels compelled to pay at all. *Everyone wins*, he always says.

The one in my hands is rose gold, in a pink case with bunny ears. I can't bring myself to remove the case because this was Mabel's phone before she dropped it behind the heater and forgot about the thing forever. The case stays on until the ears get in my way.

I look down. My fingers have trailed, again, to the sleep switch. They press it without my permission. The screen wakes halfway with the time and date, my timer counting down below. We kept going over our 24-hour limit, so with such a bounty before us, I decided a countdown, not a count-up, would be better. Hopefully, by tomorrow I'll feel okay parting with this phone. I've always been sentimental. Emil even more so, though you'd have to dig to believe it. My brother can't let go of anything. The past always haunts him, especially the parts he can't forgive.

Almost as if I'm watching someone else's fingers, I see myself wake the phone, so app icons zoom into view.

"Are we close?" Emil asks me.

"I wasn't checking the map."

He glances over, keeping his hands on the wheel. Eyes back on the road, he says, "You're a fucking addict. That's what you are."

"Excuse me?"

He looks at my lap as if there's a giant slug there. "The phone. You're addicted to it."

"We just got this phone. We just got *all* of these phones."

"I don't mean you're addicted to *that* phone. I mean, you're addicted to *phones*."

"Yeah. I'm really into calling people. I can't stop. I need help, man."

"You know what I mean," Emil snaps. Apparently, this

is his last word on the issue because I witness the return of his stony expression. I watch him for a second, wanting to get my brotherly tongue-lashing out of the way. When it seems he might be finished, I return to the screen.

I open the photos app. Before leaving Shady Acres, I took my most thorough tour yet. Went into every open room, including those marked STAFF ONLY, scoped every entrance and exit, and entered every public bathroom, including the ladies'.

As I suspected, the same artist I'd been admiring before had created warning signs all over the complex. Photos of them all are now on my camera roll, or Mabel's. Looking through them is harkening back to a simpler time — before we entered the melee, clawing for the neck of one of the nation's most well-known faces.

In the first-floor bathroom, a sign by the toilet showed a blocky man on the floor by a cartoon shitter, reaching up for help. It read, IF YOU SLIP, PULL THE CORD. A simple message requiring no illustration. The drawing seems to have been added as a fuck-you to the toilet-slippers of the world. Can't stay on the can? Then live underneath it with shit. We'll get to you if we can. I hope the cartoon man got his business done first. Pooping from the floor, possibly while injured, sounds worse than our present errand.

I swipe to the next photo. This was where I discovered the illustrator's subversive side. As I ventured into more and more obscure places, I found signs that rode ever closer to a disturbing edge. On the front door, the PLEASE COVER YOUR COUGH sign was almost pleasant. Could almost be in a church. But deep in the kitchens, where only the cooks could see it, I found a sign warning the cooks to PRACTICE SAFE SKILLS. Two illustrations on that one. The first showed a woman holding her left wrist with her right hand, mouth open in horror, the hand sketched on a countertop beside a massive cleaver, the wrist-stump spouting blood. The second showed a chef in an apron with his face on a hot grill. A second chef, behind him, holds the first against the scalding surface, mouth agape in laughter.

"There's science to it, you know," Emil tells me.

"To what?"

"To addiction."

"I'm not an addict."

"It's not even your fault. It's built into those things. Do you know about infinite scroll?"

"I'm going to guess that's a way of scrolling that ends very quickly. No, no, wait. It's *infinite*."

Emil shifts in his seat. The car's focus wobbles a little, rattling the phones in the cupholder. "Infinite scroll is when you scroll down in your Facebook feed but never need to hit 'Next page.' It just scrolls forever. Facebook didn't used to be that way."

"So?"

"So it's like slot machines. You know about slot machines?"

"Where are you going with this, Emil?"

"You used to have to pull a lever on slot machines. You also used to have to put coins into them."

"And now you don't?"

He shakes his head. "Now, most places give you a card. It's insert and go. There's just a button, no lever. If they can get thinking out of the way, they know you'll sit there for hours tapping that button. A lever takes too much effort. Each pull is a reminder of your risk, that you're flushing away your future one quarter at a time. No coins because every time you drop another one into the slot, you look into your cup and see the level going down. You can see how much you're losing."

Emil looks over to make sure I'm getting it all before he continues. "Casinos employ the world's best behavioral psychologists. Casinos keep you zoned out. There's no readout to show you how much you've spent, or how much you have left. Cards refill onto your tab automatically. They bring you food and drink, so you never need to leave the machine. No clocks or windows. Floors are always a maze, so it's that much harder to leave. If the casino is below street level, escalators will take you down to the casino floor, but there will only be stairs going up. If you want to leave, you have to climb, but coming back down is easy as pie. It's an engineered experience. Every little trigger that tells a gambler to slow down or stop, the casino smokes out and eliminates."

I shrug. "And this is relevant why?"

"Because that shit in your hands works the same way. 'Infinite scroll' is trading slot arms for buttons to make falling into a trance that much easier. It's trading quarters for cards, so you don't realize how much of your life you keep pissing away. You can think you're in charge, but the makers are training you to do exactly what they want you to do."

I should know better than trying to get a word in edgewise by now.

"Notifications remind you to check on things that don't matter and never will. You keep picking it up because you get a dopamine hit every time. The games are even worse. Addiction is a modern part of game design. Not on how to beat addiction, but how to create it. They give you a sample for free, then let you pay when you've gotta have more. They eliminate friction, so there's nothing between you and a purchase. No confirmations to make. *Tap, tap,*

tap, and suddenly your bank account is empty. Suddenly you're all alone, old, and you missed half your life staring at a screen."

"You're being dramatic," I say.

"Am I?"

I check the map, then set the phone aside.

"Where the fuck are we?" Emil asks roughly.

"Approaching Tallahassee."

"I fucking hate Florida, man. Hate it."

"Beaches. Sunshine. Lots of retirement homes."

"Hospices in denial," Emil says. "Shit flows downhill. People come here and wait to die."

"Or to live out their retirement in paradise," I say.

"I can't think of anything worse," Emil goes on, looking through the windows with a scowl. "Running out the clock in America's dick."

I know better than to fuel this particular fire, so I go silent and, knowing what's good for me, keep my hands in my lap, away from the phone. I've got a system. I take a lot of pictures, but doing it on a digital camera, as Emil suggests, leaves evidence inside our luggage. So I take them on our stolen phones instead, uploading them to a fire-walled cloud server whenever we're near a wifi signal. I'm careful, scrubbing the metadata and deleting the originals. Our stolen phones always meet a horrible end.

Emil hates it all, but he knows I can't live without a history. Or a past. Our lives are mostly faceless. We're holes in society's tapestry, notable more for our absence than our presence. Thinking about it too long gives me existential horror. The idea ... no, the *fact* ... that our profession means we have to be unpersons — folks who were never really here. That, I can't bear. Without a past, I've got no future. Without a future, I don't exist.

In my quietest moments, I'm obsessed with the idea of

a legacy I cannot have. I want to leave a mark to prove I was here, but I'm a ghost. Less than nothing. I've had a positive impact on nobody. If people look back on me, they'll say, *Robert could have been something. He could have grown into a fine man if he hadn't come to such a terrible end.*

I think of a bag of spilled M&Ms, three of the red ones settling beside each other in a tiny little monochromatic circle.

I think of a casket's interior that's way too tight, that I can only fit if I curl up fetal.

I think of Senator Bisset. The impact he's had on everyone. Of the fact that very soon, he'll never impact anyone else, ever again. We should chat, Bisset and I. We've more in common than our differences.

"You're doing it again," Emil says.

"I'm not doing anything."

"I know you, Robert. You're so fucking dour."

"*Dour.* Did you get a Word of the Day calendar?"

"Don't change the subject. You're always like this."

"How?" I ask.

"If you'd turned out different, I'd have been different, too."

"So you blame me. For the fact that you're a hired killer."

Emil says, "I like being a killer. I blame you for making me think about it way too often."

I've heard this before. Emil wants steak without killing the cow. High-brand sneakers without considering the kids who worked their fingertips to the bone in sweatshops abroad. He wants wealth without fucking the poor in their dirt hole. The world is the problem, never my brother. Emil's a man of action. The rest of us are just varying amounts of standing in his way.

"Turn here." I pitch my voice, making it neutral. Too

friendly, and he won't understand how badly he's pissing me off. Too gruff, and he'll keep arguing to knock me down. Emil is always in charge. Poor Robert is only a puppet.

Except that I can reach Emil when I need to. When it comes down to it, I'm steering the ship from belowdecks while my brother stands behind the big wheel topside, pretending he controls our rudder.

"I thought you said Tampa."

"I said Florida."

"Tampa is Florida."

"So is Tallahassee. Turn here."

Emil does as I say, but with too wide a wrench on the wheel. It's like he's trying to kill us just so he can make another fucking point. If we died, that'd show me. There's no more question of who's right and who's wrong when both brothers are in the ground.

But I don't comment. Emil can have his victories as long as I have mine.

Tires roll on lumpy pavement. The sound is a strident hum, somnolent and entrancing.

"I don't want to fight," I finally say.

"Then shut your fucking mouth."

I turn on audible navigation after that, knowing that as much as Emil hates Siri's voice, right now, he hates mine even more. Staying silent is the best way to keep our peace. My brother loves his denial. If he pretends that something hasn't happened long enough, his reality eventually adapts.

"In one hundred feet, turn right onto Pecan Street."

"Fuck your mom," Emil tells Siri.

"You'll have to unlock your iPhone to do that," Siri replies.

The man we're meeting is Hojo, half-Japanese with no

last name, just like our realtor foes. He couldn't possibly look more white, but all around the house he shares with his grandfather are photos of a boy who looks like Hojo smiling between a Japanese man and a blonde woman who seems like she might have been stolen from a shampoo commercial. Either Hojo is telling the truth and got all the Caucasian genes, or he's staged an elaborate con without any purpose. To compensate for his whiteness, Hojo practically bellows his Asian heritage from the rooftops. Even in Japan, we never met someone so fervently Japanese.

He opens the door wearing a kimono that comes dangerously close to showing off twin bags of skin. He's also grabbed a weapon, supposedly to do battle in case we turn out to be foes. But really, he's holding it to show off. The weapon is a four-foot samurai sword. Behind him, the living room is hung with paper lanterns and a parade dragon's head.

"Oh, it's you. You have breakfast? I'm making breakfast. You want bacon? I've got bacon."

You don't actually have to speak around Hojo. If you're willing to wait, he'll answer his questions without you.

He ushers us in. Closes the door behind us, sticking the sword through the sash binding his kimono.

"Long drive? I know, you can't tell me. You're on a job, right? I heard from Heinzie."

"What did Heinzie say?" Emil asks.

"Not to help you."

"Not to help us specifically, or not to help anyone?"

"Please. Who else am I gonna help? Nobody, that's who. Is Rock in this toss-up? He is, isn't he?"

An old man emerges from the back. He's slightly stooped, leaning on a cane. He's from Hojo's Irish half and, according to a few of the framed photos, once had burning red hair. Short in his prime, he's even shorter now. I've met Grampy three times, and the man hasn't remembered us once.

"Who's there?" he rasps.

"Nobody, Grampy. Go back to bed."

"I wanna go to the store."

"I went to the store yesterday, Grampy."

"I mean the video store."

"There's no video store there anymore, Grampy."

"But you watch movies!"

"Online, Grampy."

"I want to get some tapes. Take me out to get some tapes."

Hojo sighs.

"I have to poop," Grampy announces and enters the bathroom.

I don't ask because I know. In his room, Grampy has a top-loading VHS player that was made around the time the sun formed from a cloud of hot gas. Beside the player sits a stack of glossy boxes showing oiled men with feathered hairdos and purring topless women with enough pubic hair to make their panties look like pillows.

"You staying long? Sit."

We sit. All the furniture in Hojo's house is covered in plastic slipcovers. He hasn't redecorated since Grampy's wife died, laying his own decorations atop the old ones instead. The resulting style is what might happen if a kitschy Japanese restaurant collided with a big-box craft store.

"I'm making sausage and melons," Hojo says.

I think, *So is Grampy,* but say, "Okay."

"You want any?"

This question isn't immediately answered. We're both caught off guard, unsure of how to reply.

"No thanks," I say.

"You want any?" Hojo asks Emil.

"No."

Hojo pushes into the kitchen, which has batwing doors like a saloon. The springs are broken, so without pushing them back together, they stay open. We watch as Hojo shifts fruit around on an island made of chipped Formica. He plucks a honeydew from an over-large basket and sets it on a cutting board, then removes the sword from his belt.

"So Heinzie told you not to help us," Emil says.

"Not to help any of you."

"But you don't seem surprised to see us."

"I called ahead," I tell Emil.

This is a breach of protocol. Hojo was bugged once by the FBI and went upriver for a prison sentence that turned him into an anal receiver. He's only trusted conversation in person ever since. Fortunately, he's always home. Hojo is the most connected person we know who never really connects with anyone.

"You called ahead," Hojo echoes.

"That means you must be willing to help us anyway."

Hojo uses his sword to slice a melon down the center. It reminds me of that game *Fruit Ninja*. I'm tempted to rush the kitchen and start throwing all his melons and apples and oranges into the air, just to see if he can bisect the little fuckers before they hit the ground.

"For the usual price," Hojo says.

"Why?"

"Fuck you. I don't work for free."

"I mean … Why are you helping us if Heinzie said not to?"

Hojo sets the melon down, then comes to stand before us, raises the sword with both hands on the grip.

"Maybe I'm not helping you. Maybe I'm helping

Heinzie. Or maybe someone else to take you out of the running." His hands tighten, knuckles turning white.

Emil holds up a hand and is about to say, *Now wait just a second*, but then Hojo guffaws and re-enters the kitchen. He's immediately slicing fruit again, turning the huge sword so he can use the point to make delicate little designs in the melons like a chef stocking a high-end buffet.

"You're after Bisset," he says.

"Heinzie told you?"

"No. It's obvious. Heinzie refused to give details, but he *did* go out of his way to call and tell me not to help because sure as shit, *someone* would be in touch. He tells me there's a huge toss-up going, then reads me the roster so I'll know exactly who not to help? *Shit*. I even heard Blackhawk is in this one. Is it true? I know it's true. Who else is controversial enough right now? Who else does half the country want to kill? Bisset, that's who."

"Heinzie called and told you not to help," Emil speak-shouts into the kitchen.

"That's right."

"So why are you helping?"

"Because he called me."

"I called you too," Emil says before I can point out the same thing.

"Yeah, well." Hojo stops there, so this must be a finished thought I'm just not understanding.

Emil shifts beside me. The plastic dust cover makes noises like opening leftovers covered in shrink wrap.

Hojo calls out from the kitchen, "You want oatmeal? I'll make you oatmeal."

"I'll have some oatmeal," I say.

"You want some oatmeal?" he asks Emil.

"Fuck oatmeal." This feels unnecessarily aggressive as

if oatmeal insulted Emil in the past. *You think you're so hot? I've got wheat germ, bitch.*

Hojo emerges with fruit but no oatmeal, delivering what we didn't want.

"Use a coaster," Hojo says, furnishing the coffee table with fruit.

"I don't want any," Emil says.

"My house, my rules."

I'm pondering this when the bathroom door opens, and Grampy emerges.

"I can't get my dick under the toilet seat," he announces.

"What?"

"I already took my Cialis. If I bend my dick beneath the toilet seat, my tip just cleans the underside."

"I'm not in charge of your dick, Grampy," Hojo says.

"I'm not complaining. It feels good."

Then Grampy retires to his room with a tent in his pants, the issue apparently settled through means unknown.

Hojo sits opposite us. I'm immediately convinced there are no boxers behind that tiny kimono, and of course, he's right across from me. Now I'll be distracted for the rest of this visit. Waiting to see if he flashes me is like waiting for the killer to strike in a horror movie. I have a sudden urge to shout, "Don't go in there!" but manage to keep my wits.

"So," he says. "Bisset."

"Can you help?" Emil asks.

"*Will* you help," I clarify.

"The question isn't '*Can* I help,'" Hojo says. "The question is, '*Will* I help?'"

"Jesus Christ," I say. "Where's my oatmeal?"

Hojo's been tapping his chin while I've been speaking, doing his best impression of pensive. Hojo's a strange-looking cat, hardly intellectual, with eyes too far apart like a gazelle or a horse. In the animal kingdom, he'd be prey, not predator.

"So, will I help?" Hojo shrugs. "The answer is maybe."

"We'll obviously pay," Emil says.

"Obviously."

"We have cash, of course."

Hojo shrugs as if to say this is neither here nor there. He's playing cool, but Hojo's always been a mercenary. Nominally, he's on nobody's side. In truth, he undermines Heinzie whenever possible. Heinzie is slow about it for some reason, always believing Hojo is a supplier and nothing more. Eventually, he's going to figure it all out, though, and when that happens, it'll be sword versus gun. Smart money would bet on Heinzie, but for some reason, I think Hojo has tricks up his sleeve.

I start to stand — to get the money and break the stalemate — but Hojo raises a hand as I slap my palms to my thighs.

"Bisset is in L.A. this week."

I sit back. "We know."

"He gets threats all the time. He's used to them, as Zero."

I hadn't considered that. Only four years and everyone's gotten used to Senator Simon Bisset, forgetting who he was before his election. Half of me understands; like Emil says, the world's attention span is a fraction of what it was before the internet. Outrage, these days, comes and goes like the weather. But the truth is, Bisset didn't always go by his real name. A year before his first Senate run, he was better known as Zero, the supposedly benign hacker behind MoonBase.

MoonBase comes off as the birthplace of memes, but

even today, it's the germinating point for the most antiso-cial of subversives. Zero created MoonBase back when folks there were the only public pathways to the Silk Road and the larger Dark Web. Officially, Zero — like Hojo — never took sides. Unofficially, folks like me always wondered why someone neutral would create an anony-mous website where people who meant to burn the world might gather.

"That's coming from internet trolls," Emil says. "Mouth breathers who live in their parents' basements. They aren't credible threats."

Hojo nods, a considering frown on his lips. "Maybe, maybe not. Everyone wanted to know who Zero was. Rumor said someone had dirt on him. Was going to the FBI about it. MoonBase was on fire about it back then, and users started digging to see what they could find about him. Unearthing secrets is a game to those people. So MoonBase regulars started to chatter on boards like Solores and Giffley, but what did we learn after it was all out in the open?"

Hojo isn't waiting for an answer. "Zero had several aliases on every board of notice, including aliases of some of the same folks supposedly trying to work out Zero's identity. My sources tell me the FBI was a cunt hair away from opening an investigation as part of a larger probe into the Dark Web, but Zero came out of the closet. Popped his own cherry. That pissed a shit ton of people off. In a way, robbing those basement-dwelling mouth-breathers of their secret was like spoiling the end of a movie. Of course, most of what they say about him is hot air. But it only takes one crazy to make his life difficult."

"So you think Bisset has dealt with real, on-the-ground stalkers," Emil says.

Hojo nods, opening a laptop between us. He types

something, then spins the machine so we can see the results. He stands to come around, and of course, I get a flash of his dick. Goddammit, Hojo.

There's a photo covering most of the browser window — one of many plucked from a Google Images search for *Simon Bisset*. Hojo uses a long fingernail to tap a woman in the shadows to the senator's left.

"That's Selena Karkaroff. Some people say she invented Systema, which is what Krav Maga would be if it went to the gym and bulked up. It's bullshit, of course, but it's safe to say she *re*-invented it."

"She's a fighter?"

"That sort of legitimizes it, but sure." Hojo shrugs, then turns back to the photo and taps another person near Bisset — this one in the shadows, barely visible. What I can see looks like Mister Eko from the TV show *Lost*, just as stone-faced and terrible. "This is Djembe. No known last name."

"What kind of a douchebag doesn't use a last name?" I ask Hojo.

"Djembe, when he's in the U.S., goes by the name 'Carl Weathers.'"

"Carl Weathers?"

"Not the same Carl Weathers who played Apollo Creed in *Rocky*. I looked it up."

I glance up at Hojo to see if he's joking. *Rocky* feels a billion years old, and this man only looks age twenty-five or so — thirty at most.

"And?" Emil asks.

"And I'm not sure what impresses me more, the fact that a U.S. Senator has two of the most legendarily dangerous people in the modern world as his bodyguards, or that the intelligence agencies all know who they are and look the other way."

Hojo taps the screen. "Both of these people are in every picture you'll find online of Bisset. They never leave his side, and rumor swears he and Karkaroff have a thing, meaning she doesn't even leave his side when he's sleeping. Both would be facing extradition to their respective countries — Ukraine and Nigeria — if there wasn't a suspicious amount of red tape between their current job with the senator and deportation. Everyone just … lets it be. Whether that's Bisset's doing or something else, I don't know. But I will tell you one thing."

Hojo taps the screen again. "If there's one person who has the connections to keep these two around and make sure their records stay clean — the *real* connections, under the surface — it's Zero. And that's what scares me."

I look over. You don't hear Hojo admit emotion often and never fear. Showing even the slightest alarm in our business is like wearing a shirt with a bulls-eye. There's a thin line between conducting civil business with a man like Hojo and simply cashing him out and robbing him blind. It's all attitude and artifice. Reveal a chink in your armor, and you might as well go shopping for a tombstone.

"*What* scares you?" Emil asks.

"I know a lot about Bisset — probably why Heinzie figured he'd better reach out and warn me that folks like you might come knocking. Not because I'm interested in the senator himself, per se. I'm more interested in what his existence — smack dab in the middle of our government — says about the world."

"What does it say, Hojo?" I ask.

"Politicians have always double-dealt. Promised one thing and done another. But … look at Kennedy. JFK put his dick into every wet and willing hole right under Jackie O's nose, but the media had a gentleman's agreement — sort of a code of honor. It's not that nobody knew about the president and Marilyn. It's that nobody *discussed* it. Today, everyone talks about everything."

I feel my muscles tighten. What I think Hojo is about to say, I've heard a thousand times from my brother. Hojo, so he can show us the laptop, is on the couch with us now. I'm surrounded by people who feel differently than I do about the way things are. If they realize it and start their bitching, things are going to get a lot less comfortable for me.

Hojo keeps going. "More and more, people make important decisions — about their leaders, for instance — based less on qualifications and more on something like a sideshow performance. It's no longer about who can do the job best. It's about who is the most entertaining. Politicians still put on a show, but now everyone *knows* exactly what it is. Gone are the days when everyone believed leaders were perfect even though they were adulterers and criminals. Now, we know what they are, but as long as they're amusing? Well, then something like a total lack of integrity no longer matters."

It's strange hearing Hojo talk about integrity. He has it, but it comes at a price.

"But we're beyond electing movie stars and pop culture figures with Bisset. He isn't a man with flaws who happens to look good on paper. No. Bisset actually looks *awful* on paper. Zero was never tried for anything criminal because nobody could prove he had anything to do with what the users on his website were up to. But he's still infamous, a disruptor, a loose cannon with some publicly stated opinions that are eyebrow-raising at the very least. His bodyguards are killers, but he's blocking their deportation from so far up, those with the power to deport don't even try.

"But that's not even the worst." Hojo eyes my brother. "Is it, Emil?"

"Are you talking about Float?"

Hojo reaches for an envelope. It has our last name on it, almost as if he prepared it for us the second he thought we might be coming.

"I'm talking about the fact that Senator Bisset has a cousin he likes very much who's a lot more accessible than Bisset himself." He taps the envelope, then adds, "Right here in Florida, not two hours away."

SIX

Float
_____

FLOAT.

I saw Emil's eyebrows raise when Hojo said it on the couch, then waited for Emil to turn in my direction. He never did, and it's felt like an undetonated bomb ever since.

Sixty minutes on the road so far, and I'm still waiting for what's coming to me.

"Lot of birds around here," I say.

"Edge of the Everglades. What do you expect?"

"I'm just saying there are a lot of birds."

"Why do I give a shit about birds?"

"You got a problem with birds?"

"Ever since that little brick shithouse started talking about their assholes back at Heinzie's, yeah, I've got a fucking problem with birds. Thirty years, I went without knowing they fuck and shit from the same hole. What are they, Caprice?"

"Who's Caprice?"

"Now you with the goddamn birds. Cranes, gulls, fucking nightingales, for all I know."

69

"I don't see any nightingales," I say.

"FUCK YOUR NIGHTINGALES!"

I wait for more, but that's all there is. One ejaculation of bird-related anger, and then he's back to driving, hands at ten and two, eyes on the swamp road ahead. We're on some sort of berm or levy, just a foot above water so thick with vegetation, you'd need a fan boat to get across it.

We had grandparents in Sarasota, near Tampa on the gulf side, and visits were fun. Only since have I learned how many people regard the state not as retirement in paradise but as a backwater with a dark side. Entrenched. Disconnected. Isolationist.

Don't-tread-on-me.

Florida's middle has scared the shit out of me ever since. If we break down, will the hillbillies help us or see us as too outsider to be worthy of saving? We have our guns, but the overalls crew will bring numbers. It only takes one swamp-cutting machete to end our lives — and if they toss us into the muck while we're still losing blood, how long will it be before the predators come?

I pick up a new phone from the bundle in the cupholder. This one is new for us; I tossed the last one into the aforementioned gator soup ten miles after yanking its battery. The thing takes its time to power up, hard erase, and finally start downloading my photos from the cloud. Those pics are my woobie, keeping me calm through the tension. But picking up the phone — and I'd have known this if I'd taken a half fucking second to think — was a mistake from Go.

Emil is already at me. "Jesus fucking Christ. You can't leave it alone for a minute."

"What?"

"That fucking electronic leash. You think you control it? That shit controls you."

I've heard this rant before, but this time its overwhelming force comes from out of the blue.

"Fine. I'll put it away."

"Now that it's on. Now that you've told all those computers where we are."

"Relax, Emil. I turned off the GPS. Turned off all location services."

"You think they don't know anyway?"

"Who?"

"They."

"Oh, for fuck's sake. Emil …"

"Macy Palumbo," he says. "You know Macy?"

"Of course, I know Macy."

"She and that kid of hers were sitting around one day looking for something to do, and the kid, Deuce, he's like, 'Let's play *Jenga*!' So they played *Jenga*."

"You know, Emil?" I say, rolling my eyes hard now. "That's a great story."

"Later that day, she starts getting ads for *Jenga* on her Facebooks. It listens to you whether you're using it or not."

I decide to rebut him obliquely. "There's just one Facebook, you know."

"Why don't you just shut the fuck up, Robert?"

I hold up the phone. "I'll shut up, sure. But let me tell the Facebooks first."

"You know what I—"

"All of them," I interrupt.

"Oh for—"

"How many Facebooks are there? Gotta be at least six or seven."

"Fuck you, Robert. Just fuck you with a spinning fan."

"I'll tell the Twitters, too. In fact? I'll just tell everyone on all of the internets."

"You know why I get it wrong? Because I don't fucking

care. I know all the terms like you do, and suddenly I'm like all the other shitbrains out there."

"What shitbrains?"

"Head bent over that little screen. Typing with my thumbs. Taking selfies." Emil gives me a duck-face, popular with the selfie crowd since *selfies* became a word.

"This is great, man. Tell me more about *Jenga*."

"I got more to say about *Jenga*. You bet your ass."

"Then, by all means." I compose myself, turn as far as I can in the passenger seat, fold my hands primly in my lap, and wait for Emil to shower me with all his superior, big-brother bullshit wisdom. He's two years older, after all. Knows the ways of the world that I, being junior and immature and stupid, can never know. "Lay it on me, Oracle."

Emil scowls. "You think you're so fucking smart. *Look at me — I know all the stupid mindless shit that everyone else knows!*"

"Everyone but you."

"'I don't know how to manage a team or change a tire, but I know how to make it look like I'm wearing an eyepatch using this dumb fucking thing that doesn't remotely matter!'"

"It doesn't matter to *you*," I say, more seriously. "That doesn't mean you have to shit all over everyone for whom it does matter."

He starts grumbling, just like an old man who suspects kids might be on his lawn. He mutters, "Empty, vacuous crap. Things in this world used to mean something."

"That's a great story, Grandpa."

"Now everyone's got a fucking opinion. And everyone's gotta *broadcast* that fucking opinion. Everyone's looking for something to be outraged by, without ever actually doing shit to change it. 'Earthquake in Somalia! Those poor people! Let me put a semi-transparent Somalian flat over my profile picture … that'll change the world!'"

"Oh, and you're changing the world?"

"Goddamn right, I'm changing the world."

"How?"

"I'm going to put a bullet in the head of the mother-fucker who invented Float."

"Oh," I say. "*There* it is."

"There *what* is?" Emil asks.

"You think I didn't see that little look you gave me when Hojo mentioned Float?"

"I didn't give you a look."

"Right." I laugh. "You also don't have an intrusive, high-fucking-handed opinion about *me* being on Float, right?"

"Of course, I do, Robert. Of course, I have a problem with it. You shouldn't be on *any* social media. You're a goddamn *hitman*."

"Nobody knows who I am."

"*Everyone* in our circle knows who you are, asshole. *Everyone*. There's not a single fucking person I know who hasn't heard every single story about you. The same goddamn stories, over and over and motherfucking over."

"Then maybe you should stop me. Log in for me. Close my account."

"I would if I could stomach it."

"What's *that* supposed to mean?"

"You're being stupid." Emil has gone from outrage mode to lecture mode — maybe all the way to conde-scending. "Think about what you're arguing for a second. There's already too much openness in the world, only it's not even real. It's only *surface* openness. Nobody eats a danish without sharing a photo of it anymore. Without 'checking in' so people know *where* they're eating that danish. Or who they're with. Tell you what, Robert. How about we stop and get a danish at that Dunkin' we passed before we started driving down this state's puckered asshole, and you can take a picture with one of your arms around each of us — me on one side, the danish on the other. You can share it. On Float. With the caption, *Killing senators makes me HUNGRY!*"

"I don't share anything like that, and you know it."

"But people know who you are."

"An *exaggerated version* of who I really am," I correct him. "The real Robert Hicks isn't on Float."

Emil laughs derisively.

"Nathan Patel has a Float profile for his dog."

"So?"

"The dog isn't even alive anymore. Jesus, Emil. Nobody assumes what's on any of social media is real."

Now I've done it. Emil takes his eyes off the road and one hand off the wheel so he can turn and properly point in my face. "See, that's where you're wrong. If everyone knew it was bullshit, there'd be no problem. At a costume party, there's no problem because everyone knows it's only pretend. Nobody sees the Grim Reaper on Halloween and freaks out. Social media is different. I suppose technically if you really pinned people down, we'd all agree that it's not real, but it still works the same as the news."

"Oh, great. I get your news rant, too?"

"The news isn't real, Robert. It's a tiny slice of what's actually happening in the world, and whoever's in charge gets to decide what they show and how they slant it. There's no 'fair and balanced' on either side. Those in charge of the media get to tell the story their way, just like how victors get to write history books from their point of view. If people truly understood that, we'd be okay, but they don't. People believe what the TV tells them. They believe what the internet tells them. They believe what their *friends* say the internet told *them*."

Emil pauses, and I hope that's it.

But of course, it isn't.

"From every side, we're being fed bullshit that fuels someone else's agenda. They want us to be afraid, they show us what will make us afraid, so we'll give them anything just to feel safe again. They want us outraged, so they show us outrage, expecting that we'll support whoever takes action. Bored housewives clean before they share photos of their clean house. Gym rats dehydrate, do crunches, and oil up before displaying their abs. Perfection is an ideal, only nobody ever reaches it. We only think they do because everyone wants to look their best, so they lie and show the world what they want it to see."

"Emil …"

"Plastic fucking world. Nobody has any flaws, except that everyone does. Everyone is happy, except that they're all really miserable. Everyone's doing super, and meanwhile, they're fucked. Nobody talks about the gnawing pain we all feel deep down — the hollow, existential certainty that nothing we do even matters. That the philosophers were right, and we're flotsam in the stream of something that doesn't remotely care and that we'll never understand. Nobody looks it in the eye and admits the pointlessness of it all because they'd have to turn around and look in the mirror first. People polish their turds until *they* eventually believe they're diamonds. You and me. Brother to brother. Having that is the only thing keeping us from total despair."

I usually fight back at these rants and had my knives all sharpened to do so. But the way Emil ended that last bit is sadder than a rant. It makes something drop from the pit of my stomach, just like it's dropped from the pit of his.

"Jesus, Emil."

"Fuck you, Robert."

He pulls over. I'm not sure what this is, but I don't like it one goddamn bit.

"What's going on." It's not a question, just a statement as dead as Emil's picture of the universe.

"Give me that."

Emil means the phone. I tuck it back. I've taken new photos of the Everglades already, and they have yet to sync.

"Give me the phone, Robert."

I extend it halfway. He snatches it before I can pull it back.

Emil exits the car, then I do the same. The levy has steepened, the road now four or five feet above the swamp below. I can see green-brown logs not far off; some have bumps at one end that I'd swear were eyes. Supposedly they're only fast over short distances. If any of those lizards come closer while we're out here, if for some reason I can't get back into the car, I just have to stay ten feet back. They lunge, then stop. At least that's what I found online when I looked it up.

Emil moves to the front of the car. I skirt the berm, noting with alarm just how close to the edge this road has forced us to drive and follow.

He throws the phone onto the gravel, then removes a pistol he must have grabbed from the back seat. It's not the 9mm. It's the .45, giant as a hoss.

"Emil, it's—"

I can't finish before he shoots the phone to shrapnel. Three times, bang-bang-bang. And he's an assassin, remember. Every shot hits its target.

The phone is bits and pieces once he's finished.

"Feel better?" I ask into the quiet. Thank God we're in the middle of a hobo's butthole. They must shoot swamp rats out here all the time — and in frontier America, the smartest citizens know better than to ask questions when shots are fired.

It takes Emil a moment to respond, and in that moment, I wonder if it's finally over. If he's finally broken, and this thing we do has finally come to an end.

"Bisset created Float," he says instead. "If half of what Hojo said is true, he's got backdoor deals with most of the outlets out there. That means none of your little outline playgrounds are safe. You want to tell the world you bought a danish, you push it down and keep your fucking mouth shut. Do you understand me?"

I consider cracking wise, but Emil's holding his gun and has that look in his eye. He might shoot me. Or himself.

"Sure, Emil. Sure."

"We have some of his network." He looks back at the car, meaning all the info Hojo sold us. "And we know his weakness." He looks forward to the semi-known place this nowhere road will lead us.

"You bet. Whatever you say, brother."

"We're going to get to him first, Robert. You and me. Brother to brother."

"Sure thing, Emil." I think he might hear the worry in my voice, that he'll take my sudden and unflinching agreement as patronizing rather than genuine. But he doesn't. When it comes to me, Emil has always had massive blind spots.

"We're going to find him and kill him. Together."

"Of course we are."

A long moment passes. When I look back at Emil, I'd swear there's a tear rimming his eye.

"This is all that matters," he says.

"Sure."

"We're not just talking, Robert. We're *doing*."

"I know we are."

He heads back to the car, but before he gets in, he looks me right in the eye.

"You and me, brother. We're going to save the world."

SEVEN

Serendipity Or Chaos

TWENTY MINUTES LATER, I'm trying to decide if this job is lucky or unlucky, a good thing or a bad thing, serendipity or chaos gone bad like months-old milk.

We kill people for money, but this time our target is someone Emil would have wanted to kill anyway. If the bounty were rescinded, I don't think he'd want to turn around and go home. After speaking with Hojo, all the questionable shit about Bisset has blended with fresh information that digs his senatorial grave deeper. Truth is, either Bisset or Emil is a dead man. Emil will end him, watch him get killed by someone else, or die trying. I know this as if I were inside his skull instead of my own.

I can see in Emil's right eye (the only one visible in profile as he drives and I sit in hands-folded silence) just how hot this particular fire has gotten. His hands, dutifully at ten and two, are peach sausages interrupted by bone-white knuckles. His teeth aren't visible, but I know they're gritted. I see tiny muscles flexing on and off, unable to decide if they want to lie down or clench hard enough to sever his tongue.

"You okay, man?"

Emil doesn't seem to hear me. His attention is fixed inward on this one chance to eradicate all he sees as wrong in one symbolic swoop. It's as if someone dug all the badness from the depths of my brother's soul, then put it in a charcoal suit and power tie and taught it to filibuster.

Normally, a man can't fight the things he feels have wounded his past: a lifetime of insults and snubs, parents who didn't love him or know how to show it, bullies of all ages and stages, missed or failed opportunities, and choices he'd rather not believe were his own, but instead subconsciously blames on someone else.

"Emil. Are you——?"

One of the phones rings. We've got maybe a dozen in the car, and it's not the active one, so it takes me some time and a fair amount of confused searching before I finally find it. By the time I narrow the field to the cluster inside the console, my time is up, and the call's gone to voicemail. Fifteen seconds later, I find the culprit, knowing by the *Missed call* notification on its lock screen. I hold it up for Emil to see. Or *not* to see, since he's too busy staring mentally unstable daggers at the road.

I roll down the window, holding the phone with a napkin from the glove compartment.

"What are you doing?" Emil asks.

"Throwing it into the swamp. We can't use the thing if it's——"

"Christ, Robert. Really?"

"I just wiped the fingerprints. Whoever's calling will assume the phone got lost. Nobody's going to call the cops to triangulate on its last known position."

"I mean, maybe that call is for us."

"It's not the active phone. I have our numbers ported to this one." I hold up a loose iPhone from the cup holder.

The phone rings again in my hand. Emil plucks it away from me, looks at the screen and the phone itself (green rubberized case, scratch across the front), then hovers his thumb above the screen.

"What the hell do you think you're doing?" I ask before he can touch it.

"Answering a call."

"You can't do that!"

Emil does it anyway. Then he presses the phone against his real face containing his real DNA using his real fingers with real fingerprints on the ends. Even I use speakerphone and napkins when I'm able.

"Yeah," Emil says.

I hear someone's voice, far and tinny.

"Yeah." Pause. "Fuck. You're sure?" Pause. "On it." Then he hangs up without saying goodbye.

"What the hell, Emil?"

"That was Rumy."

"*Your* Rumy?" Meaning the woman Emil has loud sex with whenever he's agitated, the way an angry man hits a punching bag to vent anger. I quickly learned to leave when Rumy visits. Plaster falls from the ceiling, doorknobs rattle, and you'd swear there was murder afoot. When Rumy's not bellowing like a woman being burned alive, she's calling Emil nonsensical names like *Fucktwat* and *Assfart*. Either Rumy is so lost in passion she can't think straight, or she's incredibly uninventive. The kind of person whose passwords are all *Password*. The kind of person who names a dog Fido or Spot.

"You know a lot of Rumys?"

"I mean … But … *This* is the active phone." Again I hold up the one in rose gold, strewn with sparkles.

"Will you fucking relax? That's her phone. She gave it to me for this trip."

"Why?"

"I don't need you to do *all* my thinking for me, Robert. Believe it or not, some of my brain still belongs to me."

"But …" There are so many questions, but I let them go when he pushes forward, ignoring the look that must be on my face right now.

"She says someone was snooping around our place. Just an hour ago."

"Who?"

"Don't know. Man. Tall. Black hair."

"Did she say what he looked like?"

"She said he was wearing a hoodie and kept the hood up. She never got a look at his face. Just saw a nose. Big, like Sean's."

"Sean who?"

"I think it might have been that guy Blackhawk."

"You mean the *assassin* Blackhawk?"

"You know a lot of Blackhawks?"

I consider asking more, but there's really no point. Emil is convinced, so I suppose I'm convinced.

"Okay," I say.

"So he's after us. Probably one of Heinzie's side bets. After this job is over, maybe we solve that problem."

"By killing Blackhawk?"

"By killing Heinzie."

"Oh. All right." I suppose it's okay. Heinzie has never been a friend, and there's not really anything redeeming about him. He's not even a good criminal. Everyone knows he's into hardcore torture porn that's a bit too real for fiction, but he buys it from a chronic public masturbator named Slim, who spends literally half his time in the town jail for exposing himself to schoolchildren. Heinzie has always been a necessary evil, but after this job, he'll lose his value. I'm okay with dusting the guy, and maybe we'll just go ahead and handle Slim while we're at it.

"But right now," Emil continues, "we've got another problem."

"What's that?"

"Rumy says he was in our garage."

"Probably whacking it to those Victoria's Secret catalogs you insist on saving."

"Rumy says he had a stepladder out, in the middle of the garage."

"So, whacking it from up high."

"I'll bet he was cloning our garage door opener."

"Holy shit! Now he'll be able to whack it over your catalogs whenever he wants!"

"Goddammit, Robert. You're really not figuring this out?"

It comes to me. Most assassins are arrogant and feel they know the best way to do their thing, but we've been learners since we were little kids. Anyone who knows new stuff that might help us get better, live better, earn better, kill better — we lap it up like a kitten drinking cream.

Six months ago, Hojo set us up with a B&E specialist named June, who taught us all about garage door openers. You wouldn't think that'd be a sexy topic, but a lot of openers these days are tied to the home's wifi using a plug-in dongle, allowing the operator to open and close the door by way of an app. A good hacker can reverse-engineer the pairing process, then use it to triangulate on any manual openers out in the field — anywhere at all, so long as they're close enough to a cell tower for service. It's complicated, and I remember little of it, but the details don't matter. Point is, if Blackhawk knows what he's doing, he now knows where Emil and I are. He'll probably have figured out we went to see Hojo and maybe even where we're headed now.

"Fuck," I say. "When?"

"Yesterday around three."

I can't believe what I'm hearing. *"Yesterday?"* And to think, the conversation I heard was so civil and short. You'd think a guy with his life to lose would shout over something like that, but thanks to our previous pit stop, Emil seems to have blown his emotional wad for the day.

"I know. She apologized. She had to rush off to a hair appointment and meant to call when she was done but forgot."

"Her hair? Her goddamn *hair.*"

Emil doesn't answer. He knows I hate Rumy and seems to know I'm too spent for another fight. Remember Peg Bundy from *Married With Children*? Rumy's that.

I look at the road, then around the car. I'm far from panicked; you learn to squash hard-edged emotions doing what we do. Logic has to shine through. But I'm agitated. And concerned. I want to punch Rumy right through her fucking beehive the next time I see her.

My first idea, as my thoughts gel, is to throw the opener out the window like I'd been planning to do with the iPhone, but our pursuer already knows enough that tossing it now won't matter. And besides, digital openers are standard now, including in this car. There's no plastic remote clipped to the sun shade. You program the remote directly into your system. Like an increasing number of cars on the road today, Emil's is more computer than machine.

"Did the guy see Rumy?" I ask.

"She doesn't think so."

"Then maybe it's not a problem."

I look at Emil and know that he's thinking the same

thing I am. If Blackhawk doesn't know that *we* know he was at our place, he'll believe he has the upper hand. He'll think he knows where we are, and therefore can catch us by surprise. But we know what he's up to, thanks to Emil's fuck buddy. And that, if we play it right, gives us the upper hand.

Of course, there's still a problem.

"We need a new car," I say.

We've got a guy for that, but there's no time. If Rumy saw Blackhawk in Napierville nearly twenty-four hours ago, he'll have triangulated and be on his way already. I'm shocked that we haven't been sniped. Must be the swamp and its total backwoods assholery slowing him down. There's nothing out here but XXX moonshine and corn-hole. Not the kind you play with beanbags and a slanted board.

"Yeah," Emil says.

"Chance the GPS?" I ask, picking up our current phone.

"No choice. He already knows where we are. The cops need a warrant and cause. Lawyer can't keep us out of prison anyway if we're dead."

So I turn on the GPS, noting the signal's weakness. It's a bit disturbing, really. You get used to that digital tether, and it unnerves me whenever I know we're truly off the grid.

But it still shows me the road, a tiny town, and what's ahead.

"There's a Sloppy's up there." Then I point to the distant ghost of an overpass. "I think that's the state route. Go one exit south."

Emil wrinkles his nose. "Sloppy's tastes like unwashed vag."

"Appropriate, then," I say, thinking of Rumy.

EIGHT

The Heaping Plate

VAG OR NOT, Sloppy's is actually the perfect place to steal a car.

The most popular car on the road is the Honda Accord, and I counted six on the short walk from our parking stop to the fingerprint-infested front door. The crowd is firmly lower middle class — especially so since this particular Sloppy's is in a truck stop — and lower middle class is the Honda Accord of social strata. Drive a lower-end Accord out of a place like this, and you're easing into the fattest part of all possible bell curves. Despite the fuckery, I'm actually relieved. Emil's car is too nice, and even swapping plates at every state line wasn't (in my opinion, anyway) enough to make it vanish. We're two clean-cut types with hundred-dollar haircuts driving a car that costs six times the national average. At least after we steal something more mainstream, we'll disappear the way we should have from the start.

"This place smells like a bricklayer's asshole," says Emil one step inside the place. He glances up at the menu, says,

"Fuck any place with a burger called the True American," then walks out without another word.

I follow him across the parking lot to another restaurant. This one sit-down instead of fast food. It's called The Heaping Plate, and it looks like the place delivers on its promise.

We stop in front of the hostess stand. A bronze plate, even more finger-smudged than the doors, reads PLEASE WAIT AND THE HOSTESS WILL SEAT YOU. Cheap glossy menus sit stacked in a cubby stuck to the side of the stand. The laminate has peeled at the corners and taken the paper beneath with it on every one of them. It's like they've all bloomed the way lilies bloom, except that instead of pistils and stamens, the bud is packed with microwaved mediocrity.

The hostess could be on a poster for overworked single mothers. No question, she has kids and hates them all just a little at the end of her day because the look she gives us is the sort of maternal stare that's had just about enough of this bullshit.

"How many?"

"Two," Emil tells her. Then he turns and gives me a look that says, *What, does she think we'd invite* more *people to this walk-in rectum?* "Not in the middle. Against the wall or a window."

She takes us to one of those half-booths that looks like it should apologize to its subjects.

"Not here," Emil says as she gestures.

"Okay," she says. It almost elongates into a sarcastic *Oh-kaaaay*, but she manages to bury her irritation enough to keep things brief. "So … You want …?"

"I don't like to sit with my back to people."

She looks around. The booth is by the wall, just like Emil asked.

"This is right next to the fucking kitchen."

She doesn't even look, let alone smile or apologize for the nothing she's done wrong. Instead, she leads us to a corner booth and sets two menus on the table. I won't be eating if this woman is our waitress. There'll be piss in my coffee, without question.

"Shelby will be right with you." And then she's gone.

Emil opens the menu using only two fingers and a thumb on each hand. It's important that everyone in the place know he'd rather not be here.

"Meatloaf," Emil says. "I *knew* there'd be meatloaf here."

"You have a problem with meatloaf?"

"I don't give a fuck about meatloaf. I care about what meatloaf *means*. Meatloaf on a menu says, *Sit down and eat what the fuck we give you because it's all there fucking is.*"

"There's a lot on this menu besides meatloaf."

"Fucking brick made of pig assholes," Emil goes on. "Can't decide what the hell it is."

"We could have eaten at Sloppy's."

"Fuck that place even harder. They might microwave all their meat here, but at least it used to be alive."

"I'm not sure that I'd call that *living*. We've both seen the documentaries."

Emil pitches his voice to imitate what I have to assume is a Heaping Plate line cook. "'*What the fuck is that? Oh, who cares. Toss it in the meatloaf, and the assholes out there will never know.*' There could be cats in meatloaf for all you know. Oh. And Jesus fucking Christ. Salisbury steak. I thought that was illegal to serve outside of middle school cafeterias suffering from budget cuts."

"It's all there was, Emil. We're in the middle of nowhere, and you didn't want Sloppy's."

He folds his menu, then folds his hands far away from it. "Fuck it. I'm not eating."

"That'll show 'em."

"Show who?"

"Whoever owns this place."

"I don't give a fuck what—"

"You sure? Because you're putting on a helluva show here. Talk a little louder, will you, Emil?"

"We're here to steal a car, not shovel mediocrity down our throats."

"Fine. But I'm hungry."

"Not for food, though? Usually, when people are hungry, it's for food."

"You're such an elitist prick. What, the beef here isn't Kobe enough for you?"

Emil half-rolls his eyes, crosses his arms, looks away, and mutters, "There's no beef here."

Giving Emil any attention at all when he's like this is throwing kerosene onto a fire, so I pretend he doesn't exist. I'm sitting in this booth by myself, talking to my invisible friend. When the server comes over, I'll order, and she won't see Emil. *That's* how determined I am to ignore his little tantrum.

I flip to the breakfast page, deciding that breakfast is usually safe. Bacon and eggs can be Grade F and get left in the warmth to fester past their expiration date, but both are hearty foods, able to survive quite a while under even extreme neglect. They'll fry it in years-old grease, and I might be queasy, but it won't see the end of me. Not like the meatloaf would.

There's a picture of the meatloaf. Bad choice. Food ages like six months once photographed. The loaf seems to be a gray chunk of congealed upchuck. I'm less sure that it's food than the molded leavings from a dryer's lint trap.

Emil taps my arm. He has to do it twice since I'm pretending so hard that he doesn't exist.

"Hey."

"Eat or don't eat. Like I fucking care."

"No. Look."

I lower the menu, then Emil's finger, low and on the sly.

"Not now!"

I swivel back. "Then why'd you tell me to look?"

"Have you never been in public before? When someone says to look, you don't immediately stare."

I usually have a tank's tolerance for Emil's personality, but right now, I feel wafer-thin. So I break character to piss him off, turning again in his indicated direction and staring hard enough to make out the fine print on the Heimlich poster near the bathrooms.

Emil reacts, so I yell at the patrons, "OH MY GOD LOOK AT THE SHIT OVER THERE!"

He hits my arm. Not a slap   a closed fist.

"Ow!"

"What's wrong with you?"

"First, you say look. Then you tell me not to."

"Why do you have to be an asshole?" Emil hisses.

"Nobody's even paying attention. Nobody hears me or cares." It's true, too. None of the people around us so much as raised their heads. A truism about life: the more you find yourself in the humdrum, the more hypnotized the people around you tend to be. Nobody cares enough to acknowledge oddity or make waves, seeing as all they've got going is a crappy job and a spouse who probably sleeps through sex. I could pull someone from a booth right now and shoot their head from their neck, and it's doubtful anyone would even look my way.

"You done?" Emil asks.

"If you are."

"So look," he repeats.

I look again. I see chipped tables, peeling linoleum, and a stain on the wall whose origin I can't remotely fathom. There's really only one thing of note in view, and knowing my brother as well as I do, I'm sure it's what he means for me to see.

A woman, sitting alone. Late twenties, tiny boobs, wrists strung with cheap costume jewelry, ripped jeans, dark hair the size of a two-floor condo. White tank top, no bra, nipples puckering the fabric like a pair of bullet points — two key elements in the grade-school outline of her personality. She looks like she missed the bus for Tiffany's 1983 mall concert tour and has been here, in a time warp, ever since. Exactly Emil's type, down to her boyish chest. Just like Rumy.

"And?"

"She was looking over here a second ago. Right at me."

"Okay." I pick the menu back up.

"Robert. Go to the bathroom."

"Here? But I just bought these pants."

He hits me again. "Go to the fucking restroom. Get out of the booth for a few minutes."

"Why?"

"Because she thinks I'm with you."

I put my hand on the back of my booth, then turn my entire torso to slowly survey the room. I finally return to Emil, sarcasm queued like the next round in the chamber. "You know, I think that too."

"Fuck off for a bit."

"What, are you going to diddle her right here in the booth?"

Not that I doubt it. Emil is bold and far too confident

with women. And no offense to Tiffany Tour over there, but I'm betting she's trailer park enough to allow it.

"No, I …" Emil trails off as a mustard-colored shape intrudes on our peripheral vision.

I look over to see a short, round woman in a server's uniform. A tiny rectangle on her chest reads, SHELBY.

She only speaks in run-on monotone sentences. "Hi I'm Shelby I'll be taking care of you today can I get you something to drink."

"Coffee."

"Yeah," Emil says, blinking away this sudden change of topic, from boners to food, that angers him. "Just the coffee and water for me."

"So just the coffee and water and no food," Shelby says.

I see a twitch in Emil's eye. She's forcing him to say the words.

"Gimmie the waffle." He also seems to have decided that breakfast is safest.

"And I'll have the #1 breakfast combo," I tell her. "Eggs sunny side up."

Emil seems intrigued. "What's in that?"

"Flour egg water I can ask the kitchen."

"Not the waffle," Emil says. He opens the menu, finds the combo on his own, and says, "You know what? Fuck the waffle. Make it *two* #1 breakfast combos, *both* sunny side up."

"You want two #1s anything else."

"Toast," I say. "Wheat toast. Dry."

"Aaand," Emil says, scanning. Now that he's past his elitist crap, he's getting hungry. But instead of saying more, he closes it again. He's on and off a diet forever. It's annoying every time we eat. "Forget it," he finally says.

"Anything else."

"No."

"I'll put that in you need anything else you just let me know okay," Shelby says, done with us.

Emil stacks the menus and sets them to the side after Shelby leaves since she didn't take them. Now they're next to a rice-filled salt shaker and sugar sifter in which the sugar has turned to stone.

"Probably going to get salmonella poisoning," Emil says, muttering to no one. "Should have had them make the eggs scrambled. That shit isn't even eggs. It comes out of a box." He looks to the kitchen door through which Shelby disappeared, seeming to wonder if he should chase her with a correction.

But then she's back, occupying that same corner-of-the-eye position as before. Only when we both look over, we see it's not Shelby. It's Emil's girl.

"Let me guess," she says. "You're not from around here."

I mutter something that's clearly meant to brush her off, but she ignores me, waiting for Emil's response, not mine.

"Not really," he finally says.

"My friend didn't show up. I hate eating alone. Is it okay if I join you?"

Emil leaps to comply so fast, it's like his dick is controlling his logic. Which, I know from painful experience, it probably is. He ticks his head at me. "Scoot in."

"Emil, no." Then I look at the girl. "I don't mean to be rude, but we have business to discuss."

The girl slides in next to me anyway. I didn't preemptively scoot because I thought I was at least fifty percent in charge here, but apparently, I was wrong. She smells like bathroom vending machine perfume, and she gives me a face full of tits before I manage to get out of the way.

"Emil. Seriously," I say, now jammed in next to the sugar and salt.

"We've got some time," Emil says.

"I know I do," the woman says. "I'm Renee."

"Emil." He reaches across to shake her hand, but she takes it like a silk hankie.

"Emil?"

"Yeah. Emil."

"What an unusual name." She practically purrs.

"I'm Robert," I say, but again she ignores me.

"How's that spelled?" Her eyes are boring into my brother.

"E-M-I-L."

"That's a cute name."

"Cute?"

"Sexy, even."

"You know," Emil says, "I had a babysitter as a kid named Renee."

"Oh yeah? What was she like?"

"Goddammit, Emil. We have things we need to talk about. Like where we're going next. Like who we … you know … need to stay ahead of."

"Later." Then to Renee he says, "She was tall and leggy. Wore those little ragged jean shorts with the pockets hanging out. I always had a crush on her."

"That's sweet."

"Fucking hell," I say.

Emil turns to me. "Hey, why don't you go take a powder."

"You mean to the bathroom?" Renee asks, thinking Emil must have meant her.

"I just meant that—"

"I think that's a great idea," she says, a wide smile blooming. She glances toward the rear. "Now?" There's a glint in her eyes, and it's clear she's getting this wrong. I'm supposed to leave, not her. But she's all lusty now like Emil's invited her for a rendezvous in the stall.

She gets out of the booth, but my brother's clearly not getting it. He can't switch gears, seeing as the suggestion was meant for me. He looks up at Renee, confused.

"Well, we have food coming."

"Yeah," I agree. "We have food coming. And you probably do, too."

Movement under the table catches my eye, Renee's foot rising to brush Emil's.

"You've gotta be kidding me," I say.

So, to keep myself from screaming or puking, I get out of the booth while Renee's already up. I throw a stare at my brother, then visit the filthy restroom. I splash my face with water, take a leak, and wash my hands. Somehow I leave feeling less clean than when I came in.

I get back to the table and find Renee on Emil's side of the table with her hand in his lap. They stop whatever they're up to, but only because my brother is eyeing my return. Renee is still getting handsy and giggling, and Emil has to forcibly move her hand.

Shelby arrives, glances at Renee, and seems to decide none of this is interesting enough for a comment. She's carrying my coffee and Emil's water and sets both in the middle of the table. Emil reaches for the coffee, either forgetting he didn't order one or being a fucker.

The waitress looks at Renee. "You want another coffee or what?"

"Sure." It's clear Renee knows she's ordering on our tab and that she expected as much and doesn't give the remotest of shits.

"I'm sorry," says Emil — a man who never apologizes. "I'm being rude. Take this one."

He pushes his own coffee — *my* coffee — into her hands. I'm surprised to see that her nails are short and that there are calluses on her palms. I expected salon hands, but she actually looks like she might know how to change a tire.

She turns to me. "Hand me a Sweet'N Low?"

Bitch. She could easily reach it herself and without even disturbing my space.

I reach, but Emil, now sandwiched between her ass and the condiment caddy, reaches faster. With delicate, bird-like motions, Renee shakes the sweetener down in the packet and rips off the top, then blows to open it wider. A flirty move, like running hands through her hair — something else she's done constantly since she intruded. Showcasing her brightly colored lips, puckered as if for the world's tiniest blowjob.

"Look," I say. "I don't mean to be rude, but—"

"Then don't," Emil interrupts.

"Don't what?" Renee asks.

"Don't be rude."

When she reaches for his crotch again, I reach for my coffee — now Renee's — and drag it back to my side. She looks at Emil, not me.

"If you're not going back to your own table, at least get back over here so you won't be tempted to lay your hand on his dick."

Now she's looking between me and Emil.

"Just …" Emil sighs, giving up. "Just do what he says."

She seems confused but follows Emil's gesturing hand to my side of the booth. Next minute we're back like we were, only Renee has taken her new position as a prompt to restart her foot-diddling.

"I think I might take that powder now." She leans in, eyes grazing to the bathroom and back again. I want to shiver. Fucking in a bathroom here must be like getting it on inside a troll's intestine. You wouldn't have to put it in anyone's asshole to come out with a shit-covered dick.

"Good. You two go bump uglies. I have to catch up on the world anyway." I know what I'm about to do is a mistake, but I'm far beyond caring. I slipped our active phone into my pocket when we left the car, and now I pull it out and start working it with both thumbs.

"Hey, look," I say of the screen. "Says on Float that Kim Kardashian's ass now has its own zip code."

Emil reacts at the trigger word. It happens without his brain's permission or his cock's. He's up in a blink, half-standing and constrained from tackling me only by the intervention of the table between us. He slaps at my phone, hitting the glass instead.

Water goes everywhere, including (satisfyingly) right into the tiny purse Renee's been mothering in her lap. She screeches, exiting to avoid the wave. I want to laugh. Her hands are up and flapping, and with the crotch of her jeans now darker than the rest, it looks like she's pissed herself.

"What the hell?" she blurts.

Emil is out a second later, glaring down at me. I smile. I've still got the phone, still tapping every time he takes a breath.

A big trucker type rises from another booth, closing fast. There's no hesitation on this one. He's Dudley Fucking Do-Right, just waiting for his chance to come to the aid of a lady in distress.

He glares at Emil, who's half angry and half befuddled next to Renee.

"There a problem here?" he demands.

"No," Emil says. "No problem."

"I'm not talking to you, buddy. I'm talking to the lady."

Lady. It's a laugh. With Emil occupied in a standoff that he could easily win but won't try to (we're keeping a low profile, after all), I slip out of the booth and stand a few feet away, as if I'm not any part of this.

"It's fine," Renee says.

But she pulls back when Emil reaches to help her. That makes me want to laugh even harder. She's blaming Emil for knocking over the water, not me for provoking him. It's like Christmas came early.

A waitress that isn't Shelby arrives with a second coffee, apparently covering while Shelby's busy with something — probably smoking three or four cigarettes at once while wondering where her life went barreling off the wrong cliff. A pock-faced Hispanic man wearing a hairnet holds a tray full of food behind the waitress. Two #1 breakfast combos, but no toast. Of course. Fucking Shelby. Can't even get my order right.

"It's no problem," says the Hispanic man, unfolding a restaurant stand and setting the platter full of food atop it. "I'll grab a rag."

"It's okay." Then Renee looks right at Emil while speaking to the man and the waitress, "I'll just move to the dry side."

She sits where Emil was, staring up at us. Then there's someone else behind us, and he's got a mustache that even porn would probably reject. His short-sleeved white collared shirt tells me that he must be the manager.

"Is there a problem here?" It's like he and the trucker went to the same school of chivalry.

Emil considers them all: the trucker, the waitress and the man with the hairnet, the manager, Renee, and all of the staring diners. I can see wheels turning in his head, but we both know what has to happen. We're two killers, meant to walk like ninjas and never leave a trace. Obviously, we can't make more of a scene than we already have. One way or the other, we need to get out of here.

"No." Emil turns on his heel and marches for the door, grabbing me roughly by the arm as he goes.

"It was nice meeting you," Renee calls, her voice mocking.

I turn to look and see the waitress giving her both of our meals, as the manager informs her that it's all on the house.

NINE

A Leaf In The Breeze

A HALF-HOUR LATER, we're cruising along the top of a levee road exactly like the last one, Emil now driving the least-shitty Accord on the lot. I argued for going elsewhere, considering the stink we'd already made, but the decision was out of our hands. All four of our tires had been slashed.

This, I blame on Emil. I have to assume it was done by one of Renee's quiet dining room admirers, and we gave them time to do it by stopping to buy less conspicuous clothes in the truck stop store. It couldn't have been hard to pick Emil's car out from the rest. We stuck out, despite our best efforts to dress down. Rural Florida seems to have its own dress code, and a pair of rich assholes from up north hassling a lady? It'd be more than enough for half of those hicks.

"I'm hungry."

"Shouldn't have fucked things up for us in there, then," Emil says.

"Me?"

"You."

"You're the one who spilled the water."

Emil shakes his head, then pounds a fist on the wheel. "They gave away all our food. For fucking free."

"Of course they did. She was pulling a two-bit scam, Emil. You're smart enough to know better. Too bad your dick bought it — hook, line, and sinker."

"Fuck you, Robert. Don't talk to me."

Fifteen seconds pass. Then Emil opens his mouth again. "Just what the fuck's your problem?"

"So you're talking to me now?"

"All I wanted was a little ass. I haven't had sex in two months. *Two goddamn months,* Robert. Fucking jobs, back to back … Goddammit. I would have been finished in seconds. Back before the food arrived."

"You weren't, though."

"Because you kept cockblocking."

"What, you think she was actually going to fuck you?"

"Of course, she was going to fuck me!"

"It's a goddamn scam! You hear me?"

"A scam for what?"

"It doesn't matter! Probably has six cents in her bank account. Ten bucks is a lot to these people. She gets a free meal, and that's all she needs to call it a victory."

We fall back into silence. I'm tempted to pick up a phone and start playing games to pass the time. I'm also considering picking up one of the phones and logging onto Twitter or Facebook just to see what's happening and maybe piss Emil off. I'm a bit wary of Float now, at least. I can't help feeling now that every time I'm on there, Senator Bisset, Zero, is right over my shoulder.

Not that it's stopped me. At The Heaping Plate, right after we sat down, I sneaked one of the phones into the bathroom. I know enough not to post, but there's no harm in reading what's there just so I can stay on top of things.

But I keep my hands in my lap and say nothing.

"Hand me my ChapStick."

I look over, wondering if this is Emil talking to me again. What happened at the restaurant is his fault without question, but Emil's great at denial. He'll invent just about anything if it protects his mind from his emotions. This is all my fault already, I'm sure, and with time the story will shift until I'm entirely to blame.

It's happening already. Right now, I'm wondering if I should have let them play. Maybe we'd have left the restaurant fed, inconspicuous, and without raising flags for the cops that were likely already called, for a stolen Accord at a truck stop in the middle of Fuckall.

Good thing the cops here don't pay attention and that authorities don't respond well to backwater emergencies. A great poet once said, *911 is a joke.* He also wore a clock around his neck.

Emil asking me to fetch his lip balm is as close as I'm going to get to a declaration of peace, so I take it. We both learned the ways of life from our father. You don't resolve issues as a man. You just kind of mutually agree to look somewhere else, and maybe the problems will go away by the time you look back.

So I open the console between us.

"Not in there."

I look in the open compartment below the radio and air conditioner controls.

"Not there, either. This isn't our car, dipshit."

Of course, it's not. We stripped everything personal from Emil's car before stealing a new one, then drove it into the swamp on its rims. We bought the thing through a fence, and neither of us have prints on record.

"In the back," Emil says.

I look to where we threw all we took from the old car — a banker's box full of belongings, like an office worker's final take after getting let go.

"Where?"

"In my holster," Emil says, now sounding annoyed.

"You want ChapStick, right?"

"That's what I said."

"ChapStick. In your shoulder holster."

"What the fuck do you think the little extra compartment is for?"

"Not for ChapStick."

"Just get it, Robert. I left it in the back seat before we went into Sloppy's."

"That compartment is meant for lipstick," I tell him.

"Should be on the top of the shit in that box now. I put it in last."

"Or mascara," I say.

"Robert."

"But mainly, it's for douche. In case you need to wash out your pussy."

"Oh, you don't get chapped lips?"

"I sure don't keep ChapStick in my shoulder holster."

"It's just convenient. I get dry."

"We're in Florida."

"I get dry when we're in Arizona. In the desert. What the fuck's it matter to you?"

"I guess you need it." Pause. "After sucking all those dicks."

"That's real enlightened of you, Robert. Real woke."

"I'm not here to be woke. I'm here to tell you that a hitman who carries ChapStick in his holster is a joke. A fucking embarrassment."

"And you're doing that by equating embarrassment with homosexuality?"

"Now you're just being absurd."

"If I wanted to suck dicks, I'd suck dicks," Emil says. "No matter what you think about it."

"Then, by all means. Let's suck some dicks. That'll show me. That'll prove you're a modern man."

"Robert?"

I look over. Emil hits me in the chin with a closed fist.

"Now get my goddamn ChapStick."

I reach back and rummage for a second. I slip the tube of lip balm from a compartment that, now that I'm thinking about it, I'm not sure what it's for. Maybe Emil is on to something. I could keep all kinds of close-at-hand things in there.

I hand it over without a word. A half-minute passes before something dawns on me. I look back, front, back again. Then I have it.

"Emil. Where's your gun?"

"You mean the rifle?"

"I mean your .45."

"What about it?"

"It's not in the holster."

"You think I'd just leave a loaded gun in the back seat? Of course, it's not in the holster."

"So, where is it?"

Emil loses his smarmy expression. He reaches for the small of his back, but his skin has already told him there's nothing shoved back there, between his upper ass and the Honda's seat. You get used to the feeling of carrying a gun behind you, but that's in a chair or a booth. Car seats tip down. Try to ride with a gun behind you while driving, and it's like a robot pervert is trying to get friendly behind you.

"Shit."

"Did you leave it in the old car?" I'm trying not to be angry, but we're at least an hour away — and that doesn't account for the car itself likely being halfway to the bottom of the Everglades by now. I'm not diving for Emil's gun in alligator water, but we can't just leave it there. The car is one thing — clean when we got it, now impervious only to the most microscopic of forensics probes. But the gun has been used for murder, and a routine ballistics investigation could pair the weapon with bullets fired from its chamber.

I hope Emil's in a swimming mood because if that's what happened, he's going in the drink whether he likes it or not.

"No."

"Good. Because—"

"I think I left it inside."

For a moment, we hear only tires on gravel.

Then, "Tell me you're kidding."

All of his arrogance and swagger are gone. Every tiny little bit.

"In the booth?" I ask. "It fell out?"

"Not quite."

Now he's reddening. And I understand.

"You took it out."

He says nothing.

"You took it out to impress that girl."

"She said she liked bad boys."

"She didn't say anything like that."

"And she noticed it first. She was … touching it."

"When?"

"When you went to the bathroom."

I close my eyes, hoping this will undo itself by the time they're open again.

But, no. Emil still looks embarrassed to the pit of his soul. My brother knows he fucked up and is now waiting to see how badly I shout at him for it. As if I'm the one who likes to yell. I'm quiet, practically invisible. When the two of us stand side by side, people only notice Emil.

"She wanted to hold it," he says.

"Well. That makes it all right."

"I pulled the magazine. I'm not stupid."

"No. Never. This is so completely, entirely, without question *not stupid*."

"She said she's always wanted to shoot a gun. She said I seemed dangerous."

"You are dangerous, Emil. Jesus fucking Christ."

"It felt harmless."

"So you just let her keep it?"

"No! Of course not. I took it back when you came out. Got the magazine, too."

"And where did you put it?"

"Back in my pants."

"Uh-huh. Where's it now?"

"It must have fallen out. I …"

"Maybe she took it."

"Why would she do that?"

"I don't know, Emil. She's a con artist, remember?"

He's deflated. There's no fight left in him for now, no matter what I say.

"So we go back," Emil says. "We go back; that's all."

"We can't go back."

"You just said we had to go back."

"That's when I thought it was in the car. If your girl-friend has it … "

"The gun could have fallen out at any time. We don't know she has it."

I'm starting to snap. This whole mission, Emil's been sloppy. Ever since we found out Bisset was the target, he's been off. My brother has this fuck-the-world thing going, and he hates my social media addiction more than most people hate their cable company. After this new and inexcusable gaffe, I'm starting to worry. Emil is *never* messy with his work. He dots I's twice and has a fact-checker to make sure all T's get crossed. The idea of leaving a hot and loaded weapon behind — or maybe even getting it snatched by a danger-happy floozy — is so far beyond Emil's normal, I have no idea what to think.

"Forget it," I say.

"What?"

"You heard me. Forget it. The gun's a loss. We need to let it go."

"So you don't want to go back?"

"Think about it for a second, will you? Those rednecks were about six inches from grabbing torches and pitchforks on our way out. Half had gun racks in their pickups out front, and I saw rifles in most of the racks. Everglades folk handle things themselves. They don't call the cops."

"All we did was—"

"*You*, Emil. All *you* did."

"—was spill a glass of water."

"Uh-huh. Then girlie got free meals and probably some untraceable weaponry. I'm sure you kept your mouth shut. Just stayed perfectly silent while you were showing off your gun?"

No response, but I can read his face.

"We're not going back. We're supposed to be subtle, but you practically lit a trail of gas for them to follow. In and out, invisible. That's how it's supposed to be. What's wrong with you, Emil?"

"I just wanted some company."

"I'm your company."

"Yeah, Robert, well, sometimes you're not enough."

He says the last bit angry, but then the rage evaporates, and we're left with this embarrassing little standoff. I can't remember the last time I heard Emil admit to an intimate need — let alone an emotional one. He's usually iron and brick, verifiably human only if you check his DNA. I don't know how to feel about it. I should be compassionate, seeing my brother vulnerable, but he strikes me as unstable instead. Truckstop companionship isn't companionship. And before, when he shot the hell out of that iPhone, I'd swear his eyes were wet. The bad guy with a soft spot ... or, I'm worried, the bad guy who's losing his shit at the worst possible time.

"Maybe we should bow out."

"Of what?" Emil asks.

"The toss-up."

That changes something in him. In a blink, my brother's indecision is gone.

"Emil? I'm just saying we could—"

"It's just a gun. No serial numbers."

"Fingerprints," I say.

"When she gave it back, I wiped it down to get her prints. I didn't touch it after." Emil nods as he processes this. "It's fine. Like you said. We have to leave it."

"Unless she reports us," I say.

"She won't."

"How do you know that?"

"Because it made her hot," Emil says.

Just like that, Emil's back in charge. Again I'm second banana, my dreams of leading us no better than a leaf in the breeze.

"It's still a trail. Between this, the mess we left behind, the fact that we're now in a traceable car ... "

"It's fine," Emil says.

"And you," I add.

"What about me?"

"What's with you, Emil? You're not yourself."

Emil answers curiously. "Bisset is mine, and nobody else's."

TEN

A Bird Of Prey

It's dark in the bayou, and for some damn reason, no matter how far we drive, we can't seem to get out of it.

"We're being followed," Emil announces.

I look back, turning fully in my seat.

"Black SUV," Emil says. "I saw it at the last turn."

"There's nothing back there, and I can see for miles."

Emil's fixed to the rearview. I look again, but whatever he's eagle-eyeing looks like dead space to me. He stops by the side of the road and waits, then starts again and turns into someone's driveway. It's four minutes before I speak up.

"You're tired," I say.

"I'm not tired."

"Of course you're tired. Every time I woke up last night, you were already up."

"Then you should be as tired as me." Emil is talking to me, but you'd never know it from the outside. Whatever nonexistent phantom he imagines is behind us, it's like he thinks it'll catch him peeking, even though it's not even in our line of sight, so far as I can tell. My brother won't move his eyes off of the road.

"Bisset's cousin's place isn't far. Can we please just get this over with?" I don't like the idea of kidnapping, but Hojo was right; this is the lever nobody else knows. While all the other killers trip over themselves to get through the senator's L.A. security, we'll hold his favorite person and let him come to us. It's the best way in, and we'd be there already if we hadn't stopped. I estimate three days on this job, from hostage's start to a bullet in the senator's brain. Three days is forever, holding a captive. The sooner we start, the sooner it's over. Yet Emil keeps taking the long route.

"Shh," Emil whispers, killing the headlights. With the windows open, all I can hear are crickets and frogs. "Do you hear that?"

"No."

More silence. Emil holds up a finger. But then there's just the slightest hint of something in the otherwise neutral air. A manmade sound, too regimented to be organic. A car door opening, perhaps, or closing. Wheels on gravel? There's only a quarter moon to see by, and it's possible my imagination is getting the best of me.

"They're staying back if they're following me." Emil looks around, seeing all this nothingness. "Just watching. If they wanted us, there'd be nothing to stop them out here."

"Okay." I listen again. My mind wants to flip-flop, sure there's nothing all over again. Nighttime doesn't spook me, nor does the darkness. I live in it and have since I was a kid. I'm at home, and it's only Emil's occasional paranoid overreactions that tempt my resolve.

I get out of the car. This driveway seems to go nowhere. No home, shed, business, or road. Just a little dead-end in the middle of nowhere, like a place the world forgot.

"Robert!"

But I ignore him, walking into the road's gossamer center. I listen hard again, going so far as to put hands behind my ears. I squint into the distance, trying to make out what I can by the scant lunar light. My eyes adjust within minutes. I can see flotsam in the shallow water, including logs with unblinking eyes. Reeds and cattails make the swamp look almost like a meadow. It wouldn't be hard to drive off the road. We've driven by two half-submerged wrecks already, both accidents apparently not worth salvaging.

I squint into the distance, where Emil was pointing.

"Nothing," I say.

"There was a car. There is a car. Black, so you can't see it."

"If it's black, how can *you* see it?"

He doesn't respond, but I've known my brother long enough to anticipate his answer. Emil reaches conclusions first, then looks for proof later. It's not a bad trait in an assassin; justifications can come after the kill. But it makes him impossible to convince when he's wrong. In his mind, he knows the SUV is there, and this is us trying to find proof it exists instead of the other way around.

"Emil, let me drive."

"I drive," he says.

"Yeah. I know. But." I come up beside him, shoving with my hip. "I'll drive this time."

Emil returns to his seat, then looks up at me. "I drive."

"Then let's get to the cousin's house. Post haste."

"Not if we're being followed."

"We're not being followed, Emil."

"You were right. We're leaving too wide a trail, and now someone's onto it. It might be Blackhawk."

I doubt it. He has a reputation as an ambush shooter, sniping his targets from a distance whenever possible. We have been milling in front of our car for a while now, so I figure Blackhawk, if he were close, might pick us off where we stand. If there's someone back there, they're just seeing where we go. That speaks of bottom-feeders, if anything, in pursuit to overtake us at the last minute and earn this collar. That's me trying to play along. Trying to believe my brother isn't having an episode like he has in the past.

"The best way to get through this is to keep right on going," I say.

"That will lead the black SUV right to his cousin."

"Emil …"

"We need a new car. This one's been compromised."

He starts the engine, then does a 3-point turn to head us back the way we just came from.

"Emil. Wrong way."

"There was a trailer a few miles back. Bunch of run-down trucks in the yard. We'll slip in and trade up."

"And get some hillbilly chasing us? I don't think so, Emil."

He's ignoring me now, speaking mostly to himself. "We'll kill the engine in the glades. Then walk in, break into a truck, put it in neutral, and roll it out. Start the engine in the road. They won't even know what happened until morning. If that."

I light the screen of a phone in my lap to check the time. It's a new one. We traded out the old when we left the restaurant because a refresh felt wise. Most of the dashboard illumination in this car is broken, making my backlit screen the cabin's only light. The shadows on Emil's face make him look like a bird of prey. His hands are tight on the wheel, eyes hollow pits of ochre.

"Emil," I say.

"We just need to give them the slip."

"Emil."

"It's not a big deal. A few hours' delay. Then we'll have him."

"The cousin, you mean."

"Bisset," Emil answers.

"Bisset is in L.A."

Nothing more. I watch Emil's profile, seeing now that the shadow hasn't made him a bird of prey so much as the picked-clean skull of something horrible.

"You okay, man?" I ask.

"I didn't do anything wrong. It wasn't my fault."

"It doesn't matter whose fault it was."

We're both silent. Headed back, apparently. To steal another car and avoid pursuers I can't see, no matter how hard I stare into the darkness behind us.

ELEVEN

Back Into The Frying Pan

It wasn't my fault.

I picture Emil at twelve years, two older than me, looking up at our father like he always did when in trouble, waiting for the belt or worse. Emil only had two modes back then, same as now. When faced with wrongdoing, he never evaded. Emil fights and justifies, but he never denies. It's either that or flat-out acceptance, with an edge. I remember Emil trying to dodge the blame just once, leaning on that particular ethical crutch a single time, claiming that the disastrous error wasn't his doing.

It wasn't my fault.

Emil, playing with his tablet on the front stoop of the home we rented and shared with the crack dealers next door. The cheapest of tablets, so crappy and scratched that even in our shit-poor neighborhood, it had no value to thieves. We could be outside in daylight; the place was, for all Dad's failings, at least that safe. The devils came at night. But while the sun shone, we were supposed to be outside playing or inside studying.

Dad was a helicopter deadbeat, the rarest of parents.

117

Most of the time, he left us alone, but sometimes he insisted we work to better ourselves in ways he never had. Dad spent half his paycheck from the machine shop on beer. When I find it within me not to hate him, it's the other side I think of. Misguided and absent as he was, Dad at least valued education in that sideways value system of his.

We'd made a little corral in the yard so our cat Timmy could get some air and we could enjoy the company of another living thing — one that wasn't drunk or sleeping off a hard day's night — while Dad kicked us outside. Timmy was an orange tabby missing most of an ear. Dad said he was a fighter, that he'd had that ear chewed off by Mike Tyson. It was one of the few things he joked about successfully, though until we looked it up, we didn't get the joke.

Back then, it was Emil who glued his addicted face to a screen.

Don't take that fucking cat outside. Don't you fucking dare.

So we had, if only to prove we weren't slaves to our father's inebriated will. We'd done it before. Timmy was great outside. He seemed to know he was on furlough and that without his best behavior, we'd take him back in. But you had to watch him. Timmy was a cat, and felines can jump plenty high enough to escape a corral made by a couple of kids.

We had a deal. Emil was the older brother, so he would watch the cat. Timmy wasn't a total jailbreaker; he leaped out most often for one of our laps and a purring session. Emil would make his escape and call the cat over.

Until the day Timmy found Emil distracted by his tablet and came to me instead. Only, I was near the street. Standing up instead of sitting to create a lap for him to lie in.

There was a car. The squealing of brakes. And later, there was Emil with stone-cold eyes, regret shoved deep down because he couldn't let himself believe Timmy's death had been his doing. *It wasn't my fault,* he told our father later. But it had been, and Emil damn well knew it.

Hearing those same words now sends a chill down my spine.

I keep sneaking peeks at Emil beside me, but unless I turn on a light or wake the phone, he's only shadows behind that burned-out dashboard. Headlights are our only illumination. The only proof we're here at all.

For months, Emil woke up sweating, unsure of where he was. Dad had run off by then, and without a mom or other family, we ended up in the system. At least they kept us together, and it was in the group homes where Emil found his spine. He entered soft and graduated hard. By the time he was eighteen, he'd broken me out of the home, and we lived on the street. Lived fairly well; Emil got his first kill without blinking.

The other bums stayed away from us after that. Knowing what other professionals say about us now: *Emil is crazy.* It's a reputation we encourage. There are worst things for an assassin than being feared.

"Here it is," Emil says.

The headlights move before the car seems to, twin cones cutting through the darkness like swimmers. Emil pulls us to the side at a wide spot, now just swamp on one edge and a humid jungle of untrimmed overgrowth on the other. Scattered shacks in a mess, maybe half of them legal, with land owned and documented down at city hall.

The rest are squatters. Campers. Men and women, dangerous in their attempts to disappear.

Emil looks back the way we came. The moon, already

low, is now behind a tree. He stares for long enough that I'm tempted to call his name to break the silence.

"I think we lost them," Emil says.

Personally, I couldn't say. I've already looked both ways a dozen times, and there ain't nothin' out here but us and the creatures. No motors, no sounds of tires or feet, certainly no headlights or motorized shadows. It took a lot longer for Emil to assure himself than it took me.

"Let's get this over with," he says.

We're in luck. Behind the scrub is a shed, and far beyond it, the spark lights of a mobile home's windows and the whine of a muffled generator. Illegal homestead, with a single feeble power line strung along the road, but the trailer at the end of this dirt path hasn't tapped into it. Can't if they want to stay off-grid. Now, it's all camouflage. The generator's purr will mask our sounds, and I can see from here that the blinds are all pulled. There are three cars around the shed, two of which look like they might be movable. I have my fingers crossed that either has an engine ... or that the engine if one exists, will turn. Out here, cars are as ornamental as they are functional. If these folks want to go to town, they might do so on bike. Or, knowing this part of the swamp, they might never make it to town at all.

"The Chevy," Emil whispers, pulling his face back from the dirty driver's-side glass. "It's an '85, and it's got three pedals."

I nod, understanding but superstitiously unwilling to speak. An older car is more likely to be manual — and the third pedal, the clutch, confirms it. It's hit or miss when it comes to hot-wiring for both of us and damn near impossible for cars with chipped keys. But for a manual transmission, we just need to get the thing rolling. Pop the clutch, and we're home free.

Emil holds the door handle, then looks at me with hope in his eyes. He squints as if in concentration, then pulls. The door makes a low mechanical sound as metal disengages and the door swings open on rusty hinges.

I look inside the cabin. With a glance at the distant house, I pop the hood, then look there, too. We can't know if it's operational until we try to start it, but everything seems in place. Gunked oil around the housings, but not so much as to portend issues. It's been run, and recently.

"Think it'll start?"

Emil moves toward the rear and says, "Only one way to find out. Get in."

It's a two-man job. One pushes from the back, and the other sits inside to steer and pop the clutch.

I consider our timing and decide now's as good a time as any. We still have our old car, but once we get this new one on the road, Emil can hop in while I drive. We can shuffle later. There will be a moment of noise, and that's our window of danger. Once the engine cranks, we've got maybe a minute before we need to either drive this bitch away or hightail it to our current car in retreat. Any longer, and the shotgun Sallys inside are sure to come running.

I get in, grateful that the seat is free of garbage. I feel the play of the wheel and test the brakes. The nose is pointing toward the driveway, so if the engine turns, I'll only need to drive straight out.

I close the door most of the way, careful to avoid a slam, then put the shifter in neutral and nod at Emil.

He heads to the rear and heaves. The wheels are stuck in the dirt, but a few strong shoves, and we pop free. The car starts to roll. I didn't realize we were on a slight hill, but apparently, we are because Emil is already trailing, the car under its own momentum.

I pop the clutch. Nothing happens.

Emil jogs up beside me.

"Pop it."

"I'm trying."

Speed increases. The car pulls ahead of Emil.

"Pop it!"

"I'm trying!"

"Goddammit, look out!"

The driveway turns, the car's momentum driven sideways by a lump in the road neither of us saw coming. I'm going faster than I'd like, my wheels no longer centered. The wheel won't turn. I hit the brake, but nothing engages.

"Watch it!" Emil hiss-shouts, ostensibly just loud enough for me to hear.

I do, but the car doesn't. It slams into the trunk of a willowy swamp tree at about fifteen miles per hour, the impact sufficient to crumple the front end and cripple the radiator. Steam off-gasses in a hiss, and my chin hits the steering wheel. I didn't think to strap in for a getaway, and the car's either too old or too beaten to have working airbags.

The door flies open with Emil behind it. He grabs a handful of my sleeve and pulls me like a Neanderthal dragging their mate into a cave. I almost slip, recover, then stumble ten feet before regaining my balance.

"The fuck's the matter with you?" Emil asks.

"The wheel and brake are frozen!"

Emil glares at me, then reaches into the car and jockeys the wheel. Pinned against the tree, the front end obeys, wheels grinding circles in the dirt.

"I'm telling you, the wheel was—"

I'm cut off by a shout from the trailer. A rectangle of light there now, not just the spark of a window: an open door, full of intermittent shadow as angry people stream out shouting.

"Shit."

We parked our original car too far away and around an unfortunate bend. Trying to reach it first would take us around the trailer, closer to these fellas and any others still lurking inside than I'd like to be. Our best bet will be to fan out and …

But no, I see now that Emil is blazing right at them like a suicide runner.

"Emil!" I hiss, but my brother can't hear me.

From this far, with us in the dark, the good news is that they can't hear us either. Or see us. A security flood snaps on a pole adjacent to the trailer, but its glow is too weak to penetrate this far. They don't know how many of us there are yet — or even verifiably that we're here. The car might have rolled away on its own.

I follow Emil and stay low. He knows they'll see us if we cross the open space, so rather than running from the problem, my brother goes for control. If he can't avoid it entirely, he'll grab it by the throat.

His shadow flanks the two men who've already emerged, then vanishes.

I sprint after Emil, not knowing what he might do.

Ducking and dodging, hearing the two who've emerged pass us on their way to the wrecked car, I hightail it to where I saw Emil disappear, noting there are still people inside by silhouettes in the window, arriving in time to see him face the back door, foot up and waiting.

"Think about this for a second, will you?" I say as Emil kicks it in.

The place is full of vats and tubing, flames, and the smell of hydrocarbons. It's a doublewide, but still not enough space. The two remaining guys inside are right there, a few feet away. One is fat and sloppy, operating equipment that's half a child's chemistry set and half an explosion at the Home Depot plumbing aisle. Another is survival skinny, like living jerky. He's wearing a Bachman-Turner Overdrive shirt and is shaking a massive triple-X jug full of what I can only assume is shake-and-bake — meth that can't be bothered with precision extraction and instead comes from the shaking of what doubles as a chemical bomb.

The trailer's air is so noxious, I immediately feel a headache blooming. It's so thick with fuel, I start to wonder if the spark of a gun's firing pin could cause it all to go in a ball of flame.

Emil points his drawn weapon at Fat Man, whose hands raise but whose eyes maintain a sinister glint. He's obeying, but only until we're dead.

Emil swings his weapon toward the man with the BTO shirt. There's no reaction. Not raised hands, not even surprise.

"Yor in the wrong place tonight, feller," says BTO. "Maybe you jus walk away."

Emil shakes the gun hard in his direction. "Get down on the ground." I hate our situation already, but when my brother says that, I hate it even more. If he wants them down, it might mean hostages. We're distance killers, not kidnappers. We work in shadows, not with the blunt force of a hammer.

"My cousin," BTO says, "he's gonna eat ya whole."

"I said get down!"

BTO smiles instead of moving, and I see he's just got five teeth.

"Do you hear me? I—"

The door bursts open. One of the newcomers, bald

with swastika tattoos, says, "We didn't see nothin', but there's fresh tracks down the …"

"Hey," Emil says.

Swastikas looks over to find he's staring right down Emil's barrel.

"So you're a Nazi?"

"Fuck you, kike."

Emil pulls the trigger. Blood paints the wall, along with a clot of grey matter like a spit wad. He swings the gun to the other and says, "I'm not even Jewish."

The second man has a gun, but he'll have to quick-draw to use it in time. I see him thinking about it, weighing his odds. Between glances, I keep an eye on Fat Man and BTO, both of whom reacted but not impressively enough. Neither are armed.

"Listen to me," Emil says. "We just need a car."

"You ain't shuttin' down our cook," says the man still under Emil's gun.

"I don't care about your cook."

"It ain't even for white folks. All our customers is nig—"

Emil shoots him, too. The shot is powerful enough to throw his jaw away like a dropped retainer. I'd swear I see brainstem before his corpse finds the ground.

"See," Emil says, "I just don't care for that language."

The two remaining men have shifted one mood to the right. The fat guy has gone from uncaring to scared, and the human jerky went from angry to furious but humbled. We've got their attention, regardless.

Then the new engine — hillbilly reinforcements apparently called by one of the runners before they returned. They burst in, and we had our standoff, and that's just about where this whole story started. Out the window, grab the MAC-10 from the spare-tire well of our Honda, back in right as the clusterfuck started.

This part, you already know.

Which leads us to the arrival of that new piece-of-shit truck with my Spidey Sense tingling, to the truck mowing down two of the five still in pursuit, to the pop of the door and a voice I'd hoped we wouldn't ever hear again.

"Get in," it says. A silhouette standing in the headlights with big mall hair.

"Is that …?" Emil half-asks me and half-asks the newcomer, squinting while the remaining meth heads keep on coming.

But of course, it's who Emil thought it might be.

But because it's better than death, for now, we do what she says — hopping back into the frying pan, better at least than the fire.

TWELVE

A Pair Of Messages

I'M INSTANTLY SUSPICIOUS.

Renee's not butch enough to drive a truck like this, though I called her demographic perfectly. In truth, I wouldn't have expected *Renee* to own a truck this shitty. I'd expect her plaid-shirt-wearing, Deere-cap-owning, enormous belt buckle of a this-week's-boyfriend to hold title. But there's no boyfriend — only Renee. So, where did she get the truck? How did she find us? And most importantly: *Why?*

Emil buys her answer once we're free and clear enough for her to offer it. She found his dangerous manner irresistible, so after we left, she decided to transcend ordinary life badly enough to find the man who offered something more exciting. She shows Emil his gun, left behind like we figured, and the fact that she hands it to him instead of shooting us is apparently good enough for my brother. Because he's thinking with his dick.

Renee is bad news. We've always been a pair, never a threesome. She represents death at worst, chaos and discord at best. How are we supposed to do our job now?

We can't tell her about Bisset's cousin, and now we're headed the wrong way.

I know how this will end. We'll miss out, maybe get shot by any and all of the assassins Heinzie's sicced on us, and Emil will be out of commission for as long as her attention span lasts. They fucked in the truck while I ran to the bathroom during our first pit stop. On the second, I stayed in the truck while she took it in the bathroom. Now, 2 a.m. with no lights, they think I can't tell they're diddling each other as they sit on the bench seat in the back. Renee comes with a sound like squeezing a ferret. It's almost disturbing.

We had to leave the Honda, luggage, and guns. There was no choice. Our wallets were in there. We have a few drop-boxes where we've stashed money and new IDs, but the closest is hours away. There's no recovery for all we lost; the best we could do was to circle back after pulling away and toss a Molotov cocktail through the open window to destroy any evidence. The fact that Renee had the makings of a Molotov is suspect enough — even if it was just an old rag and a bottle of Everclear.

Now we're in a hotel with a blinking neon sign, and while Emil and Renee giggle and slobber all over each other, I'm in the second of the queens with one of the old ladies' stolen iPad in plain view. Emil hates tablets almost as much as he hates phones these days, but I'm flaunting it anyway.

They want to fuck? Fine. I'm pursuing my hobbies, too.

I have a video editor open and am unpacking the footage I surreptitiously took last week of Emil eating fried chicken so I can turn it black and white. Open a copy of *Night of the Living Dead*, then insert the clip into one of the places where zombies eat people. It almost fits the way it fit when I cut Emil into *Pulp Fiction* as a befuddled bystander. Once done, I'll upload the finished film to torrent sites without explanation. Ten years from now, if it spreads widely enough, a group of kids will grow up believing the well-dressed Italian chowing KFC is just another one of the horde.

"Where did you find the gun?" I ask Renee.

She ignores me.

"After you found the gun, how did you find us?"

Nothing.

"And why?"

No response.

But I know the answer or at least a guess. It has to be the car we stole. This is a tiny town, if you can even call it that, and everyone must know everybody. She probably knows the car's owner and asked friends to watch the roads under the ruse of wanting to catch a thief. After that, she borrowed her boyfriend's truck and came after us. It couldn't have been easy, and that rings all my alarm bells. We're supposed to be shadows, and yet here we are like a big unhappy family. Emil's fault. One more way my usually unwavering brother is slipping.

"Can you at least tell me how long you're planning to play tonsil hockey so I can find something else to do?"

Emil peers at me from over Renee's neck like a vampire. Just a look — no answer in sight.

I stare back, and Emil stares back double, and so just to fuck with them, I pick up the active phone and snap a picture of their make-out session.

"Posting this to Float," I say, standing from the bed.

Emil's eyes sharpen, but he doesn't stop fondling Renee's barely-there tits.

"Posting it to Float and Facebook," I go on, shaking the

phone, "and then I'm going to waste the afternoon going through clickbait lists with cookies enabled."

"They can track you with cookies," Emil says. Only it comes out with all the vowels flattened because he's speaking into Renee's bare shoulder.

"What, baby?" Renee asks.

He redoubles his licking and says nothing while giving me the stink-eye.

So, fuck him. Fuck them. I head for the door. But just before it closes, I reach through the gap and grab Renee's purse. A minute later, nobody's come through to chase me, so she must not have seen me take it. That, by the rules of Finders Keepers, makes it mine.

The hotel is at least a hotel, with internal corridors instead of exterior ones. It's barely a converted basement beyond that. The whole place reeks like armpit cigarettes and water from the faucets is tinted yellow like piss. There's a public bathroom by the ice machine, but I won't go in there again. Pretty sure someone dropped an upper-decker into the tank, judging by the brown juice dripping from the topside gasket.

I picture the sign that might be posted outside that bathroom if we were still at Shady Acres: a stick-figure man with his ass over the tank, probably with a pear-shaped nut sack hanging beneath. A universal NO sign over it all.

I peek in anyway, amused. There is a sign inside, but not the one I imagined. It's hand-drawn, pretty convincing, and a thousand times better. It shows that same stick man above the tank, except this particular stick man seems to have slipped, his balls pinched between lid and tank and stretched, thanks to the fall, to the length of his forearm. I'm not sure what this particular sign says, but I snap a photo for my collection anyway.

Then to the lobby, where two winos are sleeping in the aroma of piss.

Then to the pool, where the water is so cloudy, I can't see the bottom. It stinks in here too, but at least it's quiet.

I hunt for a while before finding a pool lounger that will support my weight without snapping all the plastic straps, but eventually, I settle in under a sign declaring MUST BE 18 YEARS OLD TO USE HOT TUB WITHOUT SUPERVISION. There is no hot tub, so I assume this sign is more of a general PSA for young hot tub seekers than specific instructions about this hotel and its facilities.

After making myself comfortable, I open Renee's purse. It's one of those bags that's more luggage than purse, and it's so full of crap that I have to spread my legs and make more room on the surface of the patio chair because my lap just won't do.

Inside I find:

Not one but two gallon-sized Ziploc bags filled with strawberries.

A dwarf-sized, battery-operated hairdryer and hair straightener.

A tiny little thing that I think at first is a lipstick, but that turns out to be a bullet vibrator.

Mints, paperclips, sugar packets, and loose coins form their own sticky ecosystem on the purse floor, like the foundation soil of an old-growth forest.

And a big fat wallet. The kind you unzip lengthwise, large enough for a checkbook.

I'd only meant to piss Renee off, but with her wallet in hand, suspicions return. I unzip it and go for her driver's license, declaring her full name as Renee Star LaCroix. Her birthdate makes her thirty, and her license photo shows her in glasses. I find them in the purse, along with a small contact lens kit. She's not as local as we thought, though. Renee's address puts her in Ocala, which just so happens to be where we were headed before she side-tracked our adventure, then rather suspiciously came to our rescue.

The gun isn't in here; she gave it back to Emil so he could threaten to stick it inside her. I assume this was fore-play to chase her declared love of danger, but no matter how much I enjoy danger, I don't think I'd ever want a firearm in my holes.

How was it Renee said she found us?

Oh, that's right; she didn't. I kept asking, but they both kept dodging the question. Emil said he'd find out, but she put her hand on his dick whenever he inquired. Yet one more way in which he's slipping. As if my brother wants to be caught, wants to die.

Her phone shows a four-digit lock code, and this model has a six-digit code by default. That means she changed it, likely because she had a four-digit code in mind.

I try 1-2-3-4.

I try 4-3-2-1.

Neither works, but it's fine. People like Renee are easy.

I tweeze out her license again. Her address is 4409 Bedlam, so I try 4409 and 9044. Neither unlocks the phone, and it's now prompting me to contact support. A few more bad tries, and it'll lock me out for good, maybe even self-erase if Renee has any sense at all.

I consider the license. Then I enter 0316: March 16th, her birthday.

That does it. The lock screen vanishes, and the little square app icons zoom into view. Most of her apps are dumb games and social media. If I really want to break them up, I just need to show Emil her phone.

I tap on email, being sure to check the trash and archive. Nothing recent that looks interesting.

Then I check the texts: MOM, then BELLA. The third from the top is a five-digit number with a dash: 0-4714. Either a machine or someone with an obscured number.

Inside the numbered thread are two messages, both incoming. They suggest a conversation in progress, so I assume she's erased the history, and only these two messages have arrived since.

The first reads, SLOPPYS ROUTE 8.

The second, later, reads, SILVER VOLVO, NEW YORK PLATES.

I look up across the pool to the tile beyond.

Now I wish she'd left Emil's gun in her purse for me to find.

THIRTEEN

Third Conversation Down

I raise my foot to kick the door in, but then I realize that's just adrenaline getting the best of me.

We've already left a red carpet behind us thanks to all our gaffes: a shot phone on the Everglades roadside, the incident at The Heaping Plate in front of all those witnesses, the stolen car, the meth house, the dead men, and the fireball our short-term car became. We won't decide to retire to Bora Bora after this job is over. We'll be forced there — or anywhere U.S. extradition is complicated or nonexistent.

Kicking a door in now isn't just shining a brighter light on our presence. It's unnecessary and almost certainly slower than using the key in my pocket. It's not as dramatic an entrance, so I'll save the drama for once I'm inside.

Still, I open the door with flair: unlocking first without a sound, then shoving it open with all the force I can muster. My plan is to spend no more than two seconds scanning the room for one of Emil's many guns. I'll just go at Renee with my hands if I don't see anything in that time. My brother's usually the unstable one, but I loathe being lied to. Besides, I checked Renee's Float profile before storming up here just because, and her photo is a corgi's ass. Her screenname is *Cuz*. It's the internet at its most obnoxious — the way Emil must see all of it. I want to put her fucking mall-hair head through a wall. Pin her down and take a shit on her face.

But after I bang the door open, all I find is Emil on the bed, naked save a washcloth over his erect penis like a tiny white carnival tent. He's holding two plastic cups presumably filled from a bedside bottle of champagne. Given what I've seen of this place, it must have cost upwards of a dollar, maybe two. Lucky if it isn't toilet water.

"Hey!" Emil declares, now the world's happiest man. "It's my little brother!"

I scan the room like a predator, eventually exhausting even the dumbest options. Is Renee on the floor on the far side of the bed? Maybe under the desk?

I'm missing the most obvious place: the bathroom. "Is she in there?"

"Probably rubbing herself with ointment," Emil answers.

Unless she's a pig, she'll wash her hands. That gives me time, so I go to where Emil tossed his coat and rummage for the shoulder holster beneath.

"Not because she's got diseases or a rash or anything," Emil clarifies. "Because I fucked her raw."

I come out with his .45. I leave the ChapStick where it is.

Emil sits up. "Hey, don't get jealous. She's hot to trot. I'll bet she'd fuck you, too."

I go to the bathroom door and bang on it with the butt of the gun, shouting for Renee to get the fuck out of the bathroom right fucking now.

"Robert? What the hell's going on?"

"Get her out here. Now."

"Why?"

"Now."

He shrugs. "Renee, honey?"

She answers my brother immediately, so no problems hearing. Bitch.

"Yeah?"

"Come out for a sec."

"Hang on." I hear her flush, then the faucet comes on.

"What's up, Robert?" Emil asks.

"She's a liar."

"Okay. How?"

I bang on the door and shout again.

"Easy."

"Don't tell me easy."

Emil pulls on a robe and comes up next to me. "You're going to hurt someone."

"Goddamn right, I am."

"Maybe calm down a bit."

Fuck him. Seriously, fuck my brother. He flies off the handle all the time, and I have to deal with it. Now, this *one time*, I've got something pressing, and he expects me to be Zen. Don't I ever get a say?

"Give me the gun."

"No."

He takes it by the slide anyway.

"Let go."

"Give me the gun, Robert."

"No."

He hits me in the cheek. I stagger away, smarting while he shakes his hand to disperse the impact.

"Fine." I hand him the phone. This one's case is made to look like a blinged-out chipmunk, both its size and elaborate nature make it too large to easily hold.

"I don't want your goddamn phone."

"It's hers."

He looks down, then at the purse now dropped on the floor. Strawberries peek out, inviting us to snack.

His expression is different as he wakes the phone and looks at the code screen.

"0316," I say. "Check the texts. Third conversation down."

I hear Renee finish in the bathroom while Emil does as I say. His expression is still wary but quickly evolves. The bathroom knob is turning as he composes himself.

Renee emerges. Her mall hair is wet where it touches her skin as if she's splashed water on her face.

"Hey, baby." She offers him a wily smile, clearly illiterate when it comes to body language. "Interested in another round?"

"You dropped your phone." Emil raises the thing from his lap toward her. It's still unlocked, with the text thread still open. *That*, Renee can finally see. She slowly reaches for the phone, her eyes unsure of what to do.

"Baby, it's not—"

The second her fingers brush the phone in Emil's hand, his other hand slaps up to grab her by the wrist. His face goes ugly, features distorting like a funhouse mirror. I see my brother's teeth as words leave his lips in a snarl.

"Who are you?"

"Nobody! I'm … I'm … "

He pulls her toward him, then in one motion, flips Renee back down on the bed while he looms above. The gun, somehow, makes its way from my hand to Emil's. A half-second later, its muzzle is pressing into her forehead like a cookie cutter into dough.

"I asked you a question."

"Emil! Baby!"

He seems to want to hit her, but it's too barbaric, too close to the bone. Dad used to hit Mom before she left, declaring she could no longer stand the unending ache in her heart. We never heard from Mom after that, and ever since, I've been trying to figure out who's the bad guy. Dad for hitting? Or Mom for leaving us alone with him?

The .45's hammer cocked with the rack of the slide, but now Emil uses his thumb to flick the safety to red. "Who sent you? Who do you know?"

"I don't know anybody!"

"How did you know where to find us?" Spittle has collected on his lower lip. I'm fascinated watching, waiting for it to drop a line, descend toward Renee's face like a spelunker into a cave. "Who told you?"

"*Nobody* told me! I don't know what the hell you're talking about!"

The gun grinds into her skull, pestle into mortar. It's as if Emil's forgotten he's an assassin and believes himself an apothecary instead. Beneath blue steel, her skin begins to redden.

"BULLSHIT!" He snatches the phone and reads. "Sloppy's, Route 8. Silver Volvo. New York plates!"

"It was Melvis, all right? Melvis Horn!"

That stops Emil like a slap. Me too, if anyone had been looking my way.

"Melvis," he repeats, looking at me.

"Grampy," I confirm.

FOURTEEN

The New Thread

THERE'S no way there are two Melvis Horns living in Florida's low-hanging dick.

I've never even heard the name before. It's kind of Elvis, kind of Melvin — either a name too hip for anyone or a name so far beneath that designation, it couldn't be cool if it held a gold shotgun inscribed with Ted Nugent's face. *Melvis*. I remember thinking that name was child abuse. It became a joke between Emil and me.

Who sang "Blue Suede Shoes"?

MmmmMelvis!

Better known, in close circles, as *Grampy*. As Hojo's grandfather — on the Irish side, apparently, since "Melvis" doesn't strike me as particularly Japanese.

The slap of hearing that familiar unfamiliar name is sufficient to put Emil back on his hands, the gun finding its home on the nightstand. Whatever comes next, she can't be lying in any simple way. You have to get past Hojo to know Grampy. And to even know where to find Hojo, you need more intimate knowledge than most.

So right now, I'm not doubting that Grampy is part of

this. There's no way Renee would pull *Melvis Horn* from a random hat. No way, if it wasn't true, that she'd know which name to use in her lie. It's just like Hojo to make sure his grandfather's phone shows a bogus Caller ID.

"Melvis Horn," Emil repeats.

Renee stays on her back. Her chest is moving up and down, up and down. It might entice me if her breasts were bigger than mosquito bites. She nods, the back of her head massaging the comforter.

"How the hell do you know Melvis?"

"It's complicated."

"Then why don't you simplify it for me?"

Renee's eyes go from the underside of Emil's jaw to his gun on the nightstand. The circle on her forehead is so red and so pressed-in, it looks like she fell asleep face-down in a pile of cherry Lifesavers. She looks like a frightened animal. It's safe to say she's never had a gun on her, let alone pressed so firmly into her skin. Probably never even held a gun, the way she looks ready to piss herself.

"My grandmother was in a home with Melvis's brother."

I nod. We've known Hojo for a while, and until three years ago, Melvis had an older brother. His name was Bortrand, and we used to joke that their parents named their children while high. On drain cleaner. We shouldn't know any of this, but Emil's strategy for making business connections has always relied heavily on socializing to the point of incapacitation. He gets people drunk, then lets them spill whatever they want to. It's an underrated inter-rogation tactic and so much more fun than bamboo shoots or waterboarding.

"And?"

"She had friends there, the way they do. Bortrand was sweet on her, and Grandma indulged it even though she didn't have any real interest. So I got to know Bortrand. And when Melvis visited, I got to know him, too."

Listening, I rewind my mental clock. Grampy's eccentric now, but as little as five years ago, the man was still sharp as a tack.

"After his brother died, and after Grandma passed away, he kept in touch. Asked if he could send me letters, but he had a phone, so I taught him to text. He's no good with his thumbs or fingers — too much arthritis — but he can dictate just fine."

"Hojo's grandfather sent you after us." Emil looks at me, but I can only shrug.

Of all the people to turn on us, I wouldn't have bet on Grampy. Bright five years ago or not, he's lost a lot of his faculty today. If it's not 80s TV or porn, he's typically not interested.

Renee, sensing the change in temperature, finally decides it's safe to sit up. She props on one arm, still breathing heavy, still with that little red donut on her forehead. "Not *after* you. *To find* you."

"How's that different?"

"What would I do if I came *after* you? I know what you do. As soon as you started talking, I knew. When you left that gun, I was sure. I'm a girl. How would I *get after* someone like you and expect to stand a chance?"

"What, then?" I ask.

She swallows. "I *asked* him how to find you. All he did was tell me where you were."

"Us?"

"You or anyone like you."

"Why?"

"Because you're going after him, aren't you?"

My skin prickles as Emil asks, "Who?"

"Simon Bisset."

I go cold. Again my brother beats me to the punch. "How did you know that?"

"Because Simon's people keep shuffling him around. I know what Melvis's grandson does and who he associates with, and no offense, but I've learned something about how you people think." She pauses at *you people* but then continues when we don't react. "There are rumors. One or two might just be the same old bullshit, but they keep getting new threats. *Credible* threats."

Emil and I trade a glance. *The toss-up*. Our competition must not be doing their jobs very quietly if everybody knows the fix is in.

Emil shakes his head. They won't have the standard chat about what it all meant and which of them used the other. Emil isn't exactly the romantic type, and Renee doesn't strike me that way either. They got fucked, that's all there was to it. The ride is over, and now it's time to jettison our extra engine.

"Pack your shit and get the fuck out of my face," Emil says, standing as he looks at me. "It's time to go."

"Where are you going?"

"Doesn't matter."

"I want to go with you."

"Fuck you."

Renee shoves Emil in the chest. "No, fuck *you!* I did what I set out to do. I found you when nobody was supposed to be able to. I told Melvis how important it was, and he set me up — and don't let him fool you, asshole, he's got more marbles left than it seems. He wouldn't have helped me without a damn good reason."

"And what reason is that?"

Her mouth forms a slit. After five seconds, Emil turns to me and makes little motions with his finger. *You, too,* it seems to say. You *pack* our *shit, too.*

"I'm coming," she says.

Emil turns around whiplash fast. "Like hell you are! You got me, okay? Whatever starfucker, celebrity stalker, celebrity *stalker* stalker reason you wanted to shake the tree and find me — or someone *like me* — to fuck, you got it. You were an amusing lay, nothing more. You want danger? Fine. Go wade in the swamp with bloody steaks tied to your shins. I'm done being your bad boy."

Jilted now, her color rises.

Emil turns away as if Renee's not there, and that raises all her bile and hidden vitriol.

"*He's not even in Florida, you stupid shit!* You know that? Your motherfucking target is across the country right now, and you're playing swamp gigolo while holding your dick!"

Emil spins again, this time just a half-inch from her face. "You've got a mouth on you. You know that?"

"Fucking misogynist. Arrogant pig. A woman speaks her mind, and it means I've 'got a mouth'? Fuck you. Fuck you with that tiny little cock of yours."

Emil looks at me. I shrug. Then he turns around and pins Renee to the wall. The gun isn't back out. Yet.

"All right, you want to do this? I'd really rather not kill you. But I will if I have to."

"Let go of me!" she shouts.

But the way Emil's got her right now, Renee's never getting away.

She squirms while my brother starts talking.

"I could give a shit that you're mouthy. What bothers me is how much you seem to know about Simon Bisset. You know where his people are moving him. You know about credible threats. End to end, I'd say you have a *really excellent* bead on us and our assignment. So. Tell me. What the fuck is going on, *Renee?*"

Something strange is climbing the small hairs on the

back of my neck. You need steel will and emotional strength to play this game — or emotional absence, in many instances. But you also need instinct, subtlety of action, and logic. Much of it comes down to instinct ... and I've got the same feeling brewing in my gut right now.

I've picked up her phone. Already started scrolling. When I reach a new thread farther down her text history, I stop, open it, and extend the phone for Emil to take with his free hand.

The new thread is labeled as a chat with SIMON.

"What the hell is happening here?" Emil asks.

"Melvis said Hojo sent you to find the senator's favorite cousin," she answers with her windpipe constricted. "To find the cousin as leverage."

Emil slowly nods.

Renee worms a hand free, strikes him in the throat then knocks his face sideways with an elbow.

Emil staggers back, already reaching for the gun, but Renee simply sits on the bed innocent as pie.

Then she says, "I'm the cousin, and I want him dead."

FIFTEEN

A Matter Of Belief

RELUCTANTLY, it fits.

Overnight for the second time in this shitburg hotel, I find myself up at 4 a.m., unable to sleep. Emil would have a fit at what I'm doing, but I'm more tech-savvy than my brother and know perfectly well how to cover my tracks.

With Emil sleeping in one of the beds and Renee tied by her wrists to the other, my choices for slumber are limited anyway. I can try to slide in with Emil and hope he won't run me off the bed, sleep on the floor, or eschew rest entirely, sit in a corner, and use the tablet to do some research. Through an anonymous proxy server, of course.

And, yes, it seems that Simon Bisset has a female cousin in Florida. It's slim pickings on this info since Bisset used to be Zero, and he was a hacker second to none. But it's there, and what I find — piecemeal over the course of an hour and a half — is plenty to convince me that Renee isn't lying, at least not about that.

Bisset, alienated from his family at an early age, was all but disowned once word came out that he was the legendary Zero.

Zero battling an avalanche of legal and PR battles, gradually reshaping his image before the dumb American public, as Emil would say.

Rob them blind and rape their system, then come back with a big smile and fake promises, and they'll elect you senator.

Emil has no faith in the crowd or the way things are. When people should be discerning, they're gullible and stupid. When things go tragic, and people should stand by you, no one does. We're two kids from the foster system who grew up believing in nothing. No wonder Bisset's machinations are so transparent to us.

Only one person seems to have stayed Bisset's true family.

I sleep in the chair. Emil is already up when I wake, with a plate of food from the continental buffet downstairs stacked on a Styrofoam plate. Four danishes, plus a waffle shaped like Florida, dry like he always eats them.

I look over at Renee, eating fruit with her freshly freed wrists. A small bowl of oatmeal that looks like it's already been digested, studded with rabbit turds that I have to assume are raisins.

"You let her go."

"Renee has promised to behave." He looks at her. "Haven't you?"

She gives him a look that's not far from adoring, maybe a little amused, and I realize she's either nuts, or they've gone right back to fucking while I've been in Dreamland. "Renee has promised to behave," she repeats.

I'm not so sure. Her story checks out, but she's still crazier than an elephantitus clinic. First, she wants to kill a cousin who, by all accounts, likes her very much. Second, she stalked and found us, then planted herself in that booth with some odd knowledge ahead of time that we were on our way.

That part, I still don't understand. Grampy might know what Hojo told us and where we were headed, but I don't see how he could have known about *that* specific parking lot at *that* specific time. Still, *he* did, not her; it's right there in his texts. It does nothing to calm my nerves. I felt followed already, and Renee revealing herself as the person in pursuit doesn't make it any better.

"She's not going with us."

"She's *absolutely* going with us," Emil replies.

"She absolutely is," Renee echoes.

"She's crazy."

"She's the *right kind* of crazy," Emil says.

Renee leans over and hugs his arm. It's so hokey and so transparently manipulative, I want to leap across the room and punch this woman in her throat.

"Did you ask her why she wants to kill Bisset if she's his favorite cousin? You know — the cousin we were planning to kidnap specifically *because* she meant so much to him?"

Emil turns to Renee and quietly says, "Hey. We need to head out soon. Why don't you wash up."

"Join me?"

My face curdles like milk.

"Later."

It's a little less passionate than she was clearly hoping for, but Renee still gets up and leaves without protest. Emil waits until the shower starts to look me in the eye.

"She's not dangerous. We went after her."

"That's not a logical conclusion, Emil. You pinned her down with a gun; that doesn't mean she isn't crazy."

"Fair. But it does mean she's not the craziest one in the room. I'm not planning to give her a gun."

"And you'll tie her up at night?"

"What is she, a dog?"

We match eyes.

"Fine. Maybe we can get her a second room. Lock her out."

"And if she runs?"

"She's not gonna run."

"What makes you so sure?"

"She broke her neck trying to get to us, so why would she leave once she's found us?"

I shake my head, hating every bit of this.

"What's the problem, Robert?"

"The problem is, she wants to kill him. She's a murder waiting to happen."

"*We're* a murder waiting to happen."

"She's a stalker."

"*We're* stalkers."

"She's nuts, Emil. She lied."

"*We're* nuts. *We* lie. We've been through hell and back together. We've been beaten up and shot and threatened and killed."

"Well, not *killed*," I say.

"So, really, I don't see why this is so terrifying."

I can't articulate, so I shift on the comforter like a dumbass. My mind, unable to settle on a reframe, starts to spin in its usual useless way. I wonder what Santa looks like naked. I want to scramble an egg without breaking the shell. I picture myself crossing a rope bridge like Indiana Jones, except that it's not a high canyon, it's the trading pit at the New York Stock Exchange.

"Look. She's saved us time. We were going to find her anyway, only we didn't know it was her. She's saved us at least a full day of searching, maybe more. And I don't know about you, but I wasn't looking forward to a kidnapping. This way is easy. She *wants* to come."

I glance at the shower door. Now I'm wondering what Renee looks like naked. She's not remotely my type. It must be the mania. Those loose marbles perpetually rattling around inside my skull.

"What?" Emil says after I'm silent for too long.

"Hojo told us to nab her because it'd give us leverage against Bisset."

"And now we *have* leverage against Bisset."

"Because we'd be threatening her. Because they have a *good* relationship."

I sigh.

"Fuck off with this, Robert. Seriously. Fuck right the fuck off."

"It's not what we were expecting."

"It seldom is."

"Why is she here? Why does she want to kill her own cousin?"

Robert half-bites his lip. Whatever he's thinking of saying, it's something he's not supposed to tell.

But finally: "He raped her, okay?"

I sit back.

"Psychologically."

I sit forward again. "The fuck?"

"You ever hear of something called Cloud Eleven?"

I don't really want to admit it, but yes. You'd have to be a Float OG to know Cloud Eleven, seeing as Bisset himself made such a stink about erasing it from history during the PR contortions that gradually transformed Zero the Bad Guy into Bisset, the crusader.

Early on, the Float social network was one step above the wildest days of 4chan. It was quickly overrun with the worst of what middle-class western culture had to offer. Nobody was selling guns or child brides, but it was a depository for the intrusive and profane. One of the earliest popular channels — one that, with the help of memes that conspiracy types say came from within the organization — was a cam feed called Cloud Eleven. There, you could watch remote access streams of people who didn't know they were being watched. But in those early days, there was really only one worth watching — and it caught on in that sub-group (and, after a feature news piece, the world) like wildfire.

"I know a little about it," I say.

"Renee was Lilac."

For a moment, the sentence doesn't make sense. Then I realize that *Lilac* is a name in this context, and everything clicks. Lilac was the voyeur vid stream that broke the world, and the software that made it possible could only have been installed by someone with direct access to Renee's computer, if what Emil said was true.

"She's claiming that Bisset …?"

"… made her internet-famous, in all sorts of compromising positions, without her permission," Emil finishes.

Renee probably made that sound awful to Emil, but seeing as I watched Cloud Eleven rise and fall, I have damning context that he isn't aware of. Despite her mediocre body and a lot of time on her stream spent watching an empty room, something about the sensationalism that Float (and, by extension, Zero) put behind Lilac's stream made it fit for a marquee.

Early basement-dwelling users drooled over Lilac, made and shared memes featuring her photos, and shared personal information about her that they claimed to have dug up using clues visible in her room and on the few occasions she took her laptop traveling. Facial recognition software would have made it easy to locate her face and blur it, but Cloud Eleven wasn't so courteous. I, like much of Float's early user base, couldn't have escaped the-phenomenon-that-was-the-invasion-of-Lilac's-privacy if I'd wanted, but I didn't see much.

I could probably pull up old stills now to verify that it was Renee we were watching, but I remember enough to know it's feasible, that she reminds me enough of Lilac to believe.

Watchers snooped deep. They found her Facebook profile and posted screenshots, blurring her identifying information, not for privacy, but because they wanted to keep it for themselves. They posted photos from when she was in high school. Photos with family, though most of those faces were also blurred. I even remember some hubbub wherein one of the creepiest Float users got Lilac's address, sneaked into her bedroom, and let himself be recorded on the livestream camera while Lilac herself was in the shower. That asshole got shut down — maybe even reported to the law — but it still took three months afterward before Renee ran across her own memes and figured it all out.

Soon after, Lilac's stream, Cloud Eleven, and half of Float's first users were gone, banned with the heaviest of hammers. The news got ahold of the story and propped Zero, now Bisset, up as a modern-day technological hero. Nobody had been able to scrub all of those Fappening photos from the internet, but somehow Bisset managed to make most of Lilac's disappear. Videos and screenshots downloaded by Cloud Eleven users self-erased, victim to a master kill switch Bisset had reportedly invented.

Forbes and *Wired* were writing stories about Bisset after that — about his mastery of the digital world and proclaiming him *the man who will reinvent the web.*

Lilac was probably the worst thing that had ever happened to Renee, while being one of the best Bisset could have ever hoped for.

Emil continues to explain. "She thinks he knew what would happen from the start. He used Renee to kickstart

Float, then used the purge that came after it was all in the open to elevate his business standing and political career. Who better to address 'the internet is forever' problem than the man who proved he can erase regrettable content with the flip of a switch?"

The water stops in the bathroom, so I lower my voice and make a statement that should probably be a question. "You believe her."

"I did some research of my own, little brother." He tosses a grape into his mouth — respite from all the sugar and starch on his plate. "It's no longer a matter of belief."

"And you want to help her."

"I want to do our job. But at the same time, I'm happy to help Renee get her revenge."

"Why?"

Emil sits back as if the hard part of this interrogation is over. He sets the plate full of frosted goodies on the desk in the corner, then tips back far enough to lace his hands behind his head, elbows out. In the sun, right now, his shadow would look like an eye atop a stalk.

"'The man who can erase the internet' can rewrite history in his favor. Can eliminate all the good things said about his competitors and change what's said about him. If you don't believe it, who cares? Just look online, little brother, and it'll sure seem like you're the only one."

Now I'm the one who sits back.

Emil eats another grape. "If that's not someone I want dead, then who is?"

SIXTEEN

Vodka Goggles

THINGS GET A WHOLE LOT EASIER.

Without the need to kidnap Bisset's cousin, there's no longer any reason for us to stay in Florida. With that cousin willingly helping, there's no reason to even concoct a ransom story, build firewalls to screen us while Bisset's security springs into action, or involve other parties that will try to stop us. Now we can get Bisset's attention with a phone call, and we don't even have to make it.

"He doesn't know she knows," Emil says when Renee steps into the hallway to make her call. "She told him about Lilac as if he might not know, then let him take credit when he cleaned it up. But it was him. He's the one who started that livestream and sent all the traffic. She's sure of it. Nobody touches her computer other than him because he's the best computer guy she knows."

From the backseat, I give Renee a visual once over. She's cute but hardly breathtaking or a hardbody. What Bisset did to her is terrible, but I reluctantly have to give his publicity brain some mad props. The fact that he used one rather average naked girl (who wasn't even naked all that often) to fan that much attention is kind of amazing. Right place, time, and bag of tricks. But isn't that what any social media phenomenon is, at its root? Something mundane (cats, wedding dances, amusing freeze-frames from popular movies), salted into pop culture until something unremarkable finally roots.

More hollow content for our hollow culture. We've forgotten the trick of living. Now we just carry on instead.

Or so Emil would say. I think that's why he got us into this line of work — himself first, dragging me inevitably behind him. Commit murder, and you change the world. Sometimes in small ways, sometimes in big ways, but always with a line in the sand. It makes a difference to those who knew the dead. It makes a difference to those who hear of it, who bundle their coats a bit tighter the next day and hold the hands of children who long ago stopped wanting to hold hands. It makes a difference to the police. To the newspaper writers breaking the story. To the Neighborhood Watch. The internet always gets it, and at that point, death becomes masturbatory: never-ending daisy chains of someone who knew someone who knew someone who knew someone who lived in the neighborhood where it happened. And even after Facebook's five minutes of sorrow and outrage, the real-life sorrow and outrage — or, in some cases, *schadenfreude* elation — still lives on to prove it was a true thing, creating thoughts and memory in a world that still has substance.

We order plane tickets online using our real identities, then pick them up at a kiosk three hours later. Neither of us has a felony record, officially speaking, so the computers don't flag us. If anyone chases this case in the proper direction, then yes, they'll find our real names and our real date of travel. But somehow, that's never been a problem, and there's no way there'll still be a senator left to kill if we do this road-trip style.

But of course, there's a fuckup. All of us walk right onto the plane without problems, but only Emil and Renee have seat assignments. I end up in a middle seat, way in the back, dodging the arms of a large woman and the frenetic elbows of a man with Einstein hair who seems to enjoy his music a bit too enthusiastically. Usually, in this situation, I'll pull out a tablet and start watching something hideous: *A Serbian Film*, without headphones. In the past, that's always bought me and Emil space to breathe, but of course, he has the tablet, and of course, Large Woman falls asleep right after takeoff. I don't even have a book. I have to sit Stonehenge still with my arms in, trying to stay invisible.

Three and a half hours later, we land at LAX to a gang war. From what I understand in the crowd's mumbling, small contingents from the Bloods and Crips both decided to take trips on the same day, then saw each other by colors in one of the exterior lobbies. Apparently, gangs don't keep up on TSA regulations because both sides, pre-security, still had sufficient firepower to cause a mess of problems.

They won't let us get off the plane after we've landed. They won't even hook us up to the jetway, as if refusing to break the hermetic seal of our giant flying Tylenol will keep us safe. If we open the door, the logic goes, we'll start inhaling all of that gang violence floating through the air. It'll go to work in our lungs. Tiny red cells fighting tiny blue ones, each side calling the other bitch and implying forced anal congress with their cellular mothers.

With the engines off, the air conditioning finally dies. Like twin reactors heading for meltdown, both of my seat-mates start generating an inordinate amount of body heat.

I feel like the meat at the center of a Foreman grill. Even from here, I can see Emil and Renee making out. There's an older woman with drugstore readers in the window seat of their row, trying to pretend she hasn't noticed what's happening right next to her.

By the time they neutralize the threat (with zero casualties, say my friends on Float — and fuck Emil's judgment about my checking it), I feel like my clothes have been run through a steam press with my body still inside them. Emil asks if I ran my head under the bathroom faucet without sarcasm, but I'm fuming too hard for an answer. Renee must sense this because when I say nothing, so does she.

"We'll get lunch," she tells me as we pass baggage claim. "On me."

"I could really use a shower first." I'm not hungry anyway. They had those little cookies on board, and when I was finally able to get to the claustrophobic restroom, I stole all my pockets would carry from the service cart stowed beside it. I also may or may not have swiped copious amounts of airplane vodka. There's a chance I won't remember any of this tomorrow.

"That's a good point," Emil says. Enough time has passed since I spoke that this seems out of the blue. Perhaps we're on a delay. Perhaps I'm on Earth, but Emil is on the moon.

It's around this time when I realize just how drunk I am.

"What?" Renee asks.

"Shower."

She wraps an arm around his waist. I guess "shower" sounds like a come-on. And by the way, "come-on" is a strange expression. It can't be a coincidence that after a successful come-on, the chances of coming on that person greatly increase.

That makes me laugh. Emil shoots me a look. It's a little wobbly out here, and the sun is too bright.

"The fuck's wrong with you?"

At Emil's question, Renee turns and looks at me, too. The guy behind me bristles, apparently thinking this animosity is intended for him. He's bald, holding a snow globe that looks straight out of an airport gift shop, and is as wide as he is tall. The kind of guy who's looking for a scrap, just to prove how scrappy he is.

Emil stares the man down, alpha to alpha. But then the rental car shuttle arrives, and we all get on. Baldy says he's going to Dollar while we're on our way to Hertz, and Emil pushes past him just to be an asshole, using Renee as a social shield. He shoves her into the window seat, sits in the middle, and drops his bag onto the aisle seat. The shuttle fills fast, and Baldy and I are left standing. He glares while Emil removes his bag and motions for me to sit. The staring doesn't stop.

"Oh, I know," Renee says suddenly, reaching for her purse. Emil, on the other hand, doesn't know or care what she knows, so he maintains his staring vigil until Baldy blinks, and I take my seat.

Once we're moving, Emil speaks up as if inspired. "Did you know that Dollar gets all the jizzmobiles from Hertz?"

Renee is on her phone, so the reaction's on me. I can't summon interest, so I stare at Emil instead.

He keeps going. "When people rent a car and fuck in it, jizz usually ends up on the seats, window, or ceiling, so they can no longer rent it at Hertz. Quality outfit like that has a no-spooge guarantee. So they sell it down. Hertz writes it off, and some hapless fuck has to sit in another man's batter."

"*Ceiling?*" I say.

"You'd be surprised."

159

I look up after sensing radiant malice to see Baldy staring down at Emil through me.

"Taking up a lot of seats for a loudmouth." He looks at me — at the seat that should have been his, but that Emil cockblocked using the bag that's now on my lap.

Emil looks up at Baldy and smiles. "Maybe I could sit on your lap."

"Or on your girl's lap."

"Go ahead," Emil says. I look at Renee, who's in a phone trance and hearing none of this. "I just met her, but I'll bet she'd give you a ride."

Baldy glares at me, still with that incongruous snow globe in one hand. "Move your shit. I've got a bad knee."

I'm not as bold as Emil, so I answer plainly. "It's only a three-person seat."

"Move your shit, or I'll move it for you."

Emil laughs.

So Baldy snatches the bag from my lap and throws it onto the floor, then does just as he threatened: his big muscular ass headed right for my lap. We're about to become best friends in the worst way possible when Emil snaps from cool to uncool, rising to crane over me and grab Baldy by his collar.

Baldy slaps him away. People are watching, waiting, observing all of this with the doe-eyed passivity that comes over people when the usual rules get broken. Anthropologists act like humans are predators, but in truth, most are prey, cowering like a beaten dog if confronted. You can steal the clothes off a man's back in broad daylight armed with harsh words, and chances are nobody — not even the victim — will say a thing.

"Touch him again, and we're going to have a problem you can't solve."

I see the hardness in my brother's eyes and what looks

like hardness in Baldy's, but this here is impervious stone meeting even more impervious diamond. Renee is finally looking up from her phone as everyone onboard holds their collective breath.

"Asshole," Baldy says, forcing a superior snicker as if he's above all of this and withdrawing out of restraint rather than fear. But nobody buys it, including Baldy.

Turns out, the Dollar booth is the same place as Hertz. Turns out, they're on opposite sides of the same building, and it's no wider than five of me laid end to end. The Hertz and the Dollar clerks are literal neighbors, standing ten feet apart at twin computers. The shuttle still makes two stops, for those who find thirty feet too far to walk.

"I know where to go for lunch," Renee says.

"I know what you did last summer," I say at the same time as Emil says, "Fine, whatever."

Yeah. I'm definitely drunk.

"What?" Renee asks.

With vodka goggles on, I decide that Renee is much *much* hotter than I realize. Emil and I were never the weird kind of close that comes with offers of threesomes, but here and now, I decide that I'll take one if it's offered. Although I'll have serious whiskey dick, so maybe not. But maybe so.

"Whatever you want," Emil says.

For the briefest of moments, I think this might be the threesome offer I've been waiting for, but then I realize that he's responding to her thoughts on lunch.

The line takes forever, and I start to feel sick as we wait. I sit and watch the twin lines inch forward: Emil and Renee in one, Baldy in the other. They keep throwing looks at one another. I'm relieved when Baldy is finished first and goes, then even more so once Emil and Renee are coming toward me holding keys.

"You okay?" Emil asks.

"I'm fine," Renee answers.

I decide that Renee is hotter than she is intelligent. With my vodka goggles on.

"Not you."

"Fine," I lie. Then again: "Just hungry."

There's a big, meaty hand on our car when we get there. The hand drops onto the door to hold it closed just as Emil is popping the lock. With nobody around now save the distant milling sheep lined up back at the rental shed, Baldy seems to have reconsidered. My thoughts, of course, are on his hand. Where's the snow globe he held for the entire ride?

Then I see it poking out of the top of his luggage, dangerously exposed in an unzipped pocket.

I consider asking about it. Is it a globe of Orlando or Los Angeles? Departure or destination?

"Where you headed?" Baldy asks.

"None of your business," I tell him.

"Maybe we can hook up. Hang out."

"That's …" Renee's confused expression tells me that lone word is all she's got.

"Maybe, when we do, I can teach you some fucking manners."

"It didn't have to be personal," Emil says. "You mess with my brother, you mess with me."

"That's …" Renee repeats, looking somehow even more confused than before.

"I didn't mess with anyone. I just told you to move your shit."

Baldy's puffed chest lets me know that this isn't a discussion. It's a show of pride between peacocks to see who has the boldest feathers. Emil, reading this, turns from the car to close the distance.

"You mess with my brother," Emil says again, "you mess with me."

Baldy's composed expression breaks like a dropped plate, becoming half-infuriated, half-baffled by Emil's belligerence. He says, "Man … *fuck* your brother!"

Another step. Now almost chest to chest. "What did you say?"

"I said *fuck* your brother! Fuck your mama and fuck your whole family right up its fucking ass!"

Emil drops the bag in his left hand, then hands the keys to Renee. He casually reaches into Baldy's open bag and retrieves the snow globe. Turns out, it's L.A. In a snowstorm — although, come to think of it, Orlando in the snow isn't much better. Whose brilliant idea was that?

"Put it back," Baldy says, eyeing the globe.

But instead, Emil slams it impossibly hard against Baldy's skull. Impossibly, neither breaks, so my brother tries again. And again. And again. By the time Baldy is on the ground bleeding into a pool with Emil straddling what I'm starting to suspect is his lifeless corpse, the globe in his grip looks more like a heart plucked from someone's chest by Mola Ram.

After perhaps a dozen hits, Emil sits up, and I remember to breathe. Renee seems to have forgotten breathing as well, so I poke her. She finally inhales, her vocalization at least half-sob.

Emil leans close to Baldy and holds the snow globe in front of his face.

"This is how they get you. Don't you know that, you fucking moron? Twenty bucks for a ball of goddamn glass." He drops it, then says to us, "Consumerism these days. I'll tell you. If I ever have kids, I won't buy them shit just because I go on a trip. Shit for shit's sake, that's how it starts."

He looks to Renee, but studying the flecks of blood all over her clothes and skin has kept her from replying.

"Right," Emil answers himself as he opens the car door, getting in with his blood-caked hands and arms.

I hope he opted for the cleaning waiver.

SEVENTEEN

From The Shadows

THE W HOTEL is an immediate pass.

Fifty million people in the streets and all major roads to the hotel have been blocked by barricades. Cops and people in black suits are everywhere. Even after stopping at a gas station so we can all wash the blood from our hands and change our clothes, I'm hesitant to go further. Guys like us tend to dislike cops at the best of times, and right now, we're fifteen miles from our latest kill. Someone will notice that body, even if we were pretty deep in the lot — even if we did request a car from the least popular category specifically so nobody would see us in the lot, and nobody other than the rental counter knows which car we chose.

I'm definitely still drunk, so I'm unsure if that's a good or a bad thing. I'm pretty sure it's bad, but hey … we kill people and worry about getting caught all the time.

It's just usually not so public.

And not usually after all the security cameras in the lobby saw us or after Emil's real name ended up on a rental agreement.

Not usually without careful premeditation, including obfuscation and a plan for covert escape.

I look at my brother as he drives right up to a police barricade instead of looping back, wondering again if he's slipping … and, if so, why. Only, I think I know why. This assignment is too close to the bone. Emil spends at least fifteen minutes of even an off day complaining about the modern world like a Mennonite thumping a bible, and now our target has thrown us into the thick of the biggest internet *thing* since forever.

That could have been good. Cathartic erasure of the man most currently responsible for all Emil hates and bonus points because the man will pollute all of politics with status updates and meaningless social bullshit. Unless he's killed. Emil said it upfront at Hojo's house: *Bisset is a problem because he owns media.*

Now I wonder if Emil's potential catharsis has turned to obsession. If what could have been a healthy motive (for hitmen, anyway) has instead become a splinter under his skin.

Or maybe Bisset isn't the problem. Maybe it's the stress and pattern-breaker of the toss-up. Maybe it's all the competition out there or the still-unrealized hint that Blackhawk is after us more than he's after the senator.

Maybe we've been at this too long. Maybe, given a different history, this isn't who we'd have turned out to be.

Emil lowers his window and speaks to the cop using a mouth he just wiped clean of someone else's blood. "We're going to the W."

"Not today, you're not. Whole hotel is closed."

"For what?"

"Senate debates."

Now I get it. Now I understand.

"We're with the debates," Renee says from the passenger seat.

"No, we're not," I contradict her.

Assassins rarely enter through the front door. We might as well be drawing a chalk line to our perch. Ordinarily, when we're not this sloppy and reckless and carrying extra big-haired baggage, taking a commercial flight as part of a job isn't a problem. It's less risky to use our real IDs when traveling than to kill someone than it is to risk TSA and the FBI deciding we're hiding our identities, and hence worth looking into.

Usually, we'd fly in, get an anonymous room at a backward hotel that still takes cash and doesn't ask questions, and do our job without a whisper. This time, though, we got off the plane, had a confrontation on a shuttle with a man who'll be found dead, soon or already, then popped up at a high-security gathering staffed by L.A. and the federal's finest, documented on every level from professional (TV cameras) to amateur (thousands of star-fuckers grabbing all they can with their smartphones). The stupidest thing we could do right now is to go through with Renee's impulsive plan.

This isn't what we discussed. We agreed to lay low, then find a way to use Renee's connections to open a door just far enough to do our job covertly. This is her attempt to lift our spirits after the unfortunate events at the airport, but it's an amateur shot. If Renee tried to assassinate anyone, she'd be tried and convicted before her hairspray wore off.

Of course, Renee and Emil both ignore me. Renee hands her phone to the cop, who looks it over.

"This is a VIP invite." The cop scrutinizes us to see if we're famous, which of course, is more sloppy attention we know better than to avoid. "If you don't mind my asking, how are you tied to all of this?"

"I'm the senator's cousin," Renee says, and I feel like shoving a watermelon through her nostril just to see how painful it is. I don't know why she gave the cop her invite. She should have just handed him a connect-the-dots, because that's what the FBI and Secret Service will do, easily, when this is all over.

The cop nods, hands the phone back, and waves for his fellows to move a barricade and open the way.

"See? Easy as pie. You guys are lucky I'm here."

"Except that now if we act, it'll be easy for someone to see who might have done it."

"It's okay. It's only recon," Emil says, but I can tell from his voice that he's thinking the same thing. Ironically, the more Renee "helps" us, the further we move from being able to do our assignment. I'll bet she waves Bisset over so we can shake his hand once we're inside. That will be precious — Emil inches away from the man we're tasked to kill and get rich doing it (a man he'd kill for free, really) yet unable to act.

He'll look that son of a bitch in the eye, then have to smile and walk away. And, because we've been seen, probably never return. We'll have to let someone else kill Bisset while we go home and wait for another assassin on Heinzie's payroll to kill us.

Which *will* happen. I'm not the only one who thinks Emil is becoming a loose cannon. Emil getting sloppy makes Heinzie's world messy … and guys like Heinzie are always looking for an excuse to sweep the floor.

"That's right," Renee says. "*Only recon*. What's recon?"

Jesus fucking Christ.

"It's okay," Emil says, more to me than her. "I have an idea."

Once we're inside (through the parking garage and past just one guard, so at least our profile isn't climbing any further), Emil pulls me aside and explains his simple plan. Renee is legitimately Bisset's cousin and apparently visits L.A. often, and according to Renee, she's even been invited to affairs like this before. Nobody will find it strange that *she's* here — and although I'm sure *we'll* be asked for ID upstairs, so far, all we've shown is the invite. So far, Emil and I are nothing more than Renee's "plus one." Nobody knows our name — and with a little luck, maybe no cameras have spotted us.

While Renee visits a pre-security bathroom, Emil spills the rest of our plan. Unsurprisingly, he's reached all the same conclusions.

We're inches from making ourselves unusable. The second we enter our IDs into the security checkpoint system or show our faces to a camera, we can't *ever* touch the senator — not today, tomorrow, or a month from now.

We'll have two choices: Abandon the assignment, leaving now or staying for lunch, and accept that one of the other hunters will get the collar and earn the bounty. I don't love that choice, but it's better than prison.

Or we can find a way, somehow, to do it today, even given all the challenges. That sounds just about impossible … but seeing as the alternative is 1) a very brief retirement followed by one of Heinzie's goons ending our lives or 2) again, prison, I'm certainly willing to at least hear what Emil has in mind.

It's also possible that drink has affected my judgment because even paying lip service to something this crazy doesn't sound like me at all. But since I'm happy and a little sick? Sure. Bring that shit on.

When Renee comes out of the bathroom, Emil lets her steer us. She's done this song and dance before, so even missing knowledge of this specific building, she still knows the protocol. We stay separate, trying while in the lobby to look like we're three people who just happened to end up in the same place rather than a trio of people together. So far, there's only the one officer outside and the lone guard in here who could say we came with Renee. Throwing caution to the wind, Emil declares we can "handle them later."

Noting the position of a security camera in the corner, Emil whispers to Renee, telling her that she should go forward on her own while we head back toward the parking garage.

Crouched in the little car's back seat five minutes later, I tell my brother, "This is never going to work."

"It'll work."

"You don't know it'll work."

"And you don't know that it *won't* work, so why don't you just shut the fuck up?"

Emil's carry-on is in the back seat with me, and investigation reveals a pocket on the outside containing three tiny bottles of Scotch. I tap Emil, slouched out of view in the front seat. He jumps, surprised. He's that focused. I suppose I should be too, but frankly, I don't feel like it right now.

Emil looks back. "What?"

I shake the bottles. "You gonna drink these?"

"They're Scotch."

"And?"

"You don't drink Scotch."

That's true. But it's also true that Scotch smells really interesting. Like something that would easily catch on fire. I crack the seal on one and sniff.

"Hey!"

"Just a sip."

"This could happen any minute, Emil. You get that, right?"

I open the back door and puke onto the concrete. When I close the door again, the acrid scent of bile stays with me.

"Goddammit," Emil says, wrinkling his nose.

"Now I *have* to drink it," I say. My stomach feels different, but what does that bloody sack of tissue know?

"Robert, that's—"

I down a bottle in two big swigs. It's like drinking gasoline, but slightly less offensive than puke. Might be my imagination, but I'd swear I feel it immediately. My stomach just emptied of pesky food, making it ready for alcohol.

"Hey!"

Emil's phone chirps. It's the one he had earlier — the one Rumy used to tell us about the break-in to our garage.

"It's from Renee," he says, looking.

"Who else would it be from?"

"It says 'BRB.'"

"Okay."

"Like the thing you do instead of getting a hotel room?" Emil says, puzzling the three new letters on his phone.

"That's Airbnb."

"So what the fuck is BRB?"

"'Be right back,'" I tell him.

"With Bisset?"

"I assume."

"There's also a thumbs-up thingy." He shows me. A small yellow thumbs-up follows Renee's three-letter message.

"I guess that means she got him?"

I hear a new incoming text.

"Now she sent me something that looks like an eggplant."

"Jesus Christ." I decide, in this crucial moment, to drink another of the little Scotch bottles.

New sound. Emil shows me the phone: PROLLY 5 MINUTES.

"What's 'prolly'?"

Embarrassing. It's like when you were a kid, and your parents mispronounced all the cool bands.

"It means 'probably.'"

"Why didn't she write 'probably'?"

"'Prolly' is shorter."

"By two letters."

"Yeah, well, two letters."

Emil turns around and stares at me. "What the fuck's that mean?"

"If you can save two letters, why not save two letters?"

"That's retarded."

"You're not supposed to say 'retarded' anymore, Emil."

"Okay. Wonderful. Then it's *rtrded.*"

"What?"

"I saved two letters."

The Scotch is flavoring my drunk. For some reason, I'm more angry than amused.

"Just be ready. Renee got a U.S. Senator to personally come down to the parking garage to fix her 'flat tire.' Let's focus on that."

I'm pretty far from convinced of that, but my argument to Emil is stronger if I pretend that I believe she was successful. Maybe what she implied (and Emil agreed) was correct: despite being his cousin, Bisset just might want to fuck her. Renee might have only needed to approach him upstairs, whisper in his ear, and flash her lack of panties. He might send a staffer to fix her tire, but not if he suspects that what she's asking for his help with is more vaginal than automotive.

"Yeah," Emil says. "Let's *fcs*."

"What?"

"Oh, you don't know what I'm *syin?* Like, my communication style is somehow incomprehensible when I fall down to the lowest common denominator? Is that, like, the problem? Like, right?" Emil pantomimes snapping a selfie with full duck lips. "Tell you what. MySpace this."

"MySpace hasn't been a thing for decades."

I swig again. Then Emil says:

"Do you think he'd really fuck her?"

"Are you kidding me?"

"But … cousins."

"Patty and Cathy were cousins," I tell him.

"What?"

"On *The Patty Duke Show.*"

Emil looks at me like I'm crazy. I don't know why. I often think about 1950s TV shows. Like *Mr. Ed.* Why did Ed live in Wilbur's office? Or, if you really want a mind-fuck: Why did Wilbur work in Ed's barn?

"You're drunk," Emil says.

"Duh. You know what? We really should capture this brotherly moment. Say fucking *CHEESE!*" I grab Emil by the collar as firmly as if I planned to head-butt him. I smash his face into the gap between seats as I sidle up beside him and extend the camera for a brothers' selfie. And, of course, more duck lips.

I get the shot, but then Emil is thrashing away.

"The fuck's wrong with you?" I ask.

"Hey, I'm not going to post it anywhere."

Emil straightens his shirt, shooting me dirty glances.

"Well. Maybe on Float. If I can find just the right photo filter to make you look *super sexy.*"

Emil reaches. "Give me that."

I play keep-away instead.

"No."

"Robert ..."

"No!"

A small sound — a dropped coin, a kicked screw, or nail — comes from outside. Emil stops struggling with his hand on my offending phone, so I seize my opportunity and yank it back.

He sits up a little taller, looking around.

"What was that?"

"Renee, probably."

Emil looks so intense, I almost want to laugh. But that's probably the whiskey talking. And if not, then maybe the vodka.

He shakes his head. His voice is so low, I have to concentrate hard.

"She'll come from over there." He points to a single light mounted over the elevator.

I broke it after we came back through. From what Renee said, security keeps a close eye on the public-facing doors, but they always allow rear entrances and exits for those being protected to come and go. The parking garage — which only invited people should be able to access — is outside of the security perimeter but only barely. It's the perfect place for senators and their people to smoke, snort coke off their dashboards unseen, or fuck their cousins. If Renee does her seduction job right, she won't have any problem leading him down here by the dick.

Emil's point is that the sound we just heard came from the other side of the parking garage. The side *away* from the elevator.

"A rat," I suppose.

"Or someone else taking advantage of the privacy

down here." He looks hard, eyes peeled for the cherry on the end of a joint or perhaps the bobbing head of an aide in someone's lap.

Emil eases his door open, minding the latch.

"I'm going to check."

I grab his jacket just as he's stepping out. He looks back at me with serious eyes.

"What if Renee and Bisset come while you're over there looking?"

"I'll be quick."

"That's not an answer."

"I'll—"

There's a ding. With the bulb by the elevator open, the only light to herald its arrival is the small display above the door.

"Fuck." Emil rushes back inside and grabs his rifle. It's not the good one, lost in the Molotov. Instead, Emil had to call his Santa Monica guy and pony up for a rush order, delivered stat. Pretty sure the thing came from Walmart. Good thing we're close-quarters for this job; I doubt there's accuracy on this pea-shooter beyond fifty feet or so.

He's not aimed by the time the doors start to open. I'm trying, but the sights on the end of my little Beretta keep doubling and going out of focus. I make myself breathe. It's okay.

He'll be distracted. We have time.

I think that until a hail of automatic fire comes from where we heard that sound, peppering the elevator doors with rounds before they're even fully open.

Emil pulls me down, then peeks up and back. From where I'm lying, I can see the star-fire pattern from something showy but impractical on a job like this — an M16, or maybe an AK-47. Bullets in bursts, rattling with the hail of metal.

The shots pause, and I chance a look at the elevator. At first, I think it's empty, standing open with no apparent intent to close again. Something fried inside; I see tiny white tendrils of smoke. The right-side door keeps blipping forward a half-inch, then quickly retracting. Either a bullet warped its surface, and it can't close anymore, or something's blocking the collision sensors that keep the doors from biting arms from their sockets.

But then I see a fat little butterball of a man dart from his hiding place like a Green Beret. He's clear of the elevator in one second, crouched behind a mammoth Lincoln a second later. He must have dodged left when the shots came, but my gut says he was ready, knowing the garage might come with bullets.

"Shit," Emil says.

"What?"

"Rock Harder."

"Now's not really the time."

Emil grabs me by the back of the head, lifts me up, and makes me look. The shooter must have seen their target exit the elevator because there was a new cough of bullets when he went, but right now, the air is calm. It's a standoff: an unknown assailant in the shadows and that little fireplug we met at Heinzie's, Rock Harder, behind the Lincoln. Nobody knows we're here, so far as I can tell.

"*Rock Harder,*" he repeats. "The assassin, asshole. Not the concept."

This is funny for ten seconds, then uncontainable immediately after. I start to chuckle, remembering what Rock looked like when he rushed from the elevator … then mentally completing the picture now that I understand what I saw.

I see it again: that musclebound shorty flap-footing across weaponized space. Rock strikes me as one of those highly specialized human machines, able to do one thing extremely well under precisely calibrated positions. I've no doubt that if you lay Rock on a bench and position him in a kiddie seat, so he's able to move a barbell just so, he's "strong." But under ordinary circumstances, I could probably walk up and push him over. He'd end up on his back with flailing turtle legs while I did whatever I wanted.

My cheeks puff with contained laughter. Emil looks over and is about to reprimand me when a stronger laugh arrives — and this one, unlike the last, refuses to stay inside my mouth.

Rock hears me and looks back without seeing. Emil has one hand back as if to slap me, then returns both hands to his rifle. He's wishing he had a handgun, I imagine, but we put all the guns other than the ones we planned to use in the trunk.

Emil mouths more than says to me, "It's okay. He's—"

Every window in our car detonates at once. I hit the seat, and Emil crumples so low he's practically in the footwell. My heart is a bomb exploding on repeat, blood rushing like it's got somewhere to go. For long seconds, I lose cognition to panic. Half of it's the drink, but half is the futile dawn of unfamiliar territory. We're supposed to be silent killers and seldom see the whites of our targets' eyes. I'm not used to trench warfare. I'm not used to feeling like this time, we both might die.

Just as I'm considering depositing a big shit in my pants, the gunfire stops.

Emil is on his back with that big rifle as ready as he can make it, staring upward at a car top that's now only partially there. We lock eyes and silently count together: *1, 2, 3*. Then I sit up, point where I saw that star-fire pattern, and am about to pull the trigger when fresh rounds shred our door from the right.

"That little fucking fireplug shooting at us, too?" Emil asks.

I shake my head, realizing the intense *Oh-Fuck* of this moment but unable to speak until it starts again — only this time, there are two automatic weapons in different places. For a while, one keeps sighting on us, blowing perfectly round paint-peeled holes in our rental. We crouch low again, knowing we can only wait and hope. Car doors are as bulletproof as tinfoil. All we can pray is that more shots come from the front. The engine block is our only true cover.

"They're shooting at each other," I say.

"Duck and whoever's trying to kill him?"

"Them, but also someone else."

Emil acts like he doesn't understand English. He peeks up, then back down when shots resume.

"Len and Kerry," Emil says.

"Where?"

"By the exit sign."

"You mean …" I point.

"No." And he points.

I realize what's happened all at once. There's no prey in this parking garage. The place is filled with predators.

Rock Harder, behind the Lincoln, armed with handguns perhaps because he's been upstairs, and small weapons are all he trusted to take inside. Maybe he stopped at security, or maybe he had other reasons for coming down. Reasons like all these other assassins, all of whom seem to have been thinking the same thing.

"Goddammit, Robert. This is your fault," Emil hisses.

"How!"

"Using those goddamn phones. Talking on your goddamn networks. Can't you be a human for a while? Talk to me, right here, instead of the fucking inter—"

The last of our windows explodes like a bomb.

New shooter, based on muzzle flash. How many of us are in here?

Quiet. Then: "Nisha?"

I almost recognize that voice. Nisha Swartha must be here as well because a few seconds later, I hear her voice. "That you, Dahlia?"

Emil juts his chin toward the door to my left. "Now. Go to the wall. There." He points. "I'll circle that way." He points in another direction, though the plan still isn't clear.

"Maybe we should stay together," I say.

Emil looks at me with disgust. I'm not functional, not really. Especially not after those last two whiskeys. He opens the door whisper-quiet without comment. I guess I'm supposed to follow.

Running low, equilibrium fails me. For a while, I'm sure I'm tracking this garage floor without any problems, but then I hit a garbage can and knock it over. Trash rolls everywhere.

I look up at Emil with an apologetic expression, but he isn't even looking at me. He's locked his gaze on something else. Len, of Len and Kerry fame, holding a pistol in my brother's face.

Len laughs as he recognizes Emil and says his name.

"Been meaning to talk to you. In the current real estate market, you should really consider refinancing your—"

Len's head explodes like a melon. I see Kerry, his wife, five feet away and just now rising from kneeling to a protective crouch. The weapon in her hand is larger and still smoking.

"Not everything is a refi situation, Len," she tells her husband's corpse.

Emil gapes at her.

"What? I'm tired of him getting all the credit. Why isn't it 'Kerry and Len'?"

Bullets pock the Range Rover behind her, so she crouches lower, now with her gun seeking aim. It's distraction enough to get away.

"Hey, Dahlia!" I hear Kerry shout — only, she's using a rather racist accent to imitate Nisha Swartha's voice. "That Duck guy is by the exit! Cut him off!"

When Dahlia Sweet rises to join this apparent battlefield alliance with whom she assumes is Nisha, Kerry fires three rapid shots and knocks her dead.

Meanwhile, I see the real Nisha pop up with a gun so large, I'm mostly impressed that she got it in here. It's for precision work, but she manages it deftly in close quarters anyway. This time it's Kerry's head that pops like a zit and her brains that hit the windshield of a big blue Mercedes van.

Nisha's pop-up attracts fire from the original shooter or someone who's flanked around to the original shooter's position. I hear stutter-fire, then finally see part of the offending weapon from behind a Camry in an overhead light: long and black, gripped by extremely hairy hands.

"That's Terry with the M16," I say.

"Terry *Bartow?*"

I nod. My stomach lurches, and I almost throw up again.

"You're drunk. There's no way."

He pops up, gets a lead haircut, and comes down, running his hands through bullet-riffled hair. His eyes are wide, mouth just a little bit open.

"So," I say. "Is it Terry?"

I've lost track of the shooters, but Emil makes two of the same circuit with his glances: the exit sign to the right of the elevator and a double-wide concrete post near the center. I'm guessing that means he thinks there are three live shooters still in play, at least.

"How many of us are here?" he asks with his ass on the concrete, both of our backs to metal.

It's rhetorical, but I count anyway. Len and Kerry are both dead, along with Dahlia Sweet. I raise a hand, then extend my thumb. "Nisha," I say. I raise my index finger. "Rock."

Emil nods. "Terry."

"The Duck," I add, raising a fourth finger.

"Kerry said Duck. She might have just been making it up to get Dahlia's attention."

Rapid footsteps: the pitter-pat of someone unused to sneaking in close quarters.

Just as I'm thinking it couldn't possibly be so unlucky as to cross our path, it does. I look up to see Terry emerge with what does indeed seem to be an M16.

His eyes widen. He wasn't expecting to see us, and Emil, with his big clumsy rifle ready, makes our presence known.

The bullet goes through his throat, and at first I think Emil simply missed the kill shot. But then Terry goes down, and Emil preys over him like a spider. I realize the idea was only to mortally wound, not kill outright.

"How did you know we'd be here?"

Terry gurgles. He tries to speak, but all that comes out is the whistle of air through a straw.

"Robert," Emil says. I look over, and he snaps, pointing at something. Terry watches this without turning his head. He looks confused. Dying will do that.

"What?" I hiss.

"Throw me your shirt."

"Fuck you! Use your own shirt!"

Terry gurgles again, even more confused.

Emil snatches a discarded napkin from my tossed trash can. Then he stares hard at me for a full three seconds before returning to Terry and pressing the napkin hard against the shear in his windpipe.

"I'm … not going to make it," Terry manages to croak.

Emil looks disgusted. "Of course, you aren't. Who do you think I am?"

Another croak — this one indistinguishable.

"Answer. How did you know we were here?"

"Why … help you?"

"Because I can make your wound stop hurting." Then he jabs his finger in Terry's wound but takes the napkin away first, so his scream is silent. He presses it back in place and waits.

"Didn't," Terry says.

"Didn't what?"

"Know."

"So why are you here?"

"Bisset."

"What the fuck about Bisset?"

Terry starts to swoon, so Emil digs into his wound again.

"Don't you fucking die yet, asshole," Emil says. "What about Bisset?"

"Here."

"I know he's here. Why are all of *you* here?"

"*You're* here," Terry says.

"I know why *we're* here. Let's talk about you."

At the mention of "we're," it's like Terry finally realizes I'm here, that I'm the dickhead who knocked over a trash can to ramp this melee up to eleven. He turns away from Emil, fully toward me. I lock eyes with him as he looks very hard at my position.

As his eyes start to go glassy, he returns his attention to Emil. "You."

"What about me?"

"You." *Swallow. Cough.* "Are fucking crazy."

Then he dies. I really *must* be drunk, because all I can think as Terry goes limp is how when the cops review this scene, they'll see three clean kills and one that took a while. I'm bothered for Emil's reputation. Without explanation, they'll assume that one of the assassins was a slacker, unable to get a clean headshot.

This feels in need of correction. I wonder if I can leave a note just so our team doesn't come across as incompetent.

New chatter boils from the stairwell as a door cracks, then re-closes. I see Rock Harder, visible to us without us being visible to him, squeezing his little muscular body between two cars.

We scamper with light footsteps. From the shadows, I hear another set, making for the wide-open exit at the garage's end. There's a scuffle, a single gunshot, then a series of sounds that read like revving an engine, prelude to driving off.

The next thing we see is a green SUV barreling toward the exit, hitting the dips and rises of the ramp fast enough to bounce the carriage and bottom-out the shocks. I hear the squeal of tires and the whine of the engine until it fades. There are no accompanying cars, sirens, or guns. Somehow — and this, I suspect, will forever stay a mystery — whoever's in that SUV managed to carve a path even with all this security and get away clean.

The door by the elevator bursts open, and SWAT types in body armor swarm like locusts. To me, still inebriated, it's almost funny. But while we still have a head start, Emil drags me up, and we haul ass.

There's a body on the exit ramp: Rock Harder. *Oh, absurd Butterball pseudonym, we hardly knew ye.*

My legs want to carry me past his corpse and into daylight, but I'm not thinking straight, and Emil is at least aware enough to know it. I have no idea how Nisha drove out without a tail, but the chances that we'll do the same — especially without a car and with a half-dozen armed men coming from our rear — are slim to none.

We duck into a utility closet instead and from there into an oversized vent.

Inside, I feel like an old-fashioned TV dinner.

Time passes.

All we can do is wait and hope we're not found.

EIGHTEEN

The Only Way Out

SILENT IN THE vent for hours, my thoughts start to wander.

I try to picture a three-sided coin. Which, really, ordinary coins have. The third side is ribbon-thin and wraps the circumference. Realized, this blows my mind.

I start thinking about seagulls and wonder if they have any feelings about their bad reputation.

I wonder if taco shells make fun of tostada shells or vice-versa. In the world of pounded corn, is it better to be flat or folded?

"Robert."

I look up at Emil. He's stark black and white like a Bergman film. The light in here is funny. The vent we came through was already mostly blocked by boxes, but my brother bought us insurance by reaching through the grate to hang a drape as well. That's the dark half. But there's also light coming from somewhere, reflected a thousand times through the sharp facets of the aluminum vent. I'm seeing half a man when I look at my brother, an equator between dim and illuminated as sharp as the demarcation on the dark side of the moon. I must look like half a man to his eyes. Together, I suppose, the two of us only add up to one.

"Yeah," I say.

"I count five dead. One got away."

"Or two, if The Duck was here."

"Either way, that's a lot of professionals."

I shrug. I don't need to confirm what he said, and right now, I don't feel like talking. I have no idea if The Duck was in that scrap or if it was the fog of battle giving us that impression. My guess is no. Only one car got away, and I have a hard time seeing Nisha and The Duck working together. I got a good look at The Duck back at Heinzie's, and that's all it took to convince me they couldn't be a team. They'd never pass for an innocent couple. Or a couple at all. Possibly a master and her pet. Maybe a special effects specialist and some sort of animatronic troll meant for a movie that hates children.

"How did they get here?" Emil asks.

"Dunno. Flew?"

"But I mean … How did they get inside? How did they get through security?"

"*We* got through security."

"With Renee's help. Nobody else is Bisset's cousin. Nobody else would have a VIP invite."

I make a face Emil can't see. Who cares? We almost died. I was almost a smear on the road. A human speed-bump through whose bloodstain future users of this garage would drive over. My legacy, forgotten.

It's fucked me up a little. I can't lose me. I'm all I've got.

"You hear me?"

"I hear you, Emil."

He must hear something in my voice, too, because his

Bergman-lit face seems to scrunch. "You pissed at me or something?"

"'Nobody else is Bisset's cousin,'" I repeat.

"What?"

"I've got a theory, Emil. Do you want to hear it?"

"Okay …"

"I think Renee was nervous or stupid, and something she said or something she did made security pay attention. I think someone squawked over the radio about a possible threat at the W, and that's what brought the others, who were using their codebreakers to listen in."

"Bullshit," Emil says.

"How is it bullshit?"

"It's too fast. There wouldn't be time for Renee to fuck up, for security to be alerted, and for all these others to run from wherever they were to here."

"Think about it for a second, Emil. They wouldn't be 'just anywhere,' waiting for their chance. They'd be around *him*. Everyone knows Bisset is here for the debates. It's exactly the crowded clusterfuck we were trying to avoid by going to Florida first … *away* from the obvious target everyone in the toss-up would zero in on."

Emil, to his credit, doesn't immediately bite back. I don't usually challenge the decisions he makes for the pair of us … and when I have, he seldom listens without being defensive. But ever since Vegas, I've noticed myself becoming more vocal and Emil more willing to listen.

Vegas. A pull of the one-armed bandit. The machine was called Wild West, and Emil won the jackpot when the wheels stopped on three silver bullets. We had lobster for dinner. Emil ordered two high-end escorts, then screwed them both when I decided, for reasons unknown even to myself, to take a long walk instead. Only when we were winding down later that night did Emil put his finger on what'd been bothering me so much — the reason those three bullets on the slot machine felt more like a curse than a bounty.

You know, he said, *it was exactly twenty years ago today that I made my first kill.*

I remembered. There was no way I couldn't.

At the risk of being a cliché, I told him, *sometimes I wonder if I'm getting too old for this shit.*

Emil grunted, never a fan of the objections I've made since this all started. But now, in the dark, like we were when Emil ruminated on his two-decade career, it occurs to me that maybe he didn't dismiss what I said that night. Instead, maybe a door was opened. Maybe, since then, I've been prying it wider and wider.

"Maybe you're right."

That turns my head. I'm not sure I've ever heard my brother say those words, in that order, ever. He's looking right at me. Into me. Through me. It creeps me out, so I look away.

I imagine an orange without its skin.

I picture vehicular homicide, a figure dead on the yellow strip down the center of a road.

I remember one of my favorite posted signs from Shady Acres, stored in my cloud photos if I want to dig it out, showing one stick figure helping another to stand. The legend read, KINDLY ASSIST YOUR NEIGHBORS, but to me, it always looked like the rear figure was sodomizing the first. On our last day there, someone painted Wite-Out over the "IST," turning the message into KINDLY ASS YOUR NEIGHBORS. It certainly wasn't me.

"Did you know that Mickey Dolenz's mother invented Wite-Out?" I ask.

"What?"

"Mickey Dolenz. From *The Monkees*?"

Emil makes a noise. Then: "What the fuck are you talking about?"

I tell him never mind, but it's true. I have no idea what the other Monkees or their families did after the 60s ended. Well, except for Davy Jones. He got that locker that sailors are always talking about.

"She fucked up, Emil. That has to be it. All she had to do was find him, make him think she wanted to fuck him and get him down to the parking garage."

"Maybe Rock was already in the elevator, and that's why they couldn't go."

"And that's another thing, Emil," I say, feeling my advantage grow. "Why the hell was Rock Harder inside the elevator — *coming down?*"

"If she was talking too loud, he might have overheard. He was upstairs, trying to figure out how to get through security when Renee told Bisset to take her down to the garage and ravish her."

"She'd be discrete," Emil says.

"… when she told Bisset that she wanted him to bend her over and ravish every orifice she has."

"I don't know that she'd say that … "

"When she said, 'Come in my hair! It's better than conditioner.'"

"Shut the fuck up, Robert."

Silence again. My displaced anger — from the loose lips I'm increasingly sure Renee used upstairs to Emil, who insisted we let her tag along — slowly dissipates. Sixty seconds later, we're two assholes trapped in a vent again. It's not big enough for both of us. Emil went first, and there's room past a constriction for exactly one person to conceal himself completely. I, on the other hand, had to settle for this vent's anteroom. When the cops came, when the FBI came, when the Secret Service came to drag away all the bodies and mop up all the blood, they must have decided Nisha was the culprit, and she got away, through means unknown.

Their investigation (as much as I could tell from inside this oven) seemed beyond half-assed. Like quarter-assed. Maybe as low as ten percent assed, relative to what you'd think would be required. All I can figure is they don't have time right now for *WHY* and therefore settled for tightening security to keep any other malevolent *WHOs* out. Bisset was never directly threatened. While he and Renee played awkward footsie upstairs in luxury, it was just the assholes down here who went about killing each other.

I use a single finger to move the drape outside our vent, just barely enough to see. Emil starts to object but settles once he sees that I'm not moving to leave and only wanting a peek.

I get a shadowed view of a utility room. Not much there.

"I'll admit it," Emil says out of the blue. "I thought we were caught for sure."

He wasn't the only one. Through the sheer fabric, I watched a trio of agents search this room. One even moved the boxes and pulled back the drape. With Emil in the only truly concealed spot, I had nowhere to go. I'd retreated as far back as possible, knowing I had partial concealment but nowhere near all, hoping with all my might that the dim, confusing light would hide enough of me. Somehow, I got lucky. Somehow, the agent looked right my way and never saw a thing.

"Yeah," I say.

More time passes. I think more strange things, but mostly I think of how I never want to hide inside a vent for five hours again. What used to be merely uncomfortable turned to stabbing pain, then numbness. A breed of agony that makes me wonder if I'm cutting off circulation and doing damage that only an amputation can fix. I'm ravenous. My lips and mouth are dry, and it wasn't too long ago that I was sure I'd spend the rest of my life in prison. Wouldn't the other inmates have fun with my torso once every ailing limb had been amputated?

"Emil."

"Yeah."

"I don't want to do this anymore."

"Maybe we can sneak out now. It's been long enough."

"Not hiding in the vent. I mean … *this*. All of *this*."

Emil reaches past me to raise the drape, giving his expression light that hasn't been there before. I wait for a reaction, knowing that what I just said is perhaps my most stern, most sincere declaration of the issue we keep circling.

One of us can't quit; it's both or neither. My saying I want out is saying I want my brother out. Emil, historically, has reacted to that in one way even while the door has begun to open wider.

So I wait for the explosion. I wait for his scorn, his derision, his condescension, his outright threats. But he hears it without responding. As if the words haven't made their way into his brain. He just looks out into the storeroom, then lets the drape fall and sits back in the shadows, again becoming mostly eyes and cheekbones. He's the reaper on the beach, eager to play chess.

"Emil? Did you hear me?"

The storeroom door opens before he can answer. Emil's finger shoots to his lips, but it's beyond unnecessary. I've been pondering capture for the entire afternoon. I wouldn't speak if he paid me.

We listen, stock still, while feet plod the small space. I

can see a silhouette, but I don't dare lean in for a closer look. We managed to get most of the boxes back in front of our vent, and the drape just looks like a rag spilled from one of them — but still, if our visitor gets the urge to snoop, he'll only have to lift the blind.

Emil's phone illuminates. He set it on our prison floor after we first climbed in and hasn't touched it since. He keeps it on Do Not Disturb, but the screen still lights up. Emil covers the screen with his hand to bury the light, but then one of his eyebrows raises, and he looks at it again.

It's from Renee: *WTF are you?*

Then a voice from beyond our curtain: "Seriously."

I sigh, unsure whether I'm more annoyed to hear that voice or pleased to finally escape confinement. But … Oh, who am I kidding? If it were a giant oozing zit outside, I'd still lick it with gratitude.

My legs are numb and weak, so I prop myself against a wall to let them resuscitate. Then I look at Renee, smile in a way I thought I'd never smile at her, and say, "Thank you for—"

Of course, once Emil exits the vent behind me, I might as well be a wafted fart. She wraps her arms around him, kisses him with way too much tongue, and palms his crotch in a manner that seems to claim it as her rightful property. I think they slobber gratitude to each other, but it's in the language of gross and saliva.

"You were in the vent?" she asks.

"So *that's* what you meant with that text," I say.

"When I didn't see you in here, I thought maybe they caught you after all!"

"Traditionally," I go on, "'WTF' means '*what* the fuck', not '*where* the fuck.'"

"We knew what she meant, Robert," Emil tells me as he grabs Renee's ass.

They put their hands crisscross in each other's back pockets. It's like we're in high school. I wonder if it's too late to crawl back inside the vent. We were making progress in there. Emil was finally willing to listen.

But now Yoko is back, and here we are all over again.

"I heard gunshots. They locked us down upstairs."

"Yeah," Emil says.

"What happened?"

"Competition."

"I heard that someone died."

"A few someones," Emil says.

Renee claps a hand over her mouth. She does it with all four fingers bent past neutral, making a flat little bow that displays her nails. Even her way of showing shock pisses me off.

"It's okay," Emil goes on. "They were bad people."

I want to say, *just like* we're *bad people*. But the way they are right now, I'd never get a response. It's too good of a gotcha — too fine of a petard for Emil to be hoisted upon later — for me to use the line now.

The dissonance is strong with this one. Emil only takes jobs he feels are morally justified. Sometimes, when faced with a less moral job, he asks for more money until it feels moral again. We're not the bad guys. We fell into this, intent on doing good.

"What happened with you?" Emil asks.

"Yeah," I add. "How did you fuck us?"

"Hey!" Emil chastises.

Renee's eyes tick toward me, but she doesn't respond to the loaded weight of my question. Instead, she swallows, and I see her gears turning, trying to recalibrate. Reframe this in a way that's not her fault. Or anybody's.

"I couldn't even get in. My invite didn't scan right, so the guard called up for authorization and talked to

193

someone for a while, and then he apologized and said I'd need to wait. They'd had a breach, I think. Someone's invite was counterfeit, and they'd just found the guy and kicked him out."

"They didn't arrest him?" I say.

"He just walked out," she answers. "They just let him go. I get the feeling he was ... connected."

Renee's grasp on the politics of crime is laughable, but there's a grain of truth in her implication. Most people think there are good guys on one side and bad guys on the other, but a network of bribes, glad-handing, and personal favors blurs that line until it's fuzzy at best. Most of the assassins I know get their intel and ultimately their kill position through whispers and bribes. If Rock didn't have a gun on him inside, I've no doubt he'd have a contingency to abort unscathed. He could have stashed weapons elsewhere, awaiting the right opportunity.

"Anyway, they sort of went into lockdown. My message must have gotten to Simon because he came down and made like he wanted to protect me or something anyway." Renee rolls her eyes.

"So he knows you're here."

"Of course. He invited me."

Emil's phone lights up again. I see it's from Rumy, but he stashes the phone — probably so Renee won't see he has another woman waiting.

I couldn't read it in time, but still, the message reminds me that we're in a pincer, with opposition both in front and behind.

We can't get out of this now. We can retire rich if we finish the assignment. Bail, and it's only a matter of time before we end up just as dead as Len, Kerry, Dahlia, Rock, and Terry.

I don't know what Heinzie is up to, but if I allow for

his meddling in the equation of what happened here, a lot of things start falling into place. He's playing both sides, and that means we have no idea how many gun barrels will follow our failure.

This assignment has left us with no other choice.

The only way out is through.

NINETEEN

Touché

Anonymous hotel, butthole of the west coast. There are plenty of shitty spots even in Southern California. You just have to know where to look.

I'm in the dark on a patio that looks out across a view of a dump, smoking. Robert hates when I smoke. Curiously, when he gets on his usual rant, he uses my name far more than usual.

Emil, you're going to die early if you keep doing that. How can you ignore all the evidence out there, Emil? You quit years ago, Emil. You're only smoking from stress. You could eat a cookie and get the same effect. You could pull up porn and whack it instead of smoking, Emil.

Fuck. It's just exhausting. I've been Robert's big brother all my life, and since pretty much the start, he's always stuck around me. These days, I don't even talk about it anymore. People say I'm crazy every time, once they know just how close I carry his sorry ass.

The door cracks. I hide my cigarette as a reflex, then relax when I see it's only Renee.

"Sorry. Didn't mean to scare you."

"I thought you were … You know what? Fuck it." I suck on the filter with exuberant relish — like I'm on Broadway in front of an audience. "I'm my own man."

She sits beside me and wraps us both in the comforter draped over her shoulders.

"After you finish, maybe we can go back inside."

I puff.

"You know. *Inside.*"

I know what she means. And I want it. There's no love here, but that makes things easy. Way I see it, we're two people covered in poison ivy, so when one has an itch, the other scratches it. That, at least, I appreciate about Renee. There will never be discussions of what this means. We fuck because it feels good.

"*Inside,*" Renee repeats as if I'm thick.

"Not right now. I'm sort of preoccupied."

"Oh?" She hugs closer. Obnoxiously so. "About what?"

"My brother. Robert."

"What about him?"

I hold up my cigarette. It's just a butt now, held high for inspection. "He hates when I smoke, for one."

"So what? He's not here."

I light a new cigarette with the first, then grind out the old one in the pot of a plant that perished at least a year ago. I puff again, almost as luxuriantly. Then, because I can't take this attempt at affection, I stand out of Renee's cover just to be free of it.

For some reason, I feel the need to offend her. To hurt her feelings, just in case she's more deluded than I am. So I walk over to inspect a tree as if it's very interesting to me, as if its fascination is the reason I stood in the first place.

Then I turn and lean with my back to it, still close enough that we can keep our voices low. Why, I'm not sure. In case Robert peeks out or decides to visit, perhaps.

"That's right," I say. "He's *not* here."

Another long puff. A glance into the darkness.

"What's on your mind, Emil?"

I scoff. "That's ... not what this is."

"What isn't?"

"Us."

"Oh, I'm sorry," Renee says with sarcasm dripping from her body language. "I thought this was about you and Robert."

And I think, *Touché*.

"Tell me," she says.

"I don't think so."

So she stands. Gets close. She doesn't touch me, and she for damn sure doesn't try to comfort me. Good thing. I can't stand sympathy. The second I see it in Renee — in touch, in her eyes, or anything else — this is over. She promised to be useful back at the W, and I suppose there's still a chance she can help us lure him into the open if Bisset didn't get wise. But even now — even as potential — Renee's a liability. I have to keep reminding myself that we don't know her. She could rat us out intentionally or accidentally. She might reconsider and lose her nerve. She's seen me kill and seems to see my inherent danger as an aphrodisiac.

But I've always operated with Robert alone, neither of us letting anyone else get close. I know he's threatened by Renee and that neither likes the other. I know I'm walking a tightrope I'd typically know better than to walk, simply by having her here. And that right there makes me think.

Maybe Robert's right. Maybe I am slipping. Maybe

I've been at this too long, and it's time to let go. Move on. Let two decades of self-punishment finally end so the next phase can start.

Yet as my mind finishes its thought, I still feel like punching myself. If anyone said to me what I just said to myself, I'd end them without thinking twice.

"Emil. Look at me."

So I do.

"I didn't tell you why I want Simon dead."

"Because he put your life on camera, then built an empire around it," I recite.

"That's what he *did*, but it isn't the *reason*. I've had my fair share of spoiled meat, Emil. Bad boyfriends I didn't know better than to leave until somehow it was all over. I've been shit on and disrespected in ways, frankly, that no man can ever understand. So you tell me. When I've been hit and insulted and stood up and yelled at, constantly, in front of all my family and friends, why would one creepy peeping Tom cousin set me off?"

I wait for the answer, intrigued against my will.

"Before he did the whole 'Lilac' thing before, he got obsessed with Float; I knew he was Zero, you understand. I couldn't not know because the two of us grew up together."

I turn toward her.

"He did something shitty and embarrassing and humiliating and cruel to me, but that's not what bothers me most. We were friends before he did it. He got what he did out of me because he knew my secrets. He knew my passwords. My habits. His familiarity with me — almost like a brother himself, really — was what made it so easy … and so, *so* painful … to betray me."

I just blink, speechless for the first time in forever.

"I didn't have brothers growing up. I had Simon. I know it's different than a real brother, and I know it must be different for two boys instead of a boy and a girl like we were. But I get it. I know how good it can feel to know someone will — or at least is *supposed* to," she adds bitterly, "always have your back. And so I know how much that bond, if it breaks or is willfully broken, can hurt a person."

She leans against the tree too, now very close, still smart enough not to touch me in camaraderie or sympathy. She does pluck the cigarette from between my fingers, then takes a long, slow drag before handing it back.

"Look, I don't know Robert. Obviously, no one can — not in the way you know him. But if I could give you some advice—"

"No thanks," I say.

"—if your bond is mostly good, then keep it. But if it's starting to cause problems … well … "

She's eyeing me, being too dramatic and silently asking for too much of my involvement in this discussion I didn't want to have. Now I'm not just frustrated with Robert and the way he judges everything I do or the fact that more and more, I feel like all I do is to satisfy *him* rather than doing what's best for *us*.

For a moment, all of that's gone, and there's just me and Renee. Right now, it's *her* I want to throttle — not because she's done anything wrong, but because she's put my mind on this. I prefer it stuffed down, where it's safe. Now in the open, it feels real.

"Just fucking say it," I tell her.

"Not everyone is meant to be together forever. And if your relationship with your brother has become more about pain than about love, then … "

"Dammit, Renee."

"… then maybe it's time to start distancing yourself. Maybe it's time to let him go his way, so you can go yours without him."

TWENTY

Delete Asparagus

I SLEEP IN A CHAIR, my coat as a blanket.

Emil and Renee came in late, both reeking of smoke, pretending they were strategizing about our next shot at Senator Bisset, and took the only bed without asking. It's just as well. I'm sure this place has bedbugs. Fine by me. I'll take stiffness over parasites any day.

Something is different. It's impossible to pin down, but I can feel it like sensing a watcher in the shadows. It's as if someone moved all the frames on the wall in the night, but only by an inch in each direction. Or rotated the furniture, but only slightly. It's as if, while we slept, a crew came in on ninja feet and repainted the walls just three Sherwin-Williams chips darker or lighter.

The blend of manifest oddity and a total lack of *specifics* on that oddity ruins my sense of equilibrium, the way those spinning corridors at science museums put an otherwise sure-footed person off-balance. I'm not still drunk, but a part of me feels that way.

Emil rouses as I'm scouting the room, trying to find

what's amiss. He glances at Renee, still asleep, and whispers low. "Are you looking for bugs?"

"All the bugs are in that mattress," I tell him.

"I meant electronic bugs."

"Do you see me holding an RF sweeper?"

Emil sits up. He looks out the window, then at me. "The fuck you say to me?"

"I'm saying you ask stupid questions. I'm not holding a scanner, so obviously I'm not sweeping for bugs. Nobody outside the toss-up even knows we're here."

I stop there, thinking of how for all we know, Blackhawk is still hot on our tail. I don't pause for long, though. Emil's bossiness — doubled now that he's showing off in front of Renee — has gotten out of hand. For once, I'm determined to have a backbone, even if it means holding an untenable position for as long as I can.

"Since when are you worried about being bugged, anyway?"

"Since we started messing with the Secret Service. Since being present at the scene of a multiple homicide investigated by the FBI."

"But they didn't find us, did they? Didn't check a goddamn *vent*."

But at this, my mind shows me the agent who entered the storeroom. The agent who, in fact, *did* check the vent. I remember those eyes, waiting to see if they'd pick me out of the darkness. Only luck has kept us alive and free for this long.

"Whatever, man," Emil says, swinging his legs over the side of the bed. I'm on that side, though, and he kicks at me when I try to peek under the bed.

"Seriously, Robert. What the fuck."

"Something seem different about this room to you?"

He looks around. His hair, thanks to the pillows, looks

like he's wearing a hat. A big one, too, like what the Smurfs used to wear. As he shifts, his hair-hat droops forward like a doo-wopper with failing pomade.

"No."

"Someone's been in here."

Emil laughs dismissively. "When?"

"I don't know, Emil. Maybe when you were out smoking with your girlfriend."

Emil shakes his head: the gesture of a longsuffering mother who's finally had enough. "Yeah. Fine. Okay. I fucking smoked. Is that what this is about?"

"Smoking causes cancer, Emil. Do you want cancer, Emil?"

"Maybe I do want cancer, *Robert*. Did you ever consider that, *Robert?*"

"Are you … mocking me?"

"Not at all … *Robert.*"

I glare at him. "You know what? I figured out what's changed."

"What?"

"You."

"Oh. Clever."

"You've been doing stupid shit ever since the start of this assignment. No, no …" I think back. "Since *Vegas*. When we got that bounty, and you threw half of it away on a round of roulette. It's like … What's it like, Emil?"

"It's like your mother."

"Real mature, Emil. She's your mother, too."

"Yeah, and she fucking *left*. She *left* and Dad wasn't going to do shit for us, so guess who had to start doing everything? You think I've been doing stupid shit? Maybe you'd like to make the goddamn decisions instead of sitting on your ass and waiting for me to tell you what to do."

"Oh, I see. So what's happening here is, I'm *waiting for*

you to tell me what to do. Have I got that right? Are you sure it's not, *You do things your way no matter what I say, so what's the point of even trying?*"

Renee rolls over in her sleep. Emil looks at her, sees that she hasn't awoken, then immediately lays back into me.

"You want to make the decisions?"

"Of course."

"You want to make some right now?"

"Better than yours," I say, nodding.

"What exactly have I *chosen* that's so displeased His Majesty? Tell me that, so I'll have proper context for seeing exactly how superior your decisions are."

"Oh, I see. Now I can't win."

"How can't you win?"

My voice raises a notch. I could give a fuck if I wake Renee. I kind of want to make my point in a stronger way than a louder voice, come to think of it. Maybe if I kick her while I talk? Might help me think.

"How can't I win! Listen to you. Listen to what you just said. You're not going to honestly consider anything I have to say because—"

"Oh, that's such self-pitying *bullshit.*"

"—you've already decided and announced to the world that what I'm about to say, whatever it is—"

"You know what the problem here is, Robert?"

"—is stupid, so even if the next thing I say—"

"You're more worried about your ego than doing things right."

"—is the most brilliant thing in the world—"

Emil rolls his eyes so hard, it's like his head is a craps table. "Trust me. Whatever you're about to say, it's *not* the most brilliant thing in the world."

"Oh, fuck you, Emil!"

"Oh, too close to the bone?" He fakes sympathy. "I'm so sorry. Maybe you should retreat to your safe space. Maybe you'd better go out on the internet and tell everyone all about how sad you are. How your mean brother always hurts your feelings."

I shake my head, more frustrated with myself and our fraternal situation than angry or bothered. It's easy to hate Emil right now, but I loathe myself more. He's a bully, yes, but he couldn't be if I didn't let him talk to me like this — if I didn't let him dismiss my every valid concern, if I didn't pretend to accept his choices when in fact I never really stopped doubting them.

"You think I don't know you're still going onto Float every night? So yeah. I was smoking. So fucking what? That affects me and nobody else. Your stupid fucking hollow obsession affects all of us."

"Oh for … How exactly does what I do on my own time affect all of us?"

"It's the goddamn internet, Robert!" Emil exclaims, loud enough that Renee, to slumber on, must be a heavy fucking sleeper. "We're supposed to be invisible! We're supposed to not leave tracks!"

"I just read to catch up. That's all."

"Except when you post."

"I never post!"

"Really. Is that true, Egon McWhaite?"

My mouth opens, but no words can escape me. Emil, like the predator he is, sees his opportunity to go for the throat. He slides off the bed and comes closer, sitting in the opposite chair.

"You think I don't know you have an alter ego? Pretty long history on Float, Mr. McWhaite. Where did you get the name 'Egon' anyway?"

I consider denial, but I'm so trapped right now that I'll

only embarrass myself. Knowing I have no defense for my perhaps-unwise social media activity as a hired gun, I look for the right offense instead. Something I can shout at Emil that has nothing to do with me, just to put him on the defensive. But nothing arises in the seconds I have, so I do what I always do and cower to my brother's aggression.

"Ghostbusters," I answer.

"So do you also have a profile for Ray?"

"No." My voice is small. Pouty.

"What about Venkman? Shit, you *must* have a profile for Peter Venkman. Bill fuckin' Murray, man. King of comedy."

"No."

"Then what the fuck is wrong with you? You might as well be leaving a trail of breadcrumbs! You wonder why we have killers on our tail—"

"That's Heinzie's fault. Not mine."

"You're slipping, Robert. Something's just not working anymore."

We stand, chest to chest like frat bros ahead of a rumble. I glance at Renee. How is this not waking her?

"We finish this job," Emil says, "and then it's over."

"Finally. That's what I've been saying for months."

"Oh, *I'm* still going to keep working. I mean it's over with us."

"Excuse me?"

"I'm sick of carrying you. Sick of cleaning up all your mistakes."

"My mistakes!"

"You bury your face in the phones we steal. You hijack a tablet first thing whenever we settle somewhere new. You care more about your stupid online 'friends' than you care about your real ones. Of which, by the way, I'm the only one."

I scoff. Some friend he is.

"All sorts of computer friends-who-aren't-friends," Emil says with disgust. "But not a single real one."

"And whose fault is that?"

Emil turns away, but twists to look back at me. "Seriously? You're blaming me for your total and complete … *nonexistence* outside of your job and the last of your family?"

"You don't let me go out! You don't introduce me to anyone!"

"I introduced you to Renee." He gestures, as if I might not be painfully, disgustedly, infuriatingly clear about who "Renee" is.

"You didn't *introduce* me to Renee. You practically fucked her at our lunch table in front of me. Then you kept right on fucking her after you found out she lied to us. Who's the problem here, Emil? Who's the one who shoots phones by the side of the road and leaves them? Who leads us into a meth lab, shoots a bunch of rednecks, and leaves a burning car behind full of guns and stolen phones? Who crashes right through the front door of our target's biggest event? Who fucking *kills a guy in a rental car lot just because he mouths off,* Emil? Do you really think *that's* a bigger 'breadcrumb' than me posting a few cat videos?"

"You got something to say, then say it."

"You're a shit assassin."

He smirks. It's supposed to show me that the insult is so far out as to be absurd, but he can't quite pull it off. His old smile is weaker now, less sure of itself. My brother's usual bravado, over the past year, has become ego propped up with justifications. He used to be the real deal, but now I think he knows what I know — that at this point his image is at least half artifice. Emil was the best in the business, back when we started. Now he's an old man by industry standards, leaning on old accolades instead of current accomplishments … and fooling no one.

Including, more and more, himself.

"You forget things," I continue. "You leave clues. You talk to the wrong people just because you get it in your head, then you open doors for people to see what we're doing. You fly off the handle and have tantrums that are probably meant to be scary, but really only show how broken you are inside. You yell so you don't have to listen. It's not about the superiority of your arguments; it's about covering up just how unsure you feel inside."

"So now you're my shrink?"

"You use sex to distract you. Rumy. Renee. That girl from the last job, with the harelip."

"She didn't have a harelip."

"And when you're not fucking, you're constantly jerking off."

"I am *not* constantly jerking off!"

"Oh, please. The number of times I've slipped on a puddle of 'soap' in the shower after you've—"

"I don't beat off in the shower. I'm not shy. I'll beat off right here. Right fucking here, Robert."

I turn away. I hear a zipper go down. I turn back to see him threatening to unbutton with a challenging tilt to his eyebrows.

"Oh, put it away."

"You're not so fucking great yourself, Robert."

But he won't get the upper hand again. Not now that I'm rolling. This has been a long time coming. For years I've been trying to push us out of this business, because for years it's stopped suiting us. Since we hit our 20-year anniversary as killers, it's like a switch flipped, and Emil's starting to realize it too.

He just won't admit it. He's built too many walls, too

many defenses. If this thing we do collapses, I'm not sure what Emil will do and it's clear he doesn't either. If it collapses without us earning the bounty on Bisset? It'll mean the end. Of everything.

What, will Emil go off on his own and open a convenience store? I can just see him working 9-to-5 in a cubicle like anyone else, going home to a shitty apartment where all he has to do is watch TV and talk to himself. I can picture him in sweats and a stained T-shirt, not pressed and dressed in swanky couture like he does now. It's as if there are two Emils, one inside the other like a Russian nesting doll. The Emil I know, and the real one underneath. Admitting I'm right about retiring means the end of more to Emil than pulling a trigger.

"I'm *not* great," I agree. "Which is the point. I fuck up and you fuck up. So who wins here?"

"I'm only 'not great' because I have to drag you everywhere with me."

"So … What? You want to go alone?"

"I won't be alone." He looks toward the bed.

"You're serious," I say.

"Right now, working with her sounds a fuck of a lot better than working with you."

"She's not a professional."

"So what? Neither are you."

"You don't love her. You don't want her forming attachments."

"I'll manage."

"If you're so goddamn impressive, why don't you do it alone?"

"Why do it alone, when I have *Renee?*"

"Fuck Renee."

"Renee," he repeats, really rubbing it in.

"FUCK RENEE!"

But I don't just shout it. I also pluck Emil's discarded shoe from the floor and throw it at Renee's sleeping form. The thing hits her square, bouncing off her shoulder after a solid hit. She grunts but does not wake.

"Hey!" Emil blurts.

I inch closer to the bed.

"Get the fuck away from her."

But I don't get the fuck away. Instead, I pull Emil's gun from his bag. It's the .45. The big one. I put it to the back of her head.

"Very funny," Emil says.

I press it against her scalp. I want Renee to wake up. I want her to open her eyes, see that she's staring down the barrel to hell, and scream. Because I want my brother to *hear* her scream. And when she does, I want to watch his face. To see Emil's reaction. She's supposed to mean nothing. If she doesn't, it's just one more clue that he's past his prime and ready for wider pastures.

"Put it down," he tells me.

I cock the hammer and rap the muzzle against her skull, harder than I need to. How is this not waking her? I'm going to have to give her a concussion to bring her back to the land of the living.

"If I shoot her, how is it any different from what we always do? We always tidy our loose ends, erase ourselves from anything we do. And, sure, it'll take a good amount of time on this one. We've been way more visible than normal. Left way more loose ends — everywhere from that public scene at the restaurant to the cars we stole that will eventually be traced back to us. Fingerprints everywhere. Travel records in our real names, using our real IDs. And that guy you killed? You didn't do it from a distance. Think your DNA won't be all over him?"

"There's a way. We'll get past it."

When Emil comes closer, I poke Renee even harder. I hear a *clunk*, like a child's wooden instrument struck with its hammer, and still she snoozes on. Maybe I don't have to kill her to make my point. Maybe somehow, she already died.

"I don't want to get past it, Emil. I want out."

"Then go. Get out."

"I want *you* out."

"Not to be twelve years old," he says, "but you're not the boss of me."

"And you're not the boss of me."

"Fine. Fuck it. I'm not your boss."

"And yet you constantly tell me what to do. You decide for both of us. Jobs come in and you say yes or no without asking me. You get hunches and we follow them, without any input from my end. You want to fuck some broad in a truck stop, then invite her along on our adventure? Sure! If Emil wants to get his tip wet, who's Robert to say otherwise?"

Emil's hands are up, palms toward me. It's like I'm rushing the finish line, and he's signing for me to stop.

"It's not like that, Robert. Renee only came along because she's Bisset's cousin. She's here because she can help us do the job."

"And we accept it. Just like that. She could be lying. Like at the restaurant? This could be one long con."

"Robert ..."

"She went into the W, and we got ambushed. She *says* she got stopped at security, but ..."

"It wasn't just us there, Robert. Think for a second. Come on. Half the assassins in this toss-up were there. She couldn't have pulled that together if she wanted to. Even Heinzie couldn't do that. Put the gun down, Robert.

You're not thinking straight, and if you stop for a second, you'll damn well realize it."

Emil sneaks a look at Renee, seeming to wish she'd rouse as much as I do — but for different reasons. He wants her to wake so she can justify her actions and join his team. Right now, despite the gun, my absurd impression is that what we're doing is rude: talking about someone behind her back. *Literally* behind her back, in my case.

I hold the gun steady for another several seconds, then carefully lower the hammer.

Emil still has his hands up, waiting for what's next. So I show him. I'm sick and tired of playing by my brother's rules, my entire existence dictated by his neurosis. He's nuts, so I end up part of his nutty schemes.

I throw the .45 at him. It rockets from my hand like a fastball, flying at Emil's face like a tiny locomotive. He dodges just in time to avoid a broken nose and the gun strikes a lamp — a frosted bowl atop a long black stalk.

My eighty-mile-per-hour blue steel bullet strikes the lamp and it detonates like a bomb. Frosted shards fly onto Emil's hair and shoulders as the heavy gun thumps to the floor.

Renee finally wakes up.

She blinks and lifts her head, saying something my mind hears as "delete asparagus."

He retrieves the gun and I'm sure he'll aim it at me, but instead he ticks the safety and shoves it into his waistband. Emil's look suggests more sympathy than fury — and that, somehow, makes me wish I hadn't thrown the gun. I should have shot her. Left one more body in our wake on impulse, like he did back at the rental lot.

"Whassv," Renee mumbles.

It's almost a word, so she must be waking. Enough, it subsequently seems, to notice the gun Emil tucked not-entirely-covertly into his waistband, the shattered lamp, and the bad juju rotting all the air in between us.

"Whas goin on?" Renee brushes long brown hair from her face and rolls to look at Emil's side of the room more closely. "What happened to that lamp?"

"Nothing."

Renee notes Emil's cold stare, then turns to see what he's regarding with such intense, mixed emotion. She sees how coldly I'm staring back and falls silent. Her movements become slow. Precise and delicate, like a bomb squad technician's.

I stare even harder at Emil, then address Renee without moving my eyes. "Seems my brother and I just realized we have some irreconcilable differences. Isn't that right, Emil?"

"That's right," Emil tells me.

Renee, looking from one of us to the other, still seems half asleep. "*What* exactly is right?"

"Doesn't matter." I stoop down to stuff the offal back into my bag, then zip it and stand again. "Take the room. Fuck as loud as you want."

I open the door before either of them can respond, but I can't resist a final dig before leaving.

"If anyone comes to ask about the sound of that breaking lamp, just tell them it's no problem. The same 'no big deal' that fucked up their lamp killed some guy and is trying to assassinate everyone's favorite senator." I chuckle, once. "Look at you, you're so professional. So clean. Definitely not leaving a fucking spotlight's worth of incriminating shit behind you everywhere you go."

"Robert ..." Emil says.

"Do it your fucking self if you're so smart," I say, and then I'm gone.

TWENTY-ONE

Rock Bottom

FUCK ROBERT.

I think it when the manager shows up with a noise complaint. I think it again when he asks how the lamp broke. Renee answers the door in a T-shirt that's all pokey nipples, tells him we were having crazy sex, then tosses him three twenties to cover the lamp before slamming the door. But really … *sixty bucks?* Considering the state of this place even in the best and cleanest of times, it's an egregious overpayment.

And again I think, *Fuck Robert. Fuck my brother for all of this.*

I think it as we painstakingly clean up the mess he made, then stuff all our shit into duffels and load the car. And Renee keeps asking me, *What are you thinking, Emil? Do you want to talk about it?* But of course not, *no*, I definitely don't want to fucking *talk about it*. I prefer to push it all down. People always say that if you bottle up your feelings, bad juju will eventually get you in the end. I disagree. Repression is underrated. Bring on denial and the nostalgic stoicism of the "strong and silent type." Like my father.

Like the men I grew up with, learning to admire as much as fear them.

I even think *Fuck Robert* as I decide, even though it's an enormous pain in the ass, to wipe the room for prints. Normally we don't have to do this. *Emil* is a real person who leaves real-person trails wherever he goes, but the assassin who lives in my skin is a ghost. As long as I don't get too close and leave bits of myself at the scene of the crime, it's no big deal for my ordinary activities (like staying in a hotel room with a cheap lay, for instance) to leave DNA and prints all over the place.

The trick isn't to *live without leaving evidence*. The trick is to *keep your bad shit separate*. Do that well, and you only need to be careful when there's a gun in your hands.

But I wipe the room anyway because Robert got in my head. Because all the stupid shit he said has attached to me like a parasite. My brother has me wondering if maybe I *have* been sloppy. If maybe I *am* losing my edge. He's got me wondering if I'm in the right place — if this life is my future. But how can it be over? How can I be washed up? I'm still a young man.

Renee comes out of the bathroom, snapping the fingertips of the latex gloves we bought like a proctologist taunting the start of a rectal exam.

"You worried about jizz?" she asks.

"Like … as a concept? Or like if I'm on a bus and I sit in it?"

She points. "Like on the bed. You left a lot of jizz there, boy howdy."

I consider, then sigh. It's true. If someone sprinkled that mattress with Insta-Grow eggs (patent pending), babies would grow. I left enough fluid in this room to fill a water cooler. No matter how well we wipe the place, my cum will give me away unless we steal the mattress or burn it. Even then, I'm not sure it'll be enough to erase me and my tiny soldiers from this fleabag motel. We really rounded the horn while Robert was sleeping. There may be jizz in the bathroom rug. Dripping from the flea market art on the walls. On top of the ceiling fan.

"Fuck the jizz," I decide.

"That's the plan," Renee says. It's probably meant to be sexy, but instead it's just gross.

An hour later, I realize we're being way too thorough for a place that's inevitably so semen-soaked anyway, and that we're really only burning time. It's an uncomfortable thing to realize, because it's the kind of strong-and-silent thing I ordinarily hide from my internal eyes. But it's true. We're only still at the hotel because my subconscious is waiting for Robert to come to his senses and return.

If we leave right now, how will he know where to find me?

"What are you thinking, Emil?" Then, like clockwork: "Do you want to talk about it?"

Renee's obnoxious urge to psychoanalyze me is like a fart in an elevator. Suddenly and completely, I want nothing more than to get the fuck out of here.

My eye spies Robert's jacket as I start the car — the one he'd been using as a blanket. I ignore Renee's offer to hand it up and grab the jacket from the back seat myself, noting its weight immediately.

I check the pockets, knowing what I'll find. There's an iPhone on the left side. Except, it's not just an iPhone. It's *the* iPhone. The *last* one from our Shady Acres haul, after the Florida car fire that claimed the rest. Its timer expired overnight, meaning this final phone has switched from asset to liability. I never explicitly thought about it, but now I realize I assumed Robert had taken the phone with him.

He was always screwing with it, obsessed with the internet no matter how furious his face in it made me.

But seeing the thing in my hand, a tiny part of me breaks. We really are severing ties. There will be no way to contact us now. No number for Robert to call, considering that my antiquated flip phone — the one Rumy uses to get in touch — is deliberately unfindable. Nobody can call my flip unless they, like Rumy, install a scrambler app and enter the unique code key that matches mine.

Renee sees me staring at the phone and says, "Emil, what's—?"

"Nothing." I open the car door, walk to the parking lot's edge, and lay the phone in a small puddle deep enough to drown it. Then, as we drive off, I run over the thing several times. As we pull onto the road and eventually a freeway, I recite *Fuck Robert* inside my head like a mantra.

Strange feelings try to settle on me, so I summon a mental sword to slay them. As a waiting black cloud tries to rise inside me, I summon my best denial and sit atop it, shoving it right back down.

"Fuck Robert."

Renee, looking out the window, turns her head. "What?"

And I tell her, "Forget about it."

I do, but it takes five exits and a missed turn to fully expunge this morning's events from my mind.

"Tell me about him," I say.

But when I don't get an answer, I realize Renee has fallen asleep. I look over and hate her for a moment. The hatred comes like a white-hot welder's torch, then dissipates just as fast. I blink with the feeling of a near miss. I'd have sworn, for a second there, that all my instincts wanted her dead.

My hand, usually so dutifully at two on the clock of the steering wheel, has moved to my chest of its own accord. A few fingers have even slipped beneath my jacket to brush the grip of the .45 in its holster.

I whip my hand back to the steering wheel and breathe. What the fuck?

"Renee."

Nothing. Just like back at the hotel, when we had our fight.

"Renee."

Fuck Renee, says a voice in my head. Then, because the voice is a wiseass, it adds *but not in the good way.*

"Renee!"

You can still kill her.

And I realize that the voice belongs to my brother.

Shoot her. Open the door, unbuckle her, and push her out. Run her over. Stop the car, pull over, and break her neck. Use your belt as a garrote. Smother her with a jacket. With my jacket. There's plenty more pussy on the road.

Fucking Robert. Here when he's not here. Still meddling after he's already gone.

I reach over to gently shake Renee, but I hear Robert in my head and my hand threatens to form a claw, so I move to outrun a threatening impulse and end up slugging her body instead.

She wakes in shock that turns to immediate anger. She twists in on herself as if to protect her stomach from the same rough treatment, but to me it looks like she's doing the same thing I did, reaching for a shoulder holster that isn't there, grabbing a nonexistent gun the way I seemed eager to draw my real one. I knuckle my eyes with my free hand the way people do in movies, wondering what's wrong with me.

"Jesus!" Renee says.

"How fucking deep do you sleep? I've said your name three times."

"I didn't know you were talking to me."

"I said *your name* three times," I repeat. "Who the fuck else would I be talking to?"

She shrugs, and I get the feeling there's more there. But she shakes her head, annoyed, and sits up straighter to look out the window.

I give her a minute or so, knowing she's pissed that I hit her arm so hard. Personally, I think that hit was heroic, seeing as it was an artful dodge from what might otherwise have been murder.

Don't act like it's so crazy, Robert's voice says inside my head. *Killing her would be far more consistent with your character than this.*

I don't send a thought back to Mental Robert, but I do consider what the voice is trying to say.

This refers to my car ride with Renee, my hotel stay with Renee, my undefined future (on this part of the mission or possibly beyond) with Renee. For the first time, I wonder if I enjoy her company — and *as* I wonder, I can almost feel the Robert in my head smugly nodding.

But that's a good thing. With Mental Robert acting all smarmy and superior, it quickly becomes *him* I fantasize about killing instead of her.

He wanted to leave? *Good.*

He wanted to end our partnership — and maybe even our brotherhood? *Fine.*

He wants to go onto the internet and waste his life talking to people he doesn't really know and doesn't care about, discussing inanity and embroiling himself in the drama of anonymous others? *Goddamn fabulous.*

Or, basically, like I keep saying: *Fuck Robert.* If he doesn't get to tell me what to do when he's here, I'm sure as hell not about to grant his memory more permission to control me.

So I shove the voice away. Watch the road until I can almost believe that I no longer have a brother.

Renee seems a little less pissed now, so I say it again. "Tell me about him."

"About who?" Exasperated, and not a sincere question. More like a hassle she's obligated to handle.

"Bisset."

"What about him?"

"That's what I asked."

"So you still want to go after Simon," she says, still in that semi-monotone, annoyed voice.

"Of course." I stop, then restart. "Don't you?"

"Of course."

"So what's the problem? Why wouldn't I still want to go after him?"

"I don't know, Emil. After the thing at the W? You could have been killed. Or caught. I could have too. And besides, you've been weird ever since. Tossed and turned all night. Mumbling to yourself. Who's Timmy?"

Timmy the fucking cat. From twenty fucking years ago.

"Nobody."

"Well, you said his name like twenty times."

"When?"

"In your sleep. Are you listening to me?"

"Maybe Timmy Foster," I lie, inventing a name on the spot with a shrug. "Kid I went to high school with. Maybe I had a dream about him."

Renee seems unconvinced, but then her doubt becomes apathy. It's no longer a matter of believing or not believing when you simply don't care.

"Yes, I still want to go after Bisset."

I need the money. I need out of this toss-up, with a victory, because otherwise Heinzie will see me dead.

And Robert. My brother needs the win. It's just too bad about all the *Fuck Robert* in the air.

"If you do," I add.

And I hate myself yet again. That's something a simpering suburban drone would say. Am I asking permission? Asking for solidarity? Maybe next I'll ask her if she minds if I go out drinking with my buddies.

Maybe Robert was right. Maybe I am becoming soft.

"I do," she says.

I glance at her and decide she didn't hear what sounded to me like servility in my voice. Good. Renee's already proven she can make me beg between the sheets, so I'm really not eager to give her any more power.

"Then tell me about him. Things you haven't already said. The W was a big mistake. Too high-profile. Whether my boss sent them or not, players were all there because it was an obvious event — the kind of thing anyone who knew nothing about Senator Bisset would know. I need to know where we can find him that wouldn't ever make the papers. I need to know the places he visits alone. Without his entourage. Or his bodyguards."

"He lives in Malibu."

Of course he does. Historically, the most powerful people have been rich white assholes, but at least the old-timers used to hide it better. Now it's fine for politicians to flaunt their wealth instead of hiding it and pretending to be everyman. The internet stripped the taboo from money and arrogance in leaders. Now, it's all about popularity — forget all about who you are beneath.

Republicans. Democrats. Independents. We're the sodomites of history, and they're all lining up behind us. Nobody's a hero. Or even worth cheering for anymore.

"Too well-known. Everyone knows about his Malibu pad."

"He plays cards."

"Everyone knows that, too."

She sighs and waves her hands. "I don't know, dammit. He … He …" Then she jabs the air. "He's a banjo enthusiast!"

That sounds like a joke, but it's true. Yet another reason to hate him.

"Hell, Renee. Did you grow up with the guy, or just read the latest article about him in *People*?"

"Well, what the fuck do you *want* me to tell you, if I'm doing it so wrong?"

"Anything the public doesn't know. Something private. There must be something — some hobby that takes him out of the house, preferably alone, preferably unguarded — that you know but nobody else knows. *Think*."

So she does. I watch her hand rise to her chin like that famous statue. I take my eyes from the road a few times to watch her cogitate, just because she looks so adorable doing it.

I mean, *hot*.

Or better yet, *fuckable*.

Like, what I mean, really, is that maybe it's time for a pit stop on a dead stretch of road so I can finally stick it in her ass. That's how adorable this is. I've got all sorts of feelings on the topic, like butterflies in my dick.

"Okay," she says.

I wait. It's the kind of okay that promises something cool.

"Okay, I've got it," and there's a wide smile on her hot — not adorable — lips. "There's a bar where he likes to play darts, called Rock Bottom. I know because a bunch of times, before I found out what he did, back when I still liked him, he used to complain about it."

"About the bar?"

"About *getting* to the bar. When he used to live in Las Orillas and was walking-distance to a little shithole where he and his cronies used to meet. I guess he liked their vibe on his old board and reached out to those who were local, and they started meeting up IRL."

I wince. Abbreviations annoy me the way "prolly" annoys me. What, everyone's too busy to say *I'll be right back* instead of *BRB*, too in-a-hurry to say *that's funny* instead of *LOL* — or, in this case, to say *in real life* instead of *IRL?*

But I say nothing. The times I broke off something Robert was trying to tell me thanks to an asinine expression must number in the tens of thousands.

"He said that the way he used to have to live, as Zero, had him all alone. He *needed* friends. *Needed* real-life connections. After he launched Float — after he used *my privacy* to launch Float but before I found out about it — he started earning a lot more money and moved into Malibu, but kept a standing monthly meetup to play darts with his buddies at Rock Bottom. Because even though he wasn't hiding as Zero, he was suddenly a senatorial candidate. A notorious one, with lots of fans and enemies. I heard about it because he said his guards wouldn't let him go anymore for security reasons — or, if he insisted, they went with him. Obviously that wouldn't fly — because the kind of guys who knew him back when he was this weird Dark God of the web might not be the most savory folks. They like to discuss things his bodyguards shouldn't know."

I'm drifting as I follow the story.

I regain my lane, reestablish our speed, then offer Renee an encouraging nod.

"So he sneaks out," she continues. "I get the feeling his

compound is pretty tight, but that if you're inside to start with, it's not too tight to get out."

"Nobody sees him go?"

She shakes her head. "I don't think so. He's got a routine. Turns off the cameras in one part of the grounds, and of course he drives an electric so he can get out of there golf-cart quiet. He has the gate rigged with a special code that doesn't trip the alarms. It also kills the cameras for long enough to get back inside."

"Don't the guards see his car when it comes to the gate?"

"Don't know. Somehow it works. He didn't give me details. He was mostly just bitching. I only know what I just told you is because he's so proud of it, and ..." Renee sighs and looks out the window, opting not to finish. But I can guess what she was about to say: ... *and he wanted to impress me.*

I get it. It skeeves her out to think of her cousin wanting to impress her, because that just underscores that whole issue of Renee's cousin wanting to fuck her.

But the rest makes sense. Zero became a legend, but he must have started the same way most tech legends do, as an introverted, socially awkward kid with a boner but no girlfriend to use it on. Kids like that can hack into the New York Stock Exchange without tripping alarms, but slobber all their secrets the minute it looks like they might have a chance to squeeze the nipple on a genuine tit.

"If we get his special gate code ..."

She shakes her head. "It's keyed to him. There's a thumbprint thing at the gate."

Of course. There are no tits involved, so of course Bisset did his home system hack with his usual precision and double-checking.

"The bar, then. Rock Bottom."

"That's what I was thinking."

"Have you been there?"

"No."

"Have you seen it? Know what part of town it's in? Which businesses are on either side? If it shares walls with those businesses or stands alone? If it has its own parking lot, or if you have to park on the street?"

"No."

I pull off the road. Into a Sloppy's, ironically. Then I reach into the backseat with my hand out, remembering that Robert isn't there to hand me anything only after I've done a little wave like a Bollywood dance. Renee cocks an eyebrow at me, but stops when I say, "Shit."

"What?"

"I don't have a phone."

She points at my flip phone.

"It doesn't have internet."

"And you destroyed your iPhone." This is said with reproach, as if I should have known better. I don't feel like explaining the whole phone thing to her, so I just point my open hand at her, flexing fingers.

"What?"

"Give me your phone."

"Why? What are you going to do?"

"I'm going to look up that bar. I need to see what we're in for."

"I'll look it up," she says.

"Just ..." I reach for her phone, but she pulls it back.

"What the fuck, Renee?"

"I said I'll do it."

I lean in to see, but she turns her body so the screen is facing away from me.

"You got texts from other guys on there you don't want me to see or something?"

"Don't be an asshole. A girl's phone is private."

"Oh, fuck off." I reach out, but again she dodges.

"Private like her purse. Or her diary."

So I wait. After a few moments, Renee settles back to straight and holds the phone so I can see. It's the Google Maps listing for the Rock Bottom Bar, showing a street-view shot of a building that looks just as run-down and shitty-watering-hole as she described. No wonder Bisset's security doesn't want him going there. You get staph just by walking into a place like that, and even the owner's kids, smoking and getting into knife fights in their pajamas at your feet, will try to kill you for stepping out of line.

I scroll through all the user-submitted photos, including and especially a very helpful 360-degree interactive panoramic. I see where the bathrooms are, but of course there aren't any interior shots. I keep thinking of *The Godfather*, when Michael's crew hid a .38 snubnose behind the toilet tank.

"This is perfect, thank you," I say.

As we drive on, I ask myself what the fuck.

I never say thank you to anyone. Ever.

TWENTY-TWO

Coppola's Lens

THE BAR IS GODDAMN PERFECT.

We first scoped it out on Saturday night, but even waiting until past eleven there's only a handful of filthy men left behind. Guys like that, they don't pay attention to anything more than ten feet away from where they're sitting. You could flog the president across the bar while a mustached man and his monkey play the calliope and none of them would so much as turn their heads.

"He comes the first Monday of every month," she tells me.

Which is so fortuitous, it's like someone arranged the whole thing. We only have to spend two nights in another anonymous fleabag motel before Target Day arrives. Then, on Monday, we check out and tool around town to kill time until it's our turn at bat. Strange; I'm already used to this new normal. I wonder about my brother all the time, but after three full days with just me and Renee, I'm starting to think about him less.

I keep my distance. Renee and I will part ways once

this job is behind us. Anything else is far too dangerous. We're only getting this shot at Bisset because his dick made his mouth say some things that it shouldn't have. Loose lips won't just sink ships for the wannabe senator. They'll end up putting a mural of blood and brain on Rock Bottom's wall. And there, but for the sake of discretion and keeping my mouth shut, go I.

After a dinner of tacos and some intentionally non-intimate conversations, we end up parked across the street from the bar like cops on a stakeout.

Renee sees me check my watch and breaks our ten-minute silence.

"I don't know what time he comes, but I know it has to be dark enough for him to sneak away."

I crane my head and look at the sky to separate false daylight from the real thing. You can't see the stars in L.A. for all the light pollution. I think that's why the city is so jaded. Whenever you look for the heavens, it's clear that no one's home.

"Still some light in the sky," I tell her.

We wait. Renee falls asleep, and slips sideways to snore against my shoulder.

She wakes on her own and asks me if she missed anything. I tell her she didn't just as a group approaches the door. She sits up straight, but they're all too short, too stocky to be Bisset.

Fifteen minutes later, a new trio arrives. They're across the street and it's dim, but any of them could be our man.

"There he is," Renee says.

"Which one?"

"In the hat."

I stare. One of the men is wearing a cap that's so yellow, he could easily work for Chiquita.

"Are you sure?"

"I know that hat." Renee is already reaching for her door latch.

I check my gun, then my other gun, in my ankle holster. I have a knife up my sleeve in case shit goes south. Hopefully I won't have to use anything but my primary. I already hate the circumstances here, always preferring a clean shot from a distance using any girl from my family of rifles. Close quarters like this, anything can happen — and changes happen fast.

To calm myself after the clusterfuck downtown, I keep thinking of that scene in *The Godfather*. I won't get a pat-down, so I didn't need to stow my gun behind the toilet ahead of time like Michael did, but the rest is the same. I'll walk in, put eyes on our man, make sure we've got who we're after. Then from five feet away at most, I'll put a bullet through his brain before walking right out of the place without even blinking. Nobody will follow and I'll bet it'll take ages to call the cops. There aren't any heroes in this town.

"You stay here," I say.

"Are you kidding?"

"Of course I'm not kidding. Someone may have a gun. There may be trouble."

"I can handle trouble," she says.

"Not this kind of trouble."

Renee looks like she might argue, but instead she climbs back into the car — behind the wheel this time. She rolls down the window and looks up at me. "Give me sixty seconds before you start shooting. I'll loop around to the other side of the street and park right outside the front door."

"Keep the engine running," I tell her.

"Duh."

Without thinking, before parting, I lean down and kiss her quickly on the lips. It's awkward. Without sexual context, the peck is more Ozzie and Harriet than Bonnie and Clyde.

"Um …"

"He can talk his way out of anything. And he'll be with friends. So don't let him start."

"Okay."

"Be careful."

I nod. I'm always careful. Except when I'm not. Except when I let some woman I don't know run my show, choosing her over my own flesh and blood.

She's lying to you, Robert's voice says inside my head.

So I punch that voice in the face. Then I tie it up, binding its hands and tossing it into the basement of my cerebellum.

The inside is quieter than I'd hoped. The two groups we watched enter comprise two thirds of the total groups in the bar. Ten people in three small clusters, plus the bartender. No music. No dancing. For the working stiffs here, no *life.* This is going to be easier than I expected.

I stalk toward the back table with my eyes on the target. I brush arms with a man standing from his stool at the bar on my way. He turns to walk in the same direction, but even that — unacceptable for someone in my position — isn't the sudden problem blaring like a klaxon.

That's not a man I brushed up against. It's a woman.

An *Indian* woman.

Which raises all my antennae at once.

Primitive knowledge swelling within me before I can so much as entertain the thought consciously.

Little things I'd noted but discarded as irrelevant click into place like a light coming on.

Like the broad, flat lips on one of the men who came in with the shorties. Lips like a duck's.

Like the way that one of the others farther down the bar is wearing a black hoodie with the hood still up, obscuring his face, with a long coat over top.

I wonder if they've seen me as anything more than a barfly. If they've recognized me. It's a stupid thought. Of *course* they know. If I saw them, guaranteed they saw me.

Just behind me is Nisha Swartha, dangerously close.

Standing now, reaching for something in his belt, is The Duck.

And on my right, now turning his head in my peripheral vision while he slips something long and shiny from under his coat, is Blackhawk, making me picture the Grim Reaper. The thing he's pulling from his coat is about the length of a shotgun. About the girth of a shotgun, cradled in black-gloved hands. With the same *ch-chk*! sound, as it's racked, that a shotgun makes. But still I see it as a scythe.

Fuck.

My brain's hyperdrive lays flat as thoughts scramble inside me at a million per second. I'm great at quick-thinking on my feet, but I've usually walked into sticky situations with at least some advance idea of what I'm headed into. But this isn't that. I came in expecting an easy, isolated, no-hassle plug of our primary target followed by a crazy payday. I got a nest of vipers instead.

All three of the remaining assassins are here, armed to the teeth and surrounding me.

The world becomes slow motion. When I saw Nisha, she saw me. I'm realizing it only now, as time dilates, as a man sipping beer in the corner of my eye freezes into a statue.

My head starts to slowly turn. My thoughts are flying,

but my body, bound by the same syrup of time as the rest of my surroundings, can only move so fast.

It takes half a minute to look at Nisha.

Another minute before her eyes glint with decision. Her *recognition* of me becomes *war* with me. We're not going to open our mouths with extended hands, shaking and smiling and saying hello. We're going to do something different, but things are tricky because whatever happens between me and Nisha has to happen in front of The Duck and Blackhawk as well.

Too many inputs and blossoming shooters.

I choose the nuclear option, which some might call the coward's choice. I see it as the only way to survive.

As Nisha draws, as The Duck sprints forward with his pistol rising, and as Blackhawk's shotgun clears the folds of his coat and finds aim, I dive for the floor.

Bisset's arrival struck this volatile situation's match: the sign all three of them were waiting for, and apparently the first time each one realized that any of the others were present. Because I came behind Bisset — into that forward-marching spotlight of attention — I'd ended up in the middle. They were all aiming at me, once blood in the water became clear to us all.

So when I dive and shots fire, the air above me becomes deadly. I hear the bar-back mirror shatter and fall to shards with the sound of gravel in a garbage disposal. Wood chips the size of daggers are shorn from the mahogany surface and sent pinwheeling through ethereal space.

Hitting my spine, unable to roll, sudden pain comes with a view. The Duck's wide face contorted in a sneer, Nisha's legendary, eagle-eyed concentration manifesting as calm in a crisis. Blackhawk is a shadow, his movements like the sweeping of a bat's wing. He's already fired his shotgun.

Bottles of liquor explode in a glitter of multicolored rain, and in the downpour the assassins — all somehow unscathed, having aimed more at me than each other — finally leap for cover.

I scuttle into a corner. I'm used to distance work, so this need to fight in close quarters is a significant handicap. I need time, even if it's only a few seconds, to think. I need to get as far away from the action as possible, if I want to kill from my sweet spot.

Back in the corner, they temporarily forget me.

I have my pistol out, but haven't fired it. That will only draw their attention.

I take in the melee. Although I'd only seen three shooters, until now I wasn't sure that's all there was. Watching from down here, I can confirm: Blackhawk (now in a corner himself, but attracting attention I don't have with repeated shotgun blasts), The Duck (double pistols, popping up like a Jack-in-the-Box from behind the bar), and Nisha (moving in sprints and taking careful aim with Dirty Harry's gun) are the only combatants.

Them and me, but I'm still quiet like a mouse.

With my three competitors occupying each other, I take six long seconds to scan the room. I'm pinned away from the door so there's no immediate means of escape, but the way I've removed myself — even for a moment — gives me time for thought the others can't afford.

And in that moment I see:

That there's a short hallway at the rear leading to the bathrooms, which in a place like this are probably labeled FELLAS and DAMES. At the hall's end, straight ahead and visible from where I'm crouching, I see an emergency exit. It's to code, with a bright red EXIT sign overhead and a wide push bar on its front.

That all the other patrons have taken cover but haven't dared to run. Amusingly, one of the men near The Duck is still holding an enormous stein, as if he might settle back and keep right on drinking his beer.

That in the dead-center of chaos, some poor hapless asshole has just emerged from the bathroom. If he turned, he'd see that all he needed to live another day would be to turn, press the bar on the exit door, and charge down the alley. But he doesn't turn, scream, panic, or duck. He stands there instead. Until, unbelievably, he leans against one of the walls, casual-cool. Hip as shit, like the Marlboro Man.

And that, as much as I don't want to see it … that's not Simon Bisset wearing the bright yellow hat. It's another man entirely, too old and nowhere near as handsome. Not only did I walk into a firestorm, I did it for no reason at all. Bisset hasn't arrived, or he's not coming tonight. His buddies might be here, but the candidate himself is not.

I look at the man in the yellow hat, simpering with a man on either side. If only Curious George could see him now.

If that's not Bisset, then it wasn't Yellow Hat's arrival that started this. It was me tossing a match into this crate of dry tinder. If I hadn't entered, the killers would have kept on waiting with their heads low and hiding, with so much attention on the new arrivals that they never thought to inspect those around them for threats. If I hadn't swaggered in with my big balls practically hanging out (no attempt at subtlety; why would I need stealth or protection if nobody was supposed to know this was Bisset's place?), this event would have likely been nothing. A meetup of killers disperses, and nobody's the wiser.

It's been fifteen seconds or so since the shooting started, though it feels like an eternity. The silhouette by the bathrooms — by the unused emergency exit — hasn't moved. I'd swear the fool in the shadows is staring right at me. Judging me. Wondering why I'm hiding instead of fighting like the others. Asking if I'm losing my edge. If I've gotten sloppy. If I'm old and used up, and should have left the game a long time ago.

Another second passes. The shotgun booms like a cannon. A window blows; two of the closest drinkers sprint to the glassless rectangle, leap, and presumably roll. Now there's just nine of us in the bar: four shooters, one false target, and four Everyday Joes who should have spent their evening anywhere else.

The Duck pulls the trigger and with his final bullet, the slide on his semi-auto locks back with the chamber open like a smoking black lozenge, now dry. He spies a shot at Blackhawk and moves to take it, but it's only after pulling the trigger when he realizes that he's out of rounds, that he should have dropped low to swap his magazine. Or he might not *have* an extra one. We, as a profession, aren't used to extra magazines, or to running suddenly empty in the middle of a fight. Our fights don't last this long. We like to use surgeon's precision, not the blunt force of a machete.

Nisha either sees or hears Duck's slide lock open, because she pivots like an anti-aircraft gun as he freezes. Everything about her is measured. She does not fire the second she's lined up; instead I feel an extra heartbeat while Nisha makes sure her aim is true. This time, deliberateness costs her. Blackhawk, who takes no such pauses for certainty, opens her chest like a lily. That last melee went to her, but this one's her last.

Nisha's back slams into a table and for a moment it

looks like she might balance atop it. But after one fat second, the last of her rigidity dies and she succumbs to what seems like an excess of gravity. Nisha sags like an overwatered plant, elicits metallic squeaks from the table's legs as they skew sideways and she starts to slide. She's a pile of laundry after that. Her body, punched through to the other side, goes flaccid and hits the ground, upending the table.

The tumult shakes the room with a bone-rattling crash, drawing Blackhawk's attention from The Duck, to which his barrel had been pivoting next. The distraction is enough for another two innocents (including Yellow Hat, whose false identity must be lost on The Duck, because Duck actually shouts after him) to make the front door.

Blackhawk aims, but the distraction has cost him. He's too slow.

Duck hits the deck and scrambles, leaving Blackhawk to try and follow.

By my math we're down to six inside, two of which are a problem. Seven, if you include Cool Hand Luke near the pissers, still watching the scene unfolding with interest.

I stand and shoot, announcing my presence.

My foot slips in Nisha's spreading pool of blood at the worst possible time and my shot goes wide, puffing plaster a good six inches from Blackhawk's shoulder.

His black-hooded face turns toward me and all I can see inside is a nose like a troll's. He's smaller than I remember, with poor posture and shoulders rounded like an old man. I don't get much time to see because the shotgun's muzzle is tracking in my direction.

I fire again, but it's only to buy me time. I need aim, but Blackhawk only needs the gist of my location since he's firing buckshot.

I dive again, weightless as something wooden explodes above me.

I brace for another shot but Duck has recovered, and is army-crawling toward where the bartender is hiding and taking pot shots from low cover. He draws enough attention that Blackhawk changes his aim again, staying low enough to assure I can't shoot him in the back.

That's when I see Mr. Cool peel himself from the wall at the back and walk right toward me. Right down the center of the bar, two feet behind Blackhawk as he rounds on Duck again. With the other assassins' attention on each other, nobody fires, or tells him to get the fuck down and stay out of the way.

Once our mystery guest exits the shadows, I can clearly see that it's my brother.

"Robert!"

I wave him down and out of the line of fire. It's a miracle that nobody's seen him. And that he just made that little firewalk down the bar's bleeding heart, easy as pie.

He comes down, kneeling beside me.

"What the hell? Do you *want* to get shot?"

He's casual. No big deal. "What? We always make it."

"Why are you even here?"

"Same as you."

"Did Renee contact you? Did you somehow get in touch?"

He laughs. *"Renee."*

"Did you follow us?"

"Always."

But he's strange. Still angry, perhaps. Despite new pop-pops from behind the bar, my thoughts turn to their old patterns, centering on my brother. Agitated by Robert. Unbelieving that he left me, that he came back, that he thought any of this was necessary or wise.

"The fuck's wrong with you?" I ask.

"I should ask you the same thing."

It's like he's drunk. Or high. Or, perhaps more accurately, the opposite of both. He has no emotions. My brother is only a dummy. A mannequin. An automaton — a facsimile of the Robert so recently departed.

Another time, I tell myself. *First survive. Then comprehend.*

"I need your help to make a hole," I say.

Robert looks back where he came from as if I'm an idiot. There's an exit right there.

"No way," I say, seeing his glance. "Try that again and we'll end up hamburger."

"The front door, then?"

"Or the window." But we both see the problem; reaching either will require at least five seconds longer than it will take for either of our foes to see us and take aim.

"What about Bisset? Are you just going to run?"

"Bisset isn't here. The guy we thought was him turned out to be someone else."

Robert doesn't acknowledge this as an answer. "What about Bisset?"

"The fuck's wrong with you?"

I accidentally kick a chair's leg. It squawks, and immediately Blackhawk spins and churns the leg to butter.

"You make cover. We're going to have to plug at least one of these assholes if we're getting out of here."

Robert shakes his head. "I don't have a gun."

I look around, then scramble toward Nisha's fallen body. Her weapon hasn't gone far, and I find it under an upturned chair. Heavy iron and long as a baby's forearm, earning the assassin my posthumous respect. It's a .44 Magnum, just like it looked. I feel a sudden urge to invite someone in here to go ahead and make my day.

I scramble back toward Robert, but he isn't there. My

heartbeat ratchets another notch as my head darts to the corners, trying to see where he's gone. That's when I realize, there's something wrong with him. My brother's off his rocker in some new way, and that means he needs my help even more than I just told him I needed his. He walked through a gunfight. He came in instead of out. He followed me in here, presumably to help, without so much as body armor or a weapon.

Even with mortal peril dogging my heels, it's the past few days that my thoughts turn to. Where has Robert been? If he's in this bar, it seems he stayed on the case: chasing Bisset after announcing he wanted no part of us. Now he's here, unarmed, soft as a pincushion.

I find myself wanting to find him and cover him with something, shielding him from reality until it's all over. Because it's hitting me now, ramrod straight after our time apart. I can't lose my brother, but it's as much about me as it is about him. If Robert were killed, that'd be bad enough. But if it happened because of my choices and mistakes, I'd lose my fucking mind.

"Robert!" I whisper-shout, peering through the increasingly smoke-filled room.

"What?"

He's beside me again as if he never left.

"Where did you go?"

"I went for Nisha's gun."

I hold up the .44. "*This* is Nisha's gun."

Robert looks behind himself, where two innocents are still cowering. "I thought I saw it go that way?"

I push the heavy thing into Robert's hand. Who cares where it went? Now he has it.

I'm about to articulate my plan when Robert speaks too loud. He's going to get us killed. "Why did you think Bisset would be here, anyway?"

"Renee's intel."

"He's not here, you know."

I squint hard at Robert. Did he hit his head? "Yeah. I *got* that. I *told* you that. And *you* didn't know either, so the joke's on both our asses."

Only, Robert didn't say he *knew*. He just repeated his question: *What about Bisset?* Under different circumstances, that could mean anything.

"He's at a charity gala."

A bullet pierces the metal table above us, leaving a hole like a tiny shocked mouth.

"See?"

Robert has set the gun down so he could pull a phone from his pocket. He's holding it up now, showing me the screen.

"I don't want your fucking phone! Pay attention, asshole!"

But it's like Robert doesn't hear me. He turns the screen back to me and begins the familiar upward swiping motion I recognize from his Float obsession.

"He's been posting photos from it all afternoon. You'd know that if you paid any attention to the internet like—"

"I don't need the motherfucking internet to do my job."

"I'm just saying."

"Well, don't."

"Don't what?"

"Just say."

"Why?"

A new bullet — single slug, so probably The Duck's, perforates the floor a half inch from Robert's shoe. He doesn't even look over.

"It's just ..." My brother looks pensive, as if we're

244

having this thoughtful discussion in a quiet library. "The way you wall yourself off? It's like a sickness."

"Where did you get a phone anyway?"

"I bought it."

"You *bought* it?"

"That's how normal people get things, Emil. We buy them."

"With cash?"

"My credit card."

I sigh so deeply, I feel like Jesus must be crying.

"Hell, Robert. You can't just—"

"I'll buy you one, after we get the bounty."

I look my brother hard in the eyes. Something's changed. He's different than he used to be. He's not the same man. His demeanor is different. He used to fight me, but the way he's acting now, it's like he already won. Like he thinks this is all done in concept, and all we need to do is dot I's and cross T's. Like I'm convinced this is my final hurrah, so we can blaze as haphazard as we'd like. Why not? The way Robert's acting, it's like we'll be on a private plane to Ibiza in the a.m., with all of this suddenly a sad little memory.

"Fine," I say. "Buy me a phone."

"You bet."

"Install all those apps. The ones I hate."

He smiles.

"But first, we need to get out of here. There's no new phones — no Float, no Twitter, no goddamn Facebook — for dead men. You hear me, Robert? Do you understand?"

He says, "I always understand you, Emil. Better than you understand yourself."

He shifts, putting one hand on the floor and rolling to his right hip. It's a pre-standing motion, so I grab his arm to stop him.

"What are you doing?"

"Getting us out of here."

"You can't just stand up. You'll be shot."

"We can't just stay low," he echoes. "We'll be shot."

"Robert!"

He stands, and I gasp. Robert's never been a good shot. *I'm* the marksman, and Robert is my wingman. What he's doing — standing in the line of fire, praying to get shots off before Blackhawk or The Duck do the same — is suicide. *Especially* with a .44 Magnum. He's not used to the kick. His rounds will end up in the ceiling.

But I'm wrong. The big gun is louder in Robert's hands than it was in Nisha's, and the first slug slams Blackhawk in the shoulder — a better shot than it sounds, because most of his body was behind a brick partition, and shoulder was all that was visible.

The cloaked man goes down beside the bar, his weapon hitting the floor. He reaches for it and Robert fires again, this time managing to hit the shotgun's barrel instead of Blackhawk's hand. An impossible shot, but also ideal. With the barrel buckled by Robert's large-caliber bullet, the shotgun is suddenly out of play. Blackhawk's body language shouts rage, but he can't play without a weapon — no matter his deadly, difficult-to-kill reputation. For a moment it looks like he'll play anyway, but he rushes for the door instead. Slower and more stooped than I'd imagined, but maybe that's just the shoulder wound talking.

Seeing the two-on-one situation, The Duck comes up from behind the bar using the bartender as a shield.

I'm still stooping gape-mouthed like the slacker Robert says I'm becoming, so I stand beside him and raise my own pistol. We're both sighting on The Duck, but his cover is complete.

"Step aside!" Duck quacks. "Let me out or he's dead!"

"Shoot through him," I whisper to Robert.

"You're such an asshole," he tells me. "No manners at all."

He fires once. The gun doesn't shake or move so much as a nanometer. Its recoil is minimal, as if Robert's arms are made of steel.

The Duck drops dead. The bartender's left hand whips up to his ear, just above where glasses would sit. I can see a small red line forming there. Scorched flesh, nearly too cauterized to bleed.

"Sorry about that," Robert says.

The bartender stares at us before finally breaking his paralysis and hauling ass for the emergency exit, limbs flailing like a Muppet. When neither of us raises our weapons again, the two remaining barflies clamber to their feet and do the same.

We're alone. Without company and without so much as music on the speakers, the joint is a mausoleum.

I walk to The Duck, collapsed in a pile like a marionette with its strings cut. Somehow — and even looking back, I have no idea how — Robert found a good enough shot to punch him through the eye. Just like Moe Green in *The Godfather*, I realize. Funny, how I keep seeing this job through Coppola's lens.

Without turning to face my brother, I say what's been on my mind this entire time — something I can face enough to ask only now.

"Why did you come back, Robert?"

"Because you needed me."

Then more tellingly: "Why did you leave in the first place?"

"Because you didn't need me then."

I squat, preparing to search The Duck's pockets.

Unseen behind me, Robert asks, "What's changed, Emil? What's changed between before, when I left, and now?"

I don't answer because it feels like a trap.

"Absolutely nothing," he says.

A split second before something hits me hard across the neck, and darkness descends like a shroud.

TWENTY-THREE

Baffled

I BLINK to see lights above, but they're diffuse and for several long seconds there's nothing to focus on.

My eyes feel coated with Vaseline and I can only see them through the haze. A shape with warm hands and a scent like lavender appears through the blur.

"Emil?"

A shape now smacking me in the face, trying to get me to sit upright.

Fucking shape. I'd really rather go back to sleep.

"Emil? Are you okay?"

The lights come into focus, a little. I realize that I *am*, in fact, more or less okay, and the revelation washes over me like a pleasant surprise. In the movies, when someone hits a person to knock them out, they go down like chloroform and wake up like smelling salts. It's a simple and straight-forward *off* switch followed by an equally facile *on* switch. But the reality of being knocked unconscious is far less once-and-done in real life. The place where Robert hit me feels like someone's stuffed a gourd between my scalp and my skull. Like the bricks never stopped dropping.

Renee is looking at me like a bird that fell out of its nest, like I'm a lost child waiting to be saved.

"Do you want me to call an ambulance?" she asks.

I roll to sitting, then consider shaking my head. The attempt — which calls forth a masterpiece of head pain — is immediately aborted in favor of a verbal response.

"No."

"Are you sure?"

As my eyes and brain relearn the trick of attention, I take a visual circuit of the bar. I see bodies, blood, and mayhem. What I don't see, unless he's hiding, is Robert. That asshole.

"Emil? There's a bump on your head the size of a lemon. You *sure* you don't want an ambulance?"

"I don't think it's a good idea to be here right now."

A softball answer. Truth is that guys like me never, ever call an ambulance. 911 is for people who've done nothing criminal to cause the problem. Paramedics arrive with the police in a situation like this.

Renee looks around at my answer, as if she only saw me at first and is just now noting the bloodbath. But she doesn't waver at all the blood and gore. The bar has turned from watering hole to a deconstructed autopsy, and she doesn't even flinch.

"Did his bodyguards show up or something?"

"*The competition* showed up."

Now she's interested. She looks at Nisha's body and spies the blood-spattered legs visible just past the bar. "Do you mean they're …?"

"… like me," I say, trying and failing to nod. "More people who want your cousin dead."

She looks around again, searching for Bisset's fallen body.

"It wasn't him," I say, grabbing my forehead and

gesturing toward where Yellow Hat had been sitting. Now that I'm awake, all my nerves are starting to fire and this headache isn't going away. It's on the sides, at the front, clawing its way down my collar and into the muscles of my neck and shoulders.

"What?" Renee asked.

"In the yellow hat, that wasn't Bisset."

"It looked exactly like him!"

I shrug, which hurts. I can tell her all day that our man wasn't Bisset, but it's like Renee thinks she can *make* it Bisset just by wanting it badly enough.

A siren screams in the distance.

Renee perks up and slides a hand beneath mine, around my back. "Can you stand?"

"I guess we'll find out."

Standing feels like shoving a jousting lance through my eyes. The effort is intense, but I manage not to scream. We hobble to the front door, and I'm determined to handle my own painful locomotion two-thirds of the way there. I shake Renee away and we cross the street to the car. I keep my head low and motion for her to do the same, but no one is going to peek out their windows in this neighborhood, despite the gunshots.

Renee drives while I medicate with an expired bottle of ibuprofen in the center console. I swallow six dry. That hurts like hell, too.

Her fingers are white on the wheel. Her face is equal parts horror and anger. Of the two, anger is dominant. I see the way the wheel's pleather wrinkles beneath her clenching hands. Fingernails pressing half-moons into her palm as they wrap around to the underside.

Out of the blue she says, "I was sure that was Simon."

"Well, it wasn't."

"I was so sure that would work. Get him away from his security. Catch him off guard."

"I don't know what to tell you."

Renee shakes her head, eyes like lasers on the flickering, fluorescent-lit road ahead. I'd swear I could hear her teeth grinding. "That was our chance. He'll never go back there now."

Obviously. She's not Robert. She's not my partner in this. She's not even a professional. So why does she have so many fucking opinions?

"So what now?" she asks, as if I'm the goddamn oracle.

"Who did you see come out the front door?"

"What?"

"You heard me."

A little shake, like a bird drying itself at a birdbath. "Nobody. What the hell does that have to do with anything?"

"*Everything*, Renee. It has fucking everything to do with *everything*. You get that those were professional assassins in there?"

"I gathered." She takes a breath. "I heard."

"And Robert."

"Wh … Your brother?"

"I don't know any other Roberts."

"Robert was *there?* In the bar? With all the assassins?"

"He's the one who hit me."

"*Your brother* was the one who knocked you out?"

"Did you think one of the dead people did it?"

"I thought one of the *bystanders* did it, before running away."

I clench my teeth, but keep my tone in check. Renee's obtuseness, right now, makes me want to throttle her. I've had a viciously awful day, and my brother wouldn't be asking such stupid questions if he'd stuck around rather than running off. Even after the hit to my head, I prefer his company to Renee's clueless inclusion.

"It was Robert."

"Did you call him?"

"No. I think he's been following us."

"Why?"

"Fuck if I know, Renee! Why don't you just shut the fuck up for a second and let me think!"

For sixty seconds it's only the sound of tires on the road.

"I'm asking if you saw anyone leave because I want to know if you saw anyone that looked like Robert leaving?"

Nothing.

"Renee."

"Oh, am I allowed to talk now?"

"Just answer the question."

"Are you sure? Sometimes I get to yammering on like a crazy broad. Some stupid dame."

"Oh, so you're going to be all butt-hurt because I yelled at you?"

"Why would he leave through the front door, right under the streetlight?" Her tone is more of a challenge, less of a genuine question.

"He wouldn't want to be seen. The others left through the back door. Knowing Robert, he'd rationalize going out the front … because what guilty person would ever do that?" I'm sure Robert would have gone through the front.

"Is he stupid, Emil?"

"No, he's not *stupid*. He's one half of the best team working right now."

Renee huffs. She'd cross her arms if she wasn't driving. "Well, *I* didn't see him."

So he did use the back door, then. Which makes me

wonder more what Robert is playing at. First he leaves our group, then shows up for the job as if he's doing it solo. But he doesn't *really* go solo; he comes to my side when he could easily have shot The Duck from behind — or, perhaps more wisely, exited without engaging once he saw that Bisset wasn't there to kill.

But then after *helping* me, Robert *assaults* me. He's always been a bit nuts; maybe our new estrangement has finally shoved him over the gulf into crazy.

I'm not sure if I should hug him or shoot him, next time I see him.

I didn't give Renee a destination, so I'm not sure where we're going. We didn't plan for a next step. We both assumed this would work — that the senator alone and away from his security detail would make him stupidly easy to hit. Instead, we got four shooters and another botched attempt with the target nowhere in sight.

"Blackhawk," I say.

"What?"

"There's an assassin that goes by the name of Black-hawk. He was at the bar. Took a round in the shoulder, but got away."

"And?"

"Robert and I already knew he was following us. That he's after us, like *assigned* us in a side deal. He must have somehow figured out what we were up to. Somehow leaked it."

"And he came in later?"

"No. They were all there, already waiting when I walked in. The room perked up when the guy we thought was Bisset came in. I didn't bother to lay low, so it was probably seeing me that got it started." Then I realize: "Blackhawk left through the front door, too."

"Oh. I did see someone."

"Didn't think to mention that before?"

"You asked about Robert."

"The fuck, Renee? Obviously I want to know about anyone."

"Well. *Sorry.*"

"And really — how do you know the earlier guy *wasn't* Robert?"

"He was small and hunched." She looks me over, seeming to note my height and build. "But I figure your brother must be …?"

I shake my head despite the pain.

"Oh. So I did poorly," Renee says.

"Forget it."

"I fucked it up. Is that right?"

"I said forget it."

"I suppose I caused all the bad shit inside the bar, too, huh?"

"So now it's a pity party? For you? I'm the one who got hit with a brick or something."

"And it's all *my* fault? Listen, asshole. I didn't ask to come on this little vacation."

Liar.

"I didn't force myself on you."

Liar.

"If you were so happy without me, you should have just said so."

I did. We both did.

"Never mind," I say.

"No, let's talk about it."

There's a gas station ahead. I point for her to stop. When she does, I exit the car and circle around to the driver's side and motion for her to open the door. She does, and I sit. By the time Renee reaches the passenger side, I've hit the lock button.

"Door's locked," she says.

"Is it?"

"Come on. Open up."

I put the car in Drive. It inches forward before I press harder on the brake.

"Oh," she says through the glass. "Oh, *fuck you.*"

She moves to the front of the car and blocks my exit.

"Move."

"No."

"Move or I run you over."

"Fuck you, Emil. I don't even have a phone."

Hers is still in the cupholder. I pull it out, open the window a hair, then sling it over the roof and into a minuscule patch of urban grass beyond. She glares at me, but when she goes after the thing, I open my door and throw all her stuff onto the concrete. I hit the gas, but she darts in front of me again.

"Funny story," I tell her, already tired of this. "Do you know what I do for a living?"

"You won't kill me."

I gun the engine and ram her midsection before hitting the brake again. "Move, because I definitely will."

"Emil. Come on." Her face changes. "You're angry."

"Yeah. I'm angry." I rev the engine again, but don't hit her this time.

"And you probably have a concussion. You're confused."

I don't know about the concussion, but I do feel confused. Confused about why I'm so angry, given that I told Renee to stay where she was and not be a hero. Baffled because I don't know if I want more to figure out where Robert went and find him again or if I'd rather go after Bisset by myself. I don't know if I'm more worried that Blackhawk is still out there (and as good as the rumors say he is, having arrived at two potential venues I'd planned before I did) or more dedicated to the assignment than ever.

I mostly just know that when this is over one way or the other, I think I'll kill Heinzie. He gave us our start. He's the reason any of this happened, after my little tailspin left me searching for a fresh direction.

"You can't get to him without me," Renee says.

I throw the car into reverse, then flatten a fleet of election signs and carom off the gas station's cinderblock corner before my automotive ass bangs off the curb and into the cross street.

She rushes forward to intercept, but I throw it back into Drive and floor the gas before she can.

Renee dwindles in the rearview until she's only a speck, still shouting and cursing my name.

TWENTY-FOUR

Conflicted

THE NEXT HOTEL is fancy instead of a dump.

I order room service, because fuck it. Blackhawk and I are the only two left in Heinzie's meat-grinder toss-up, and the weaker assassin is wounded. I can't remember if the bullet found his dominant or non-dominant arm, but either way that injury will slow him down and invite some questions.

Either I've got the advantage now and will be the one to collect the senator's head, in which case I won't mind the obscene cost of this hotel because I'll have earned so much more. Alternatively, Blackhawk will still beat me to Bisset and I'll lose, in which case my opponent will finish me off or Heinzie will call someone else to do the job … in which case I definitely won't care about my bill because I'll be in a shallow grave.

So fuck it. I open everything in the minibar, too.

I watch TV for a while. Then porn, jerking off like my dick did something to offend me. I finish twice then work for a third. The abrasions come before me, so I crack the first-aid kit for Neosporin.

Room service arrives and I instruct the server to leave the tray outside. I squat low and wait for the shadows of feet to depart. I listen, because the hallway is hardwood covered with intermittent rugs. When people pass, half their steps are invisible and half are clear as day.

When the half-on footsteps fade, I peek through the peephole and verify that no one is there. Still, I slip my .45 into my hand and hold it behind my back before opening the door.

I scan: Right, left, right. The sterling tray is at my feet.

I stoop. Pick it up.

Then before the door is fully closed, someone kicks it back at me.

With both hands on the tray and the gun tucked back into my belt, I'm defenseless.

A cool metal ring pushes against the back of my neck.

"Amateur mistake." The voice sounds muffled, like the speaker has a bag on his head. "You crazy bastard. You never put the gun away until you close the privacy lock."

I turn around to find Robert behind me. The cool metal ring turns out not to be metal at all. It's a plastic pill bottle I assume he stuck in the ice machine so it'd be cold enough to fool me.

"The fuck, Robert."

My brother's grinning because he beat me. Nobody gets the drop on me. Ever.

"We were in the next room. You didn't look to see if your neighbors' doors were ajar."

I give a tiny laugh. Then I hit him in the stomach so hard, even the soft flesh there hurts my fist. Robert strikes the rear wall of the hallway and sags to the ground. I walk away but leave my door wide open.

"Not the 'the fuck' I was referring to."

Robert scrambles back to his feet and follows me into the room, still gasping for air.

"What? Are you seriously still pissed about the bar?"

"You knocking me out? Giving me this?" I turn and lift my hair so he can see the golf ball on my head. "Yeah. I'm still pissed."

"Forgive?"

"Not yet."

"When?"

I hit him again. Same place, harder.

"I guess now."

Robert gets up, slower this time, taking extra time before moving forward. But I leave the door open, and he comes again.

"The *fuck*, Robert. *The fuck*. What happened back at the bar?"

"I was trying to help."

"*Which side* were you trying to help?"

"Come on," Robert says, looking injured. "I knew three was a crowd. I didn't want to interfere if you and Renee wanted to go it alone."

"*The fuck!*"

"Well, what was I *supposed* to do?"

"Not hit me. Or run off after you did."

"Come on. You know I can't be there when Renee's around. Wasn't it you who decided that?"

"I seem to remember you making your own decisions, Robert."

"So, what … you think that fight was all *my* fault?"

"Goddamn right it was. And I'll tell you another thing." I point hard at him. "You ever do anything like what you did at the bar again, I'll fucking end you. Doesn't matter that you're my brother."

Robert holds his punched stomach, breathes unsteadily, then nods as he walks past me.

I'm closing the door when a hand stops it. Renee, also in the hallway of my hotel, and me with a chafed dick.

"Speaking of ending you," she says as she, too, invites herself inside. "If you ever even *think* of ditching me again …"

"How the hell are you here, too?"

"What do you mean?" she asks.

"The fuck do you think I mean?"

"So now you don't want me here?"

"I never wanted you here!"

"Then who were those posts for, if not for me?"

Alarms. Flashing lights. Bad omens.

"What posts?" I ask.

"On Float, you asshole."

"I don't even use Float!" Not that that single objection erases the fuckery of her implication. The idea here seems to be that I became lovelorn, couldn't live without Renee, and contacted her through Float to come and rescue me from myself. There's so much wrong there, I don't even know where to start.

"Bullshit," Renee says. "They were your pictures."

"What pictures?"

"Pictures of us! Pictures of this trip! What the hell is the matter with you, Emil?"

Ah, yes. More shit that makes me want to punch babies. I don't take pictures. Even if it wasn't bad form for a guy like me, I find the incessant photo-happiness of the modern world more aggravating than door-to-door Jehovah's Witnesses. I don't feel the need to always be seeing my life through a lens — always be pointing a camera at myself for something to share, because *I'm* so goddamn important that everyone needs to see what I'm up to. I'd rather live my life than share it.

"Think about it for a second, will you?" I tell Renee. "You know I memorized your number. Even if I *was* some dickhead twenty-something selfie-happy cunt — and even if I suddenly *did* have a desire to break all of my rules about security and stealth by activating a new phone — why would I open a Float account to message you? Why wouldn't I just text you?"

"Are you high?" Renee looks at Robert, or perhaps just around the room in exasperation. "You didn't message me. You *posted*." She looks sorry for my stupidity when she adds, "How backwards *are* you, that you don't know the difference between a private message and a public post?"

I feel all the blood leave my body. I reach out my hand — for her phone, maybe … unless someone printed fliers to advertise my assignment as well. "Show me."

"Why?"

"Show me!"

Renee pulls out her phone, opens Float, and hands it to me — all three actions punctuated by stabbing fingers and frustrated glances. And there, plain as day, I see the pictures she was talking about on the public feed. A short message begging Renee to come back to me is right underneath them, with her screen name in cornflower blue. Apparently, that means I tagged her.

Only, this isn't my Float account. I don't have one. This account belongs to …

"Hell-ooo!" Robert sings from behind us. He's on the bed, spread out like he expects naked slaves to start feeding him fruit. He gives a jolly little wave and I want to punch him all over again.

"Shit," I say.

"What?"

263

"*You* did this?" I ask my brother.

"No, *you* did," Renee says.

"I'm not talking to you. I'm …" But I trail off, because I can no longer work my hands. They're locked closed into fists of steel. If I'd been holding a pencil, my grip would have reduced it to dust.

I close my eyes and force myself to breathe slowly.

Something odd happens as I do. Random thoughts enter my mind, the way Robert always describes.

I think of the time we were kids at the zoo, just me and Dad and Robert, and Dad, drunk at 10 a.m., told a balloon vendor all about his boys. I nodded and told the vendor I'd done something bad by getting distracted and left my brother behind. Dad burped, then said that it wasn't a problem anymore, that everything had (more or less) worked out fine. We were together now and that's all that mattered. It was sage for a drunk, so I nodded even though I still felt guilty. The vendor gave me a free balloon. Told me I was a good brother anyway.

I think of Shady Acres. About how Robert sometimes played the piano in the old folks' lobby when nobody was around to hear.

I tell myself: *Be the good brother.* Blood, they say, is always thicker than water.

"We're *on Float.*" I try counting to ten, but that doesn't calm me at all.

I make myself focus and lay it out slowly. Maybe if I take this clusterfuck apart and examine each piece individually, my biggest mistakes will be visible through the cracks. "Our pictures … of us on assignment to kill a senator … are *on Float.*"

"I felt bad about being the reason you broke up," Robert says from the bed. "We aren't friends on Float, so I couldn't send a message."

I pinch the bridge of my nose. Hard. I open my eyes and look, now flicking through Robert's posts using my thumb. There are dozens. Pictures of me and Robert or just me or just Robert, photos of Renee. They weren't all posted just today, or yesterday. This goes back to the beginning. To the very first post showing Robert in selfie mode and me with my eyes on the road, unaware that he took the picture.

The caption says, *Heading out to meet @zero with my bro!*

"Robert," I say, still pinching my nose.

He and Renee respond in unison. "What?"

"What did you do?"

Renee is still an idiot, still unclear who I'm talking to. She answers about what she's doing, but I can only hear my brother.

"You know about Cortés. When he reached the new world, he burned his ships so his men would have no way of turning back, and could only move forward, no matter what hard times lay before them."

"Fuck," I say. "Fuck fuck fuck fuck."

"What?" Renee asks.

"Get out of here, Renee," I tell her. "Come back in ten minutes, if you must."

"What? Why?"

I put a hand on her chest, shove her into the hallway, then close the door.

"Explain yourself," I say to Robert once we're alone.

I'd pull a gun on anyone else, but all I do this time is put my fingers on the grip. I won't shoot my own brother. Probably.

"We said this was our last job. So ... Cortés and the ships. I wanted you to honor your promise, and motivate you to succeed. So we could retire in style." He lifts his current phone — one he must have lifted somewhere, then hopefully cleared before using — and wiggles it at me. To Robert, this was about accountability. But to me, it feels like sabotage.

"*You* said this was our last job, I hadn't decided."

"Oh. Sorry." Robert's not sorry at all. He looks up, smiles, and says, "Well … you're decided now."

I really feel like killing something. Like socking my brother again, or throwing things across the room. But what's the point? I've hit him plenty, and breaking things draws too much attention.

I'm pacing.

"You need to erase it, Robert. Take down every picture. Every post."

"You can't remove posts from Float after twenty-four hours, Emil. It's the gimmick, like when Snapchat used to self-destruct."

"Self-destruct I can handle."

"Well, Float's thing isn't self-destruct. It's *permanence*. Sort of Zero's platform from the start — and now in the senate, if people still called him Zero."

I'm screwed. We both are. Bisset is for net neutrality and government-funded public WiFi and smartphone subsidy programs so that even the poor can access all the online nonsense people feel is so fucking important. Bisset is for declassification and disclosure, which is probably why everyone says he was behind those celebrity photo hacks a few years ago. Starlets, it seems, shouldn't be allowed to keep their tits confidential. He says he's against secrets and censorship. What I suspect Bisset is really against is *other* people's secrets, seeing as he must have plenty of his own.

He does seem to enjoy raking muck from the other end of society's garden.

Like the Lilac incident.

Like all he did to Renee.

Of course you can't delete anything from Float. It's nature's way of ensuring that every drunken gaffe and dumb decision becomes part of a permanent and searchable record.

Your mistakes on display forever. That should be the slogan.

"I'll be honest, Emil, I thought that if you could see past your own damn nose for a minute, you'd be happy about this."

Oh for Christ's sake. "Why would I be *happy* about you outing us to the whole internet? We're going to have to leave the country!"

"We were *already* planning to do that. The only thing I did was ensure you couldn't change your mind."

"It compromises the mission! For fuck's sake, Robert … you think this will make it easier for us to kill him? We need money before we run off, idiot!"

I hate how evenly Robert replies. It's like he's the rational one and I'm hysterical. "It doesn't compromise the mission. Calm down for one damn second and I'll explain."

My jaw works. I stare at my brother for a long moment, then sit on the second bed opposite him.

"Do you remember me telling you about One?"

"One *what?*"

"One," Robert repeats, his tone implying an importance I'm still missing. "At the height of Zero's notoriety — back when Bisset still *was* Zero and nobody knew his real name — a second hacker calling himself 'One' started aping everything Zero did, seemingly to prove he could. Zero's people hacked into the *New York Times* and changed the headline to BALLS OUT on an entire print run … then the next day, with *NYT's* cybersecurity tightened and apologies issued all over New York, One changed the *Times*

headline to the far less subtle FUCK EVERYONE'S MOM."

"So?" I ask.

"One constantly taunted him. A real thorn in Zero's side. Nobody ever figured out who he was. The government, maybe, trying to shake Zero's kingdom by sowing gossip and proving he wasn't the only one with skills. But here's the thing. One left digital calling cards all over the place just to mess with Zero. And all those calling cards had this on it."

Robert shows me an image on my phone. A cartoon man's face, his eyes happy and wide. It looks vaguely antiquated, like a hair gel advertisement from the fifties.

"Get to the point, Robert."

"I know it pisses you off when I talk to people online, but the truth is, I'm *good* online. I've met a lot of people. Delved deep. And it turns out, there's one act of mischief — like the *Times* stunt — that Zero never got to before time came to out himself and let the world meet Simon Bisset the Socially Constructive Citizen. Almost nobody knows about that back-burnered plan he had … but I do."

"What plan?"

"He wanted to burn a Z in the White House lawn. Z for Zero, like Z for Zorro."

"And?"

Robert pulls up a recent photo from his stream — one I didn't see before. My brother in our old hotel room, before we split, with the dark rectangle of a nighttime window behind him. There's a foot peeking from sheets in the background: my foot, or maybe Renee's.

I see three things on the hotel desk beside Robert.

The first is a small model of the White House — a tiny thing Robert must have bought from places unknown, then hidden from me.

The second is a small bag of powdered herbicide — the kind of thing you use to kill grass, possibly in a recognizable pattern.

The third thing beside Robert is a printout of that happy cartoon face: One's logo, for want of a better term.

A little quieter, I say, "You want him to think you're One."

Robert nods. "And he will. Almost nobody knows that Zero planned to score the White House lawn, but of course, One would. But here's the thing: Senator Bisset has all sorts of 'people.' He can send someone to handle just about anything for him, but this is private. Same as Renee's lead, if you hadn't jumped the gun and gone in blazing after the wrong man. We missed our chance to get him alone at the bar, but this is how we make it up. We just have to meet him somewhere. He'll want to face One, and without anyone knowing. He isn't just a hacker. Rumor says One got dangerous. I'm telling you, Bisset will want to deal with this."

"What makes you think he'll bite?"

"He already has. I messaged him. He knows our faces, but not who we are. He can figure it out, but he'll have to call in favors at the phone company to figure out who I am, and I've already threatened to expose shit he doesn't want out there if he doesn't meet us in a lot in less time than it will take to track us down. Bisset knows the clock is ticking. He'll show up wherever we tell him."

I watch him, unsure how I feel about this. *Conflicted* is the answer. I'm still furious at being pictured on Float at all, and I'm not in love with the way Bisset knows it's us who are after him. But at the same time, if Robert is right, this is our last way to lure him out alone. You aren't supposed to get second chances in this game, but my brother's given us one on a silver platter.

"You shouldn't have done it, Robert. You're forcing our hand, and leaving us without any room to maneuver."

"And no way to back out."

"I'm not ready to leave the game. I'll need a new name and identity."

"Or you could finish the assignment, collect the bounty, and retire in style like we've already talked about."

"Like *you* talked about."

"We agreed."

"We never agreed."

"You're losing it, Emil. If you don't retire now, you'll be in a box a year from now."

"I'm not losing anything."

"Look around you," he says, indicating my hotel room. "Did you pay for this with cash?"

"This hotel doesn't take cash."

"So you used a card. Showed your ID."

"We show our IDs every time we fly."

"And we have decoy transportation always set up. We take precautions and set false trails. But look at you. You walked in with a Pelican case full of guns. You still have blood on your shirt."

"Where?"

"There." He points, and it's true.

"Nobody saw it."

"You're sure?"

"Nobody knows who we are or where we've been."

"Except that cop working the barricade outside the W Hotel. Except the guys from that bar, who jumped out the window or ran out the back door."

"Nobody can pin anything on me. There isn't any proof."

"Except all the proof in this room. Except the proof all over the mattress in the last place. You're not the professional you used to be, Emil. You're not just leaving a trail for the cops to follow when this is all over. You're practically drawing them a blueprint."

I think of our exposure. My face online, above captions announcing the start of a road trip — captions in which our target himself was tagged.

"The only way out is to see the job through to the end. We meet with Bisset, pretending we're One. We kill him. We get the money. And we run somewhere without extradition to the United States."

"Goddammit, Robert."

"Once we're through it, you'll thank me. I've only forced you to do what you already wanted to do, but don't have the stones to do without me."

I could fight him on that, and part of me very much wants to.

But it's true, and I know it.

TWENTY-FIVE

Strange Hobbies

I LET Renee back into the room ten minutes later, but refuse to catch her up on what my brother has told me. She's no longer a part of this, and never should have been. It seemed like we needed her, back at the start of this. But the way things have worked out, we no longer do.

I suppose I feel bad that Bisset did what he did to her, but Renee will get hers when we put him down like a rabid dog. She doesn't need to see her revenge. She doesn't need to be a third wheel anymore, now that two of her attempts to get us in front of our target have failed.

Fail me once, shame on her.

Fail me twice, shame on me.

Fail me three times? Well, yeah, fuck that shit with a garden rake. I don't abdicate my jobs to anyone — not Robert, definitely not someone like Renee. She queued us up and dropped the ball, and Robert forced my hand. But now that we're in it, this has to be my show again. I'm in charge, solely and fully, this one final time.

Or not. I have a few ideas — and if I pull them off just right, maybe this doesn't have to be my last outing as an assassin. Robert won't like it, but my brother's not the boss of me. He may have controlled my life since we were kids just by being there, but that ends now. That ends *today*.

Robert is already up when I wake in the morning, cutting large rectangles from sheets of paper. I leave Renee sleeping and peer over my brother's shoulder before he sees I'm there.

He must have run down to the hotel's business center, because each sheet has been printed with one of Robert's photos. The signs he collects wherever we go.

To one side: CAUTION - MACHINERY. The illustration shows a man having one arm pulled off by gears.

To the other: A sign showing a figure bent over a water fountain ... to which some witty person added a second figure grasping the first's hips from behind, servicing the butthole while the lips drink water.

"Morning," I say.

Robert looks up. I surprised him, and it's clear he wasn't planning to share this particular arts-and-crafts project with me, or anyone else.

His face reddens. "It helps me relax."

"Did you sleep?"

"I never sleep," Robert says.

There's been too much animosity between us lately, so instead of responding I ruffle his hair. I haven't done it since we were kids, but even as adults Robert offers no protest.

"Did Bisset respond?"

"We're meeting at the Big Boy at ten," my brother responds with a nod.

"Tonight?"

"This morning."

I look at my watch. It's 8:36 a.m.

"He wanted daylight," Robert explains. "And somewhere public."

"As long as he comes alone."

Robert nods again. "He'll come alone. I dropped a mention of Lilac, too. I'll bet the real One knows who she was. I'll bet he knows that Bisset exploited his cousin. He won't want anyone knowing about either of the things we're supposed to discuss. Not his bodyguards, and definitely not his wife."

"What does he think we want?"

"Money."

"So he'll have a bag. There'll be a record, somewhere, of a withdrawal."

"No. I told him we want it in Pentz. Guy like Zero, his Pentz account might as well be dollars in the Caymans."

"How much?"

"A million. It felt like a nice round number. He'll pay half when he sees us — when I wave a high sign at him. I told him what we'd be wearing." Robert points to the second bed, where a loud red shirt is waiting to be worn. "Related: You're wearing that today."

"And then?" I ask.

"Then we'll go inside together and talk. I'm supposed to give him a thumb drive with an encryption key on it. Then he can permanently erase a bunch of files I've already set aside — either as blackmail if he welches on us, or as his to erase if he pays in full."

"You know how to do all of that?"

"I know how to fake it enough to pass. It'll fall apart once he sees more, though. You understand I don't actually *have* the blackmail One used to threaten him with back in the day."

"So I have to kill him in the parking lot. After the high sign."

Robert nods. "I figure half a million is enough."

And he's right. As much as I hated him pinning us like this, the plan is actually brilliant if we can execute. In addition to Heinzie's bounty, we'll now get half a million Pentz from Bisset. We get in, grab the collar, take a lot more than we'd been planning, and fly somewhere tropical where the cocktails all come with umbrellas.

Only, I have other plans. We're not quite as pinned as my brother means us to be in my version of this. What he intends as retirement, I see as a short vacation. Once the heat dies down, I'll be able to get right back to work. Assuming I can pull it all off.

I stop dreaming to find Robert looking at me.

"What?" I ask.

"I could ask you the same question. What aren't you telling me?"

Renee stirs. We both look over as she stretches and yawns.

She sees the mess of papers and clippings, along with a bit of what's on them, then looks up at me with one eyebrow raised.

"It's his hobby," I explain.

"You have strange hobbies," Renee tells me.

"Not mine. His."

I gesture toward Robert, but he's gone. The bathroom door is closed, a line of light visible beneath the door.

"Sure," she says. *"His."*

TWENTY-SIX

Dead As Disco

THE BIG BOY sits on a hilltop, and I find that a travesty.

You put great things up high for all the world to see, and reserve the very best views for the very best people. But someone got it all wrong this time. Big Boy, in his red-and-white checkered overalls and pompadour, holds his big brown burger overhead at the top of a vista that should belong to a fine winery. Or perhaps an eight-figure mansion. At the very least to a scenic overlook, not blighted by icons that weren't even in style a half century ago.

"What time is it?" I ask.

Robert looks at his watch. "9:35."

I drive us in a slow circuit of the parking lot, looking like a car that could be owned by a senator. It isn't a difficult chore. The Big Boy crowd isn't any classier than the one at The Heaping Plate, and they all drive mechanical assholes.

"He might not have brought a car."

"He'd have to," Robert tells me. "If he takes a

rideshare, the driver might recognize him. Nobody can drop him off for the same reason, and he's not walking up here or taking a bike."

I park in the back lot. We both figured Bisset would come early and scope for us, so we had to arrive even earlier.

"Does it feel strange?" Robert asks me once we're settled — when we crack open little creamers and begin adding them to our drive-thru coffee. "Being here with me?"

"I'm with you all the time."

"But this could be the last time."

"For a job, Robert. Not the last time with you."

Robert shrugs, but says nothing.

"What was it like with her?"

"For fuck's sake, Robert."

"I'm not jealous. I'm just wondering."

"She's annoying," I tell him. "When we headed out to that bar, she wouldn't stop talking. Or asking questions."

"Questions? About what?"

"About me. You know. Like someone 'in a relationship' would ask."

"But you're not in a relationship."

"Exactly."

"You're just fucking her."

"Right."

"Doesn't she get that? Doesn't she understand that it's only sex?"

"Sex and revenge," I say with a nod.

The real answer is *no*, I don't think Renee gets it at all. I thought we were on the same page when this all started. But she's gotten clingier and clingier. Hugging me close as much as reaching for my johnson. Now she wants to kiss when we fuck. And this last thing? That was the icing on the cake.

The chance that I'd take Renee with us on this final Bisset errand was slim from the start, but there was at least a chance. Then I explained it and she started asking even more of those obnoxious questions, all the while I kept thinking of what Robert said last night about my trail. Because it's true. I have been leaving breadcrumbs anyone could follow if they looked. Renee's questions, through that filter, were leaks waiting to happen. She invites herself to everything we do, so it's easy to forget she's not supposed to be here — that we picked her up at a truck stop and carried her like baggage ever since. Strictly speaking, now that we have this new plan after both of hers have failed us, I should probably kill her to erase the loose end. I doubt I will at this point, but if she knows too much when we cast her off, she'll come back to haunt us.

Plus, she has that whole "woman scorned" thing. I got rid of Renee once, and she's still pissed about it. She thinks I invited her back, but my brother did that for reasons unknown. I told her that we'd leave her in a nice hotel instead of a gas station this time, but it was little consolation. We still left to the backbeat of her cursing my name.

"Are you going to kill her?" Robert asks.

"Not unless I have to."

"Are you going to take her to Aruba or wherever with us?"

I bore my eyes into Robert's skull. "Why the hell would I take her with us?"

"Just in case you get tired of me."

"I can't get tired of you, Robert. You're my little brother."

"Just because you feel guilty about leaving me behind

doesn't mean you enjoy my being around 24/7. You proved that in L.A."

"You left us, Robert, not the other way around."

"You sure about that?"

I'm about to try and answer when a black Tesla enters the lot.

"That's him." Robert nods at the vehicle.

He must have told Bisset what kind of car we'd be driving too, because the Tesla drives right toward us. But then, just as my brother described, he stops a hundred feet away. This is probably to make him feel safe. Truth is, I could use a bullet to drill a cavity out of his second molar from twice this distance, but the target doesn't need to know that.

Robert gets out of the car and makes a complex gesture in the Tesla's direction. Bisset, for whom "being Bisset" is apparently confirmation enough for this transaction, simply nods and pulls a phone from his pocket.

A few seconds later Robert's current phone dings, confirming receipt of a half-million Pentz.

"That's it," Robert says.

We get out of the car. Robert reaches for the gun behind his back, but I can only see the sharpshooting display he put on at the last bloodbath as he does. For once, Robert was the killer. Robert was aggressive and fearless. Robert did what needed to be done, while I stayed low.

I put my fingers on his reaching arm, minding my plan. "Not yet, I want to look this asshole in the eye."

Robert looks over. Is he suspicious? Or does he think I'm just trying to grab glory like I always do, taking the shots so my brother doesn't get to?

His hand moves back, and we walk toward the senator. He's dressed incognito, wearing jeans and a T-shirt that's seen better days. Only his fancy car gives him away as he stands on his side of a hostage negotiation, waiting patiently for the swap.

"You Robert?" he asks me.

"This is Robert," I say, gesturing. "I'm Emil."

Bisset already knows our first names. Robert, burning our ships.

He looks at my brother, then back at me. "If you say so. You have what you promised?"

"Robert has it."

"Okay. And … How do I get it from Robert?"

"Give it to him, Robert."

Bisset looks over when I do. That's when I punch him in the throat, spin him around, and snatch Robert's pistol to press against his head while my other arm compresses his windpipe from the rear.

"Emil!" Robert shouts.

"Shh!"

Bisset chokes. Gags.

"Let him go!"

"What was the plan, Robert? Does it really matter if I let him go?"

But the question is a decoy. I know the plan. To move our conversation behind the Big Boy dumpsters, then shoot Bisset point-blank in the head. There wasn't supposed to be any contact. That leaves evidence — and with the victim being a senator, it won't just be local cops investigating the murder we're about to commit. Our Caribbean escape plan is outlined in rough, but it all falls apart if we leave a trail to the TSA's door.

I punch Bisset in the kidney and he finally stops fighting.

"You're carrying a laptop," I say. "Tell me the truth."

Of course he is. Bisset carries a computer wherever he

goes. It's his legend and legacy. He used to be one of the internet's most famous rascals, and today that past is a PR tool rather than a criminal offense in need of addressing. Everyone knows Bisset used to be Zero. His supporters love it. If he's not staring at a screen whenever he's not kissing babies — no matter where he happens to be — he loses street cred with half of his followers at least.

"I don't have a laptop."

I hit him again. Same kidney.

"Emil!"

I move the gun to his upper back. Better chance of muffling the report down there, anyway.

"Tell the truth or you lose a lung."

He nods. Vocalizes, though it's not quite words.

I shove him toward his car. I motion for Robert to join me in the back, while Bisset slips behind the wheel.

"Take us to your place," I say.

"Fuck you," Bisset replies.

I hit him hard with the gun barrel, racking his skull. He coughs, then spits blood.

I turn to Robert. "See if he has his home address saved on the navigation system."

"I don't," says Bisset.

"I wasn't talking to you!"

Robert raises a hand. "Think for a second. We came out here because he'd be alone. No security. We don't want to go back into the lion's den."

"And they can track me. If I don't come back, they'll know where this car has been."

"Fine. Then we do this here." I pull what seems to be a laptop bag from the back footwell and shove it forward. "Log into Float."

"*What?*"

"You heard me. It's your fucking network. You must

have a master dashboard or something. Admin-level access? Whatever lets you delete."

"Nobody can delete anything from Float! Not without taking the site down!"

"Then take it down."

"I can't do that from here. I'd have to call—"

"Then you're worthless to me, and I might as well kill you now." I'm holding an automatic, but Robert always lowers the hammer when he carries the thing just in case. I'm glad.

I cock it and his hands shoot skyward, striking the Tesla's ceiling. "All right, all right! There's something I can try." He screws with it for a second, then turns his head to see me in profile. "We need to go back to my place. It's a laptop. I don't have a signal."

"*Bullshit!* Big Boy has WiFi."

"But it's … I need a secure connection! Anything open like that is vulnerable to—"

"*BULLSHIT!*"

Robert is staring at me like I'm a loose cannon, but I'm already in this and have no intention of backing down. I press the gun harder against the back of his head (or, really, his cheek now that he's turned) and feel my hand start to shake. I see it and think, *This isn't professional. It's supposed to be emotionless. Nothing personal.*

And yet I'm so adrenaline-fueled agitated, it's as if part of me feels this man is responsible for all that's gone wrong in my life. In reality, he's responsible only for changing the internet, opening digital legislation, and basically buying himself elections through blackmail, charisma, and a fist-grip on the media.

It's worth murder in my book many times over.

There's more than enough to make my hands tremble, and my temples throb in fury.

Robert seems desperate to say something to me, but he doesn't dare. His mouth works like a fish out of water.

So I do all the talking. "I'm going to make this real easy by giving you exactly two options. The first is for you to do whatever the fuck I say, right fucking now. The other is for me to redecorate the inside of your car with bits of your skull. There's a contract on your life, my friend, and I'm only one of a bouquet of killers hired to end you. So if I can't get what I want from your smug fucking face, I'll get it from the people who want you dead. It's not something I'm afraid to do, or haven't done a hundred times before. Do you understand? Or you still got shit in your ears?"

He understands. His arrogance and bravado disappear as his head begins to bob rapidly up and down.

"Fine. Okay."

"What are you doing?" Robert asks.

"Not retiring."

"We agreed."

"*You* agreed."

"Why would you want to keep doing this?" Robert asks.

I turn to my brother. "Because when we're through, there's nothing else left."

This is who I am. This is what I believe. It's not pretty, and I don't even like it. I'm a ship missing its anchor, and no port in the world to claim as my home.

"Pull up his account," I tell Bisset when I see that he's logged into his Float administrative console.

"Okay. Sure. You bet."

I give him Robert's screen name. Bisset reads it back as he types.

"Now. Delete the entire thing. Every picture. Everything he typed. From everywhere. Because if I find out you had anything backed up somewhere later on, I swear to

God I'll find you and I won't just put a bullet through your head. I'll knock you out, tie you down, then roll you over and use a kitchen knife to cut out your spine while you're still alive."

"Jesus, Emil," Robert says.

"Do it!"

Bisset types and clicks. He keeps missing letters. I can see the thrum of his pulse in the vessels of his neck.

"Okay," Bisset says. Then he reads: "Emil Hicks."

"Robert Hicks," I tell him.

"This says Emil."

I turn to Robert and stare. "Fucking seriously?"

"What's your birthday?" Bisset asks me.

"The fuck you want my birthday for?"

His hands go back up, but only halfway. His voice is thick. He might have pissed his pants. *"To confirm!* To make sure this is the right account!"

I give him Robert's birthday.

He shakes his head, then reads me back my own birthday.

"It's the wrong account," I say.

"It's the right account, Emil." But all of a sudden Robert's voice is even. Not loud or scared or horrified or embarrassed or worried or angry at all. He might as well be reading me the daily news.

"It's the wrong account," I repeat.

Bisset says the screen name again. I make him spell it. Then I grab Robert's phone from his coat pocket and look at the Float feed he showed me earlier. And yep, Bisset is on the right account. Looking at his screen between the seats, I can see that the avatar picture is the same. As is the top post.

I turn to Robert, confused and furious. "Why did you use my information?"

"Who else's would I use?"

"Just delete it," I snarl at Bisset. "Delete it or you die right now."

"Okay. Okay. Just … please. I have to pull it up. This is only a list."

I watch, silent as he works. Bisset is a rat, and I don't trust him a bit. I'm going to kill him when we're done either way, but for now he still believes I'll let him go if he's willing to follow orders.

I lean over like a vulture. I let him see me watching, so he doesn't try anything funny. I want this done, and done right. Because if we can sweep up our real-world trail and Robert can scrub his digital one, there can still be a future for me in this career. I've waffled on whether to quit the game the way Robert wants, but in truth the idea of quitting gives me chills. I do want to stop, but even more I don't want to let it end. Something inside me is terrified of that ending, holding tight to my truths and comforting delusions.

The account comes up on Bisset's laptop screen. It's the right one. I see the offending photos, the offending status updates that tell the world too much. In my current cloud of rage, part of me wants to turn some of that anger on Robert. I can't believe all he's shared, just like all the other idiots on social media.

On Float, he checked in at the W, giving our exact geo coordinates.

He shared a picture of us at the police checkpoint outside — an incognito snap when I was presenting our VIP pass to the cop.

And he shared …

And he shared …

My mouth hangs open. I'm looking at something

hideous. Something impossibly *wrong*, shared to Float just a few days ago.

"What the hell?" I say.

Bisset hears the doubt in my voice, so he turns. He faces my gaping mouth, taking it for weakness or indecision or emotional conflict, which it is in a way.

"Look. Whatever your boss is paying, I'll double it. *Triple* it. I'm just a man. Just an ordinary guy, no matter what anyone——"

There's a crystal pop as a tiny starburst appears in the Tesla's side window. I blink, trying to understand. But then I see there's also a starburst in the passenger window as well, lined up exactly with the first one.

The passenger side of the car is also painted in blood and brain.

Bisset slumps sideways, dead as disco.

I'm trying to comprehend all of this when I realize that my brother's fled the car, that his door is open and I can't even see him in the distance. But he's not the one who killed Bisset. The angle is wrong. Robert just ran like always.

I'm never at a loss for words or action, but I am right now.

It's maybe ten seconds later that the driver's side door opens and I see Senator Bisset's killer arrive holding a precision sniper rifle.

My precision sniper rifle, which apparently didn't burn after we shook up those meth cooks after all. It was stolen, not destroyed.

My mouth won't close. As good as I like to believe I am at my job, I never saw this coming.

The assassin tucks the rifle under one arm and clears the chamber, exactly like a pro used to the weapon would know to do. The ejected shell goes into a pocket, lest it be left behind as evidence.

"Thank you," says the assassin, "for leading me to him."

It's Renee.

TWENTY-SEVEN

Pantomimes

"I WANT YOU TO KNOW," Renee says, "that I genuinely like you."

She plucks a rag from her back pocket and, keeping her distance from the car, rubs it along the grip, the stock, the oiled black length of the long rifle that ended Senator Bisset's life. The rag is a dull periwinkle and comes away stained.

"Did you ever see *Can't Buy Me Love?*" she asks.

I haven't moved. In the commotion, my .45 dropped to the floor. I can see it now, and know from past experience just how fast I'd be able to grab and fire it — especially already cocked, and the safety a quick thumb-flip away. But if Renee is who I think she is (or at least *what* I think she is) I won't be fast enough. She'll cut me in half before I can brush the trigger.

So I say, keeping my voice as calm and cool as I'm able, "The Beatles song?"

"The movie," Renee says.

When it seems she's still waiting for an answer, I slowly shake my head.

"What about *Can't Hardly Wait?*"

"No."

"*Ten Things I Hate About You. She's All That. How To Lose a Guy In 10 Days.*"

"No."

Renee slips a black Beretta with a silencer on the end from her waistband before carefully setting the sniper rifle aside. Then she raises the handgun, and I'm staring into the Beretta's sights.

"What the hell *have* you seen, then?"

Is this a real question? I'm still trying to decide if I can get away or grab my gun or do anything besides continue this conversation.

"Emil? Come on. I thought we were past this. I thought our relationship was mature enough that we could talk. And yet, I don't really know you at all. I don't even know what kind of movies you like."

"Tarantino," I hear myself mumble, tensing and measuring a grab for my weapon. "I guess I like Quentin Tarantino."

"That explains it, then." Renee sighs. "When I say *Can't Buy Me Love*, I'm talking about that trope where some teenager dates a social outcast on a bet, then falls in love with them for real and has to declare their love in front of everyone." She tilts the Beretta and thumbs the safety, which is, of course, already off. "Tarantino's never done a fake relationship movie."

"I guess not," I say, still considering my fallen gun.

"And if he did, it'd be a violent romp full of swearing and racial slurs."

"They're not really slurs, the way he uses them," I explain.

"If you say so, honky."

Renee raises the Beretta.

"What I meant, is that this thing between us? It began as a con, but just like Patrick eventually fell in love with Kat in *Ten Things*, I eventually enjoyed being with you." She squints, sighting the gun. "I know it's fucked up, but I suppose I ended up loving you for real."

"Then maybe don't kill me," I suggest.

"Work is work."

"Come on." I try for sexy and end up looking stupid. It's a ploy to shift position, getting my hand closer to my weapon. I'm going for Venus on a divan, but instead I look like I've been suddenly paralyzed, slouching without control. "You got Bisset. You can let me live."

"Heinzie wouldn't like that. And all things considered, *I'd* prefer to live, too."

Something clicks, and a moment later I understand what's happening here.

"You're not Bisset's cousin."

"Not in this lifetime."

"You're Blackhawk, aren't you? You've just been waiting to make your move."

"Swish," she says.

"I thought Blackhawk was a man."

"To quote a great cinematic warrior, 'Most men do.'"

Trying the notion on — and removing my bias that the most mysterious player around must be male — I see that it fits. She's my height with small boobs. If she wore a tight sports bra and kept her hood up, nobody would know her gender or anything about her. Blackhawk is anonymous and off the grid. According to legend, nobody's ever seen the assassin's face.

Renee's finger brushes the trigger. Now she's just playing with me. Trying to have this final exchange before wiping me from the planet. I watch it happen, thinking, trying to put the pieces together long after the puzzle left the box.

She doesn't want to shoot me. Even on Heinzie's orders, she doesn't want to shoot me, so I still have a chance. If this part were purely professional, I'd already be dead.

Give her an excuse. Anything to delay. To buy some thinking time.

I just need one or two extra seconds so I can be the one to put this to rest — *and*, I realize, to claim the collar on Bisset for myself. Renee — Blackhawk — is holding *my* gun. If I manage to kill her, I can take the credit, the money, and my life.

"I don't understand," I tell her. "You got us into the W."

"With an improvised VIP invite that was good enough to fool the cops outside, but wouldn't have held up inside."

"But it did hold up. For you."

"I just took the elevator up, used the restroom, then came back down when it was all over. At the top, just before the Secret Service checkpoint, I saw Rock Harder coming. I even smiled at him, pretending I thought he was just another guy. I told him to be careful. Said I saw someone down in the garage, skulking around. Maybe more than *one* someone. *I think they have guns*, I told him."

"You tipped the others off. At the W, then again at the bar."

Renee nods. "There are two kinds of players. Those who try to win from the start, and the smart ones who lay low while all the others fight, then swoop in after the field's been thinned."

"So you *don't* know Bisset."

"I know he's dead."

"You lied to me. The story about Lilac. About his favorite dive bar."

"I'm sorry, honey," she says, re-raising her gun. "But you lied to me, too."

My eye ticks toward the laptop, still open on the seat beside Bisset's fallen body. There are flecks of blood on the screen, along with that impossible image that stole my breath before shit went from bad to worse.

"Renee, wait."

"No time like the present," she says.

But she still doesn't fire, so I filibuster more. "At least do this honestly. Stop lying. Please. At least now, if you're going to do this, tell me the truth." I swallow vomit and make myself add, "You'll do it, if you really love me."

"Well. I wouldn't go that far."

"But … *Can't Buy Me Love?*"

"In addition to the bounty on Bisset, there's a quarter-million Pentz on you. I'm betting with that much, I can buy all the love I want."

"I shot Blackhawk in the shoulder," I say, but my chances to prolong this with talk are expiring. She'll pull the plug sooner or later.

"I don't know who you shot in the shoulder, but it wasn't me."

Again she steadies her aim.

"Wait!"

This time she lowers her gun with a sigh. But that's okay, because I see Robert sneaking up behind her. He doesn't have his gun out. Why not? He could shoot her now from a distance. One quick pull and we'd be home free, and a hell of a lot richer.

"This is getting really old, love."

"There are pictures of you on Float." I point, partially to distract her as Robert inches closer. "He's been documenting our assignment all along. You saw them!" I blurt, realization coming like a savior. "You came back last night because you said I posted for you, so I know you saw all the posts and pictures out there." I spy the laptop screen again at this, but I shove that dissenting bit of evidence out of my mind. "If you don't erase the account, you won't get away clean."

"Noted."

"But see … It's locked up already. The site timed out, and now you can't get in to erase anything without a password. But it's okay, Robert can help. He's great with computers. If you let us go, he can get into the account and take it all down. But if you kill me now …"

"Who?" she says.

"Robert."

Which makes me wonder why, if she's such a professional, she hasn't commented on the open car door or the absence of my brother. She should be looking around, lest she get jumped. She knows we came together. And they say *I'm* the one who's gotten sloppy?

Robert stops behind her.

I try to catch his eye when Renee looks away, except she never does. She knows I have a gun somewhere inside. How could I do what I came here to do without one? The fact that she hasn't asked me to find and toss it to her says more about her intended outcome here than anything else could. If I flinch, I'm dead. She knows exactly how to handle me.

I watch Robert from the corner of my eye, never centering my pupils lest Renee see me do it. He's stopped just feet behind her, but I can't read my brother without looking right at him.

I want to know what he's thinking, or more important, *what's he waiting for.*

"Do you understand? If you shoot me and can't erase the photos of—"

"Don't mansplain the internet to me. *You're* the one who doesn't understand technology. *You're* the philistine. *You're* the grouch."

"But Robert's account—"

"*Your* account."

"He opened it in my name."

"Who did?"

"Robert!"

Robert shrugs behind her.

Renee says, "It's a shame, Emil. We'd make quite a team, if I didn't have to kill you."

"You don't! Join my team!" Then I can kill her. She'll figure that part out later.

"Even if not for Heinzie, you're fucking crazy."

"So people say."

"And you could never be on a team. You're too damn alpha. Too much of a batshit-crazy lone wolf."

"I'm not a lone wolf! What about Robert?"

My brother, still three feet behind Renee, shakes his head and rolls his eyes when I shout for her to remember him. But really, what a dick. Does it matter if I remind her that he's there, if he's not going to grab her or shoot her or do anything to motherfucking help me?

"Seriously, Emil. Who the fuck is Robert?"

"My brother! Jesus Christ ... *My brother,* you dumb bitch!"

She squints at me, thinking. The gun sighs just a little, and I wonder if it's enough of a lapse for me to grab my own weapon from the floor ... seeing as Robert is apparently just going to stand there.

Except that now, he's pantomiming something. He makes a gun with one hand, holding the first with the other: a two-hand grip. Then he pretends to fire, and whips his hands apart.

What's that supposed to mean? Something for me to do? To know?

But *what?*

"I research all my targets, Emil. It's how I got into your garage before coming down here. Your security could be a whole lot better."

"So do I. But that doesn't explain why you're—"

"According to everything I could find, you don't *have* a brother. Why do you keep talking to me about—?"

"*Robert!* Robert! *Fucking Robert,* asshole! The third person in the car? The guy in the other bed? The man sitting across from me when you sat down at our fucking booth at that shithole restaurant!"

Something changes on Renee's face. I can't name the new emotions I see there.

"Some people believe that we see paradise after we die. That we're better off." Renee aims her Beretta, and I know this is it. "In your case, I think it might actually be true."

I'm really about to die. Not as a construct or abstract idea. No. This time, it'll be lights-out for real.

My life seems to flash proverbially in front of my eyes. I remember being a kid. I remember Timmy the cat, and how he met his end. I remember Dad. I remember why he left. *When* he left. I remember things I saw, and everything past age twelve is a double-exposure: one photo laid atop another. I see two paths. Two ways every moment went, or may have gone.

I see myself alone. I see myself with Robert.

I see myself with Robert. I see myself alone.

Empty chairs.

Empty beds.

Desperate as the final sands fall through the hourglass, I abandon all subterfuge and shout to my brother. "*Robert! Now!* Fucking do it, will you?"

"You're sick, Emil," Renee says. "I'm sorry, but this time it's really for the best."

Robert pantomimes:

Gun.

Hands flying apart.

Gun.

Shooting.

Explosion.

Fuck. I know what he did, but not why. I know what's about to happen and why it's a problem, but not how or when. Renee fooled me. But she didn't fool everyone.

"You were alone when I met you," Renee says.

And then she pulls the trigger.

TWENTY-EIGHT

Robert Is Nowhere

I saw it on an episode of *MythBusters* once. When a gun fires with something jammed in the barrel, the whole thing won't curl open like a banana being peeled or a lily in bloom. The round simply strikes the obstruction and throws shrapnel everywhere.

But that's not even the real problem. Even in a 9mm, if the hot gasses have nowhere to escape, they'll lance through gaps in the steel like a welding torch. You'll lose your hand if you're unlucky. The less fortunate will get a shard to the heart. The eye. The brain.

Renee gets off even easier. I see the explosion, and watch her hands fly apart. The gun, buckled but whole, hits the parking lot. Then something else hits it. Two things, actually, and both make a sound like hot dogs dropped on the ground.

Her fingers. Index and middle, if I had to guess. It's going to suck hard the next time she wants to flip someone off.

Seeing it, knowing it, and somehow sure (though I have no way of having known) exactly what's happened, I ducked back when she fired, shielding my eyes. I felt the pepper of tiny particles, but am, as far as I can tell, entirely whole.

Renee falls to her knees, left hand clutching her right wrist. She's like a partially clogged hose, spurting blood more than bleeding it. The .45 is in my hand within seconds.

Kill her.

But my hand won't obey.

"Don't," says Robert. "This is the end for us."

"She'll come back."

"She won't," he tells me.

Renee looks back at Robert, then at me. Then at Robert, then at me. Every time she looks at my brother, she looks at his crotch, maybe his stomach. Not his eyes. Not his face. It's like she's seeing right through him.

She stares at me then, still gripping her throbbing hand, her expression closer to vacant than merely approaching shock. Her jaw is slack. She's not looking at me like her murderer. Instead, she's staring at me like I'm a lunatic.

She gets to one foot and one knee, as if she means to propose.

The gun shakes in my hand. I try to force the squeeze. One quick lead fist and this will all be over, but my goddamn hand won't pull.

"Mercy," Robert says.

"She didn't show me mercy."

"All the more reason."

Renee gets to both feet, then stops to stupidly gawk in my direction. The gun has become a vibrator, better for pleasure than pain. My muscles have locked. It's as if the gun is sheathed in invisible armor I can't squeeze past.

She runs. I lower my weapon, frustrated, scared,

confused, and impotent. I climb out of the car and move to where Robert is standing. He was right in the line of spatter, yet my brother's not wearing a single drop of blood.

"You plugged the barrel," I say.

Robert nods.

"So you knew."

"As you knew."

"I didn't know. I thought she was just a girl."

"You knew," Robert repeats.

We stand in silence. There's nobody back here, and thanks to the silencers, I doubt anyone heard. We'll have to haul ass, of course, and we'll need to flee the country after a quick stop at Heinzie's to collect our money, and possibly threaten his life. You can kill businesspeople all day long and nobody looks too closely, but Bisset was a senator. The man who created Float. Millions loved him. Millions, including me, hated him. To me he's a sign of all that went wrong.

I remember how obsessed I used to be, before it all happened.

How I, like so many others, lost all my time to that bright little screen. To the unfortunate exclusion of all I should have been seeing instead.

"How did you know?" Robert asks me.

"I *didn't* know. I just said."

"Okay. Then how did *I* know?"

"The fuck should I know that?"

"Just think," Robert says. "Just play a game."

So I do. "At the first hotel in L.A. The way she got out of my grip."

"Yes?"

"That was Krav Maga."

"It was," Robert says.

"Strange, that some average girl from Florida would know Krav Maga well enough to disarm me."

"That *was* strange," Robert agrees.

But it's only part of the puzzle. Now that it's over, I'm starting to see the clues that Robert saw and I missed. Tiny affects and little shifts of behavior, the way Renee chose to say things, the deft way she handled weapons. Of course she wasn't "just some girl." She tried to hide, but it was clear from the start, if I'd paid close enough attention and not been distracted by sex, that she was one of us.

That by the time Rumy warned us that someone was coming, we'd already been found.

"She's crazy," I say without believing it. "Do you remember Timmy? Our cat when we were kids?"

"I used to, but now neither of us does."

Twenty years ago.

We hit that landmark just as Heinzie's toss-up for Bisset was starting to roll. It's not the kind of thing I wanted to remember, but I did nonetheless. The most macabre anniversary we've ever had to celebrate.

"We didn't have a cat, Emil. We both begged, but Dad always said no."

Of course. My mind goes back, searching for incorrect ends. It hits a bright red wall, painted with bottomless pain. At that I flinch back. At that, I obfuscate and startle.

"Don't," Robert says.

He moves to Bisset's car. I follow.

He opens the door. I open the door.

He picks up the laptop. I pick up the laptop.

He puts the laptop on top of the car, exactly as I do the same.

Onscreen is the selfie Robert snapped of us in the car. The one I told him not to take, then not to post. Of course he took it. Of course he posted it.

Except, I'm the only person in it. My arm is holding the phone, even as I seem so frustrated to be under its lens. Robert is nowhere.

"What does it tell you, Emil?"

I study the photo and say the only thing to enter my mind. "Someone erased you."

"Yes," Robert says. "Someone did."

TWENTY-NINE

20 Years Ago

Two YOUNG BOYS aged twelve and ten — both inseparable and unable to stand each other, in the way of boys that age — play outside a faded blue duplex with wood lap siding that's rotted underneath, where the nails attempt to find purchase, a lizard shedding its scales one long row at a time.

One of the boys in the small front yard is tall and thin. The other, still far enough from puberty that it's merely a concept, remains as horizontal as vertical. But it's okay, says the father. He'll grow tall and lean, once he gets a chance.

If he gets a chance.

The older boy sits on the stoop, his face in a tablet. Sometimes the father has things to say about that, too, but he seldom punctuates his tablet thoughts with a belt the way he does about more important matters: swearing and talking back, running in the house, breaking keepsakes, or even spilling the proverbial milk.

On the subject of the tablet, the father is more amused (maybe a little annoyed, as his childhood had no such wonders) than angry. That was the purpose of young Emil's tablet, after all. In younger days, the father needed time. To work, to drink, to chore, and to fuck the woman next door whose husband had no idea until he had all the ideas, at which point guns were drawn, things were said, and the father eventually solved the problem by finding another man to cuckold. Fortunately for the neighbor, that next man and his beautiful (but not too beautiful) wife live three states away. On the other hand, the same news was not as fortunate for Emil and his younger brother Robert, who stay behind.

But for today, for now, Emil and Robert are doing as the father asked. They're staying out of his hair, getting some of the "fresh" air outside — a word the three of them always put in air quotes. It's funny to them. They laugh. You'd almost think they were a family.

Robert — always the more inventive of the two — is not looking at a screen of any kind. He's never really gotten into that kind of thing. Sometimes Emil shows him things he finds online, and sometimes Robert is amused. But he never fights for the tablet, or plays his brother's online games. He's just not interested.

Robert looks at stars at night and plays in the woods whenever he's allowed. As an adult, Robert figures, he'll be a ranger. He'll walk the Appalachian Trail, which a cousin did last year. Emil can watch and digitally play and Facebook his day away if he wants … but for Robert, such things hold no appeal.

What's captured Robert's attention right now is the other living thing outside, contained for the moment inside a makeshift corral that started life as an outdoor pen for Emil, then Robert. It's their orange tabby cat, Timmy. In Robert's mind, it's cruel to keep Timmy inside all the time. He's a wild animal, and prefers to roam. Which he can do, to a limited degree, inside the twelve-by-twelve oval of suburban lawn. Not that Timmy needs to constrain his wanderings to twelve-by-twelve in practice. In practice, the cat eventually escapes. Every time. That's when the real adventures begin — and where, somehow, Timmy lost most of his left ear.

To pirates, Robert told the family. *That's who took Timmy's ear.*

With his big imagination, Robert does not believe he's in a small, out-of-date toddler corral in his front yard in Shitburg, USA. No, he's out on the Appalachian Trail, and Timmy is really a tiger. Robert's *pet* tiger, in fact. Robert tamed that domestic tiger easily. It's just one of his many gifts, along with whistling and playing *Jenga*.

Robert looks over at his brother. Emil used to play this game, but lately he's been pulling away. On the cusp of adolescence, Emil has more grown-up fish to fry. He's got a crush on the girl on Georgia Street, for one, and sometimes when they get on the bus he can see her underwear flash beneath her skirt. Emil is also interested in robotics. Watching birds. *Classifying* birds. Documenting his classifications on a private little corner of the internet.

Emil! Robert calls. *Emil, come play Jungle with me and Timmy!*

Emil either doesn't hear or pointedly ignores Robert. It feels like the latter, but in truth it's probably the former. He's almost a teenager, after all, and Robert knows that teenagers lose their hearing unless the sounds are being made by girls (or boys, Robert supposes; he's cosmopolitan enough to understand and support such things) or perhaps movie explosions.

It's okay, Timmy, Robert says. *That just means it's up to me and you. A boy and his faithful tiger. If Emil doesn't want to play, we don't need him.*

But it turns out that Timmy feels he doesn't need Robert either. So he makes a spontaneous decision, with his feline fickleness, that he's done with the game — that he's opting out, leaving the party, declaring it to be *passe* or at least *tout fini*. In truth, Timmy has been sandbagging on this whole "can't escape his prison" idea. In truth, he's been biding his time.

In one quick orange leap, Timmy is up and over.

Robert calls to Emil for help, knowing his brother is faster. In the past, it's always been Emil, never Robert, who's caught their fleeing cat. But, because Timmy hasn't gone far yet (and because Emil's grown a temper lately, and resents all requests that pull him from his digital distractions), Robert keeps his voice small.

When Emil doesn't hear (or, again, perhaps he hears but ignores), Robert climbs out and decides he can handle this little jailbreak himself.

That's when Timmy bolts.

Into the street, just as a car is coming.

Robert, seeing the world in slow motion, shouts for the cat — now with less come-here and a lot more alarm. Robert doesn't know it, but this is when Emil finally raises his head, meaning to shout for Robert to shut his stupid yap — or not, maybe, because Emil can hear the fear in his brother's voice as well.

Robert runs. Emil, seeing more of this and having two years' worth of broader context, understands the real peril. Whereas Robert's noted only one car, there are in fact two. The first misses Timmy by inches, barely swerving. Robert, watching, flinches hard but keeps his pace. He doesn't slow as Timmy narrowly avoids destruction; momentum alone has made that nearly impossible.

The cat stops for a second, then runs again. Robert turns on the afterburners …

… but fails to see the second car bearing down on him, drunk old Mr. McKenny behind the wheel.

There's a sound of squealing brakes, but it's far too late.

Timmy the cat sits down and lifts one leg straight in the air, then begins licking himself a feline bath.

A small shoe rolls into the gutter, and a full two minutes later — as screaming and shouting begins, as all the screen doors along the narrow block start to open and the scene begins to fill — Emil sits on the curb.

His father is at work, and two weeks from now will finally leave for good.

Emil understands this, somehow, already.

Other than the cat, he's all alone.

THIRTY

Dining Alone

MY LEGS TRY TO BUCKLE. In the Big Boy parking lot with Renee gone and Bisset dead, I'm all alone.

Again.

It's my hands on Bisset's laptop. My fingerprints on the keys. It's my face in the selfie on the laptop's screen and nobody else's. It's my arm, visible at the picture's side, that holds the camera.

My eyes that found the perfect-size rock from the hotel parking lot. My fingers that worked it into the muzzle of the Beretta while Renee was sleeping, making sure it was tight and would block as much of the exhaust as possible when the trigger was pulled. I couldn't be sure she'd use that Beretta, but I had a hunch. With all the clothes coming on and off, it felt unlikely that Renee, Blackhawk, was carrying her own weapon. Somewhere in my mind, I asked myself what I'd do in her situation, if I didn't want to reveal who I was or what I was actually up to. And the answer was, *I'd improvise.* I'd use the weapons at hand. I keep my .45 close and barely remember the Beretta ... so of course, when we left without Renee and she followed believing herself covert, it was the Beretta she'd grabbed to finish me off.

Clearly Renee wasn't an average girl. She didn't just *know* Krav Maga; she deployed it like instinct, which is the way a defensive art is supposed to deploy. The ease of her movement in disarming me, almost balletic, must have taken years of practice. *Years.* A ton of psychological experience. Readiness and waiting, like only a professional killer could do.

Although I knew it all, the top part of my brain knew nothing. Only the part of me that calls itself Robert was wise.

A voice speaks to me from across the top of Bisset's car.

"You understand?" Robert asks.

I look up. He shrugs at me in a way that's almost sheepish. He looks different now. Younger, perhaps.

"No."

"You understand," he says, bobbing his head.

My mind is a sequence of vaults, each locked within the next like a chain of nested dolls. The doors opening inside me now — all at once, and never mind the brute force of it all — have been closed for most of my life. You wouldn't think you could live a lie and never know it, but the mind is strong. The will is strong. Everyone believes what they need to.

"You ruined us, Robert. Now the whole world thinks we killed Bisset. We'll have to run."

"You ruined yourself, Emil. And now that the whole world thinks you killed Bisset, you get to start your new life."

"It wasn't always me." A voice within me knows it's just another closed vault — one more lie I've been telling myself. "You saved me in the bar."

"You saved yourself."

I shake my head. I'm talking to a man I now remember to be dead — a man who died young, and never *became* a man — but still won't believe it.

"You came to the bar through the back door."

"I came to the bar inside your skin," Robert tells me.

"You shot the last man."

"Could I make that shot, Emil? I couldn't hit a can with my slingshot when it was five feet away."

It's true. As much as the term "never" can apply to a life that lasted only ten years, Robert was never a good shot. I, on the other hand, can ruin a flipped nickel while it's still in the air. Punch a man's cortex through his pupil, barely brushing the iris around it.

"The Float account …"

"Float was before my time."

"But I hate it. I hate all of it."

"*Why* do you hate it, Emil? When's the last time you asked?"

It comes back a bit harder with each of Robert's words. I hear my own voice now more than his. I hear those words so close to my ear, they might as well be coming silent from inside me. I see my adolescence as a Hollywood set.

I remember the mourning of neighbors, all of whom were more hysterical than I, for some reason, could bring myself to feel.

I remember telling my father, the way I tell others, *It wasn't my fault*, knowing damn well that it was.

I remember a funeral with an obscenely small coffin. My father didn't take me; Miss Williams from school did. Dad had taken a business trip. Never mind that he was a welder, and hadn't left our town for legitimate reasons his entire life.

The business trip lasted for a week.

A month.

A year.

Inside me, memories fold and reconfigure like living origami. The old thoughts don't change in big ways — they're stripped down the way varnish undresses wood. A memory of Christmas with Robert in the State Facility for Boys becomes a memory of me alone, refusing even the best-intentioned requests of the others to join them. Memories of schemes plotted with my brother become memories of introversion.

A disturbed young man sitting in solitude with his pen, scribbling plans for his unlawful future.

My thoughts aren't always a two-way street. Sometimes I'm deposit-only, like the drop safe at an all-night convenience store. Now, with the mental tourniquet loosened, I recall suspecting Renee. I recall not liking her for the same reasons Robert didn't like her. Little by little, my honed instincts hoarded evidence that she wasn't who she claimed to be, but once inside those realizations vanished.

The Robert inside me plotted against her, while the Emil kept on denying it all.

I'm smarter than I thought I was. And also more blind.

I remember life on the street. Alone. Needing someone, having nobody. But that was fine, because by then my delusions had the force of solid matter.

My iPhone never leaves my side. I love taking photos of interesting signs. I enjoy the company of the elderly. I'm addicted to Float. For that, someone had to pay.

I look up. Robert's still there, but not for long. I know that now. It's hard to see; a fuzz of saline clogs my vision. He's been my right hand, almost literally. My strength when I'm weak, or my weakness when I'm strong. My tether and hot air balloon. He brings me down. He lifts me up. All that one man can do, I've turned into a pair.

I want to deny it, knowing how sick I am.

But there *is* no denying it. The walls inside are open now, having cracked the day I looked at the calendar and realized we'd had another anniversary. Robert would be 30. Even as brothers, the real man, if not for that car all those years ago, would have begun to pull away.

I know why I got into this game. I know why I got so good at it.

My legs collapse all at once, like my bone has turned to cartilage. There's no time to anticipate or plan. I'm up one moment, down the next. It's as if I've been assassinated. As if someone pierced my heart from afar, and these are my dying breaths.

Slouched against Bisset's car, I see my brother standing over me. He kneels. He's translucent, now. More not-there than there.

"I've been telling you for a long time, Emil," he says, a new and unfamiliar note in his voice, "it's time for this to end."

"I'm not ready for it to end. I still have years in me."

"I keep saying, you're getting sloppy. Leaving clues. Opening little cracks in what you used to keep drum-tight."

"I can do better."

"Brother," Robert says, "you can't. Not now. What's open can't be closed."

"Stay."

"No."

"Goddammit, Robert. Stay. You fucking *stay with me.*"

I close my eyes, trying not to see, shoving away the visions that come.

I have slept perfectly all my life. I have no history of illness or dissonance. I was not a known problem in the foster system, sent frequently to psychiatrists who recommended pills. I have a real brother. Of flesh and blood.

I am not always Emil. Please God, not that.

When I open my eyes, Robert is waiting patiently for me to stop being such a willful asshole.

So I do what I always do. I solve this the way I always solve problems. I pull out my .45 and stick it under Robert's ghostly chin. There is no resistance. If I don't hold the gun perfectly still, it threatens to drift right through him.

"Stay, or I'll fucking kill you."

Again.

But Robert shakes his head, as if he heard that last bit.

"You were good to me, Emil. Even after I was gone, you were always good to me."

"Stay," I tell him again.

But he's already gone. The gun isn't under Robert's chin. Turns out, it's under mine.

This could be so much easier, I think, not moving the weapon.

Another flash. Another repressed memory. I see myself parked beneath an overpass at age sixteen, rain like liquid grapes abated in a fat rectangle around me. My windshield is fogged, so the homeless hiding under the stanchions can't see me. But they'll hear. In a moment, they'll hear me fine.

I remember a voice then: *Don't be a dick, Emil.*

I remember looking over. Seeing that empty seat, hearing that almost-voice. I remember deciding, somewhere far beneath rationality, that reality is subjective. That the world in which we live, if we wish, can be a choice.

Robert, beside me that day in the rain. I saw myself

pointing the gun at him, not myself. Wrong, sure. But easier that way.

Don't be a dick.

I'd put the gun down. Wondered why I'd pointed it at my brother in the first place.

Then Robert said, *Let's get chicken and waffles. I've never had chicken and waffles, and everyone says it's excellent.*

We'd gone to an IHOP. The waitress had looked at me funny when I'd ordered for two, and when she brought the cups of coffee she'd put them both in front of me. Stupid bitch. Everyone always ignores Robert. I used to ignore him, even, until I grew older and got wise. That's why I didn't see when Timmy the cat escaped. It's why, when Timmy was hit by that car, I comforted Robert more than I mourned the loss of our pet.

My mind shows me one small shoe, spinning into the gutter. I hear the squeal of brakes, too late. I see the rush of neighbors into the street. The screams of anguish, even from people who didn't know … *Timmy.*

I lower the gun, now, from beneath my chin. The .45 is too heavy. When the back of my hand hits the blacktop, it falls out with a clatter.

I can still feel the press of the muzzle under my chin.

"Don't be a dick," I say aloud.

I wipe the scene, then climb back into my car.

There's an IHOP ahead for chicken and waffles, and today I'll be dining alone.

THIRTY-ONE

Las Palmas

A WEEK after Bisset's death, even the news in Cabo is airing his laundry. Lately it's been like the day at the laundromat when all the machines break. All that wash — some clean, but plenty dirty — comes out. Is hung. And swings in the breeze for all to see.

At first, the world was outraged. The planet mourned. Bisset, to many, was the second coming of JFK. He was charismatic, fair, and incorruptible. As Zero, he'd proven that he could subvert the law, so the fact that he chose to play within its boundaries meant, to many people, that he had no illegal jollies left to give. The truth turned out to be otherwise, and by day five it was all the reporters would talk about.

Old connections to the Dark Web were unusual and lucrative things for a member of Congress to have. The tastes of the powerful have always edged the border. Drugs, forbidden hobbies and collectibles, in-the-flesh perversions and videos to tease the senses instead. With Bisset as conduit, half of Washington had been patronizing the internet's filthy gutter floor. When Bisset's possessions were cleaned out, his wife discovered both the stock of what her late husband had supplied, and the cash profits skimmed on the back of every transaction.

I took my time going to Heinzie for the bounty, wanting to be sure he had no reason to double-cross me. By then, the shadier parts of Senator Simon Bisset's character were coming to light. A big shift in public opinion made everyone a little less outraged and the police a lot less interested in finding the killer. Still, I wanted backup. I took Hojo. He's awful in a fight, but he's a granddad of this thing we do. Respect alone made Heinzie play straight — a good thing because I haven't been able to shake this feeling that he wanted me gone, and would have seen to it then and there if I hadn't brought my credibility with me.

"I know you sent people after me," I whispered in Heinzie's ear, low so Hojo wouldn't hear.

Instead of confirming or denying it, Heinzie just squinted at me.

"What?"

"You usually say 'we.'" Then he added, "You fucking fruitcake."

With over a million Pentz in my hidden account and myself in Mexico, I doubt I'm in any danger. Heinzie's a disloyal ass, but he's also practical and cheap. He wanted me gone, because everyone thought I was nuts. I'm gone now, so problem solved. The fact that Heinzie didn't need to make it happen with bullets and big dollars is, I'm sure, a gift horse whose teeth he won't be inspecting.

I've talked to people I know in the police down here, where I'm biding my time before offshoring myself a bit more aggressively. Turns out, I can afford more than I realized. Forging one person through various customs with artificial docs is expensive, but not nearly as pricy as the two I'd been planning.

The police say that the Americans have shifted the investigation of Bisset's death toward an investigation of his sordid life. They say that if the senator weren't dead, he'd be facing the next six lifetimes in prison. There were blips about our battlegrounds, found littered with dead assassins, as well: the bar, the garage of the W Hotel. The public knows about that last one, the first one not so much. For now, according to my man Luis, there's nothing to worry about. The blood and bodies were cleaned. They could investigate a lot further than they will, but the feeling is that the problem is solved enough. The killers self-liqui-dated. Maybe one got away (there were fingers found severed at the scene of Bisset's assassination: the index and middle), but it was only one. With Hojo retiring and Heinzie looking to flee abroad the same as I have, this ring I've spent twenty years living inside will soon be disbanded anyway.

Still, I've been watching my steps. Being careful in ways I wasn't careful before. "Robert" used to watch all of that for me, but I'm learning to do it myself. In reality, I've been doing it myself all along, so of course I can. The hard part is to remember how when my memories are all brushed with obfuscation.

On Tuesday, sitting in a comfortable chair in room 315 of the Las Palmas retirement home just outside Cabo San Lucas, Luis comes in with that knowing expression.

"Señor," he says. *"Hay una llamada para ti en el—"*

"Jesus Christ," I interrupt. "Speak English like every-body else."

Nobody here speaks English.

"Lo siento, señor. I am saying that a phone is happening for you."

"The fuck does that mean?"

"Telefono. Yours."

I pull my current iPhone from my pocket and unlock it. It's still on the photo app. I finally got around to making a dedicated album for my sign collection. My recent favorite is also the most current: a black and white placard showing a man sitting on a toilet. There's what looks almost like a shark head in front of him, circled with a universal NO sign. Since I can't speak Spanish, I have no idea what the legend beneath it says, so I prefer to think it's something about sharks in the plumbing, and this is a warning that they'll either eat your waste or eat your balls.

"No, señor. Office telefono."

I get up and follow. The place is pretty nice for an old folks' home, proving that at least some Mexicans live better than I've been thinking or that I've been a racist asshole to assume otherwise. Possibly both. They keep the window and doors open when it's cool, which gives the place a fresh smell and strikes me as something that paranoid American healthcare wouldn't do. Other than that, the only real difference is that instead of calling the old women *grandmas*, they're *abuelas*. They all seem to like me for my exoticness, and nobody cares that I'm whiter than anyone in this place, and can't possibly be blood-related to anyone. Every one of them keeps telling me to eat more, that I'm too skinny. It's easier to do so, when I'm not loading a plate for my invisible brother.

As I pick up the phone, I think about the thousands of miles of cable and airwaves connecting me to my caller. I imagine yanking all that wire out by the roots and using it as a lasso. I picture myself using it to knit a quilt, then calling someone using my bedspread.

"Hello?" I say.

"Hello, is this Emil Hicks?"

"And who's this?"

"This is Maria Marquez, returning your call."

The Hispanic name combined with unaccented English throws me off. But then I remember calling Hojo, and Hojo connecting me to a man named Ramon, and I remember telling Ramon that if he gave me one doctor who didn't speak the King's English, I'd tie his nut sack around his neck like a bow. It was probably an unfair threat, but I needed Ramon to understand. It's bad enough to consider seeing a shrink without having to contend with questions like, *What is being your problem?*

"Oh. Right."

"Is this a good time?"

I look around. My life is now a vacation. Heinzie is gone, Hojo's got my back stateside, and despite a lot of asking around, nobody's heard from Blackhawk or a woman meeting Renee's description. Good enough for me. I know I didn't leave a trail here, and there's no point in stalking me. Heinzie is done as ringmaster, and there's no other payday in town.

"It's fine."

"When would you like to come in?"

Answer: *Never.* But now that Robert is a feeling inside me instead of a person I see, a quiet part of me promised him I'd at least sit for a few sessions. Maybe I am fucked up. And also, there's no *maybe* about it.

"You're in Ibiza?"

"Yes, we're at—"

"I'm still in Mexico. I'll get your address later." I sigh, still annoyed by this. It's hard to believe I'm the one pushing for therapy at the same time as the other half of me is pushing away. "Tomorrow, if I get in soon enough."

Pablo and Lucinda, the office workers, keep sneaking glances. I wave them out. I can do that, because everyone knows how much I'm paying to hide here.

When the door is closed, Dr. Marquez asks me about

the issues we'll be discussing. At first I flat-out lie, avoiding all mention of the real problem. She knows I'm deflecting, because I said some of the deeper stuff in my message. I hear the verbal tricks she pulls to get me talking, but after a few minutes I let it happen anyway.

Soon I'm on autopilot, telling her all about keeping company with my dead brother for twenty years as if I'm telling her about the clouds in the sky or yesterday's rain. The way I figure it, if I keep my tone casual, she'll see how healthy I am and how little I need her help. No big deal. Just a total lapse in my connection to reality.

As this is happening, I'm watching my primary abuela hobble by with her walker through the window. Her name is Margarita Leon, and she adopted me as I walked through the door. We came to Las Palmas at almost exactly the same time, and she was as overtly lonely as I was covertly alone. She makes me call her Abuela, with a capital A. She's always giving me butterscotch.

She sees me and waves. It's an arthritic travesty. She wobbles on her walker because she's only got one arm left for support, and before Abuela can get it back in place, she almost tumbles and breaks a hip. Then a wince as she strains something in her arm that's not used to going that high anymore. She grabs her shoulder as the arm comes down, then it's the lack of a second hand that almost fells her.

I rush to the door and open it, knowing she'll knock.

"I'm on the phone, Abuela."

"Si, si! You are talking to home!"

"Not my family, Abuela." I keep telling her, I don't have family left that I care to find. I also keep telling her not to wave at me, and to nod or speak instead. I don't repeat all of that now, because Dr. Marquez is still chattering in my ear, offering a stupid opinion on some of the head shit I just told her. It's hard to juggle both, and to keep each woman from hearing the other.

"I sit," she says. "I am very tired."

"Not … Oh, come the fuck on," I finish as she plants herself in one of the office chairs. There's a little bag hanging from the front of her walker, and she rummages in it for mints, or makeup, or maybe her butterscotch.

"Language, Emil."

I roll my eyes. Marquez is still talking.

As Abuela keeps searching, I cross the small office and turn my back to her. I close the blinds, so more abuelas don't walk by and want to see me. I've lost all interest in the shrink's diagnosis for the moment, but if I plan to see her in Ibiza, I suppose I shouldn't be rude or hang up on her now.

I catch only snippets of what she says, huddling to keep my words and face invisible to the elderly woman behind me.

"… dissociative personality, which sometimes …"

"… comfort of the familiar, you know, and that can be …"

"… because of guilt, but if you were only twelve years old, it's your father who should have …"

I hear Abuela stand. She really shouldn't stand so soon. Bad hip. Bad shoulders. Bad knees. I don't know why she sat in the first place.

I turn back. She looks caught, because this isn't a new conversation between us.

"Stop getting up and down," I say. "You'll hurt yourself."

She twists. Winces. Again her arm plucks up from the front bar of the walker, then lies back down.

I cover the phone again. "Did you hurt yourself?"

"It is an old injury."

"Let me look at it," I say.

"No. No, it is all right."

Still, I tuck the phone between my shoulder and cheek, then walk forward as far as the cord will allow. I let Marquez psychobabble while I use both hands to gently touch Abuela's shoulder. She hisses and draws back.

"For honest, Emil. It is okay. It is too tender to touch."

But she never accepts help. I can tell this is a problem — one I've noticed her favoring since the day we met — and I may have a superpower to help. I never studied bodywork, but Robert did. Robert, who was actually half of me all along, is quite the masseuse. I still don't know how that works (if I gave massages that I believed he gave, and just don't remember) but I do know I'm more able than I realize, and have proven it on my own aching body.

So I push back the sleeve of Abuela's nightgown and discover the problem. She doesn't have a torqued muscle so much as a half-healed, possibly-infected wound in the meat of her wrinkly deltoid.

"Abuela," I say, my brow furrowing. "Is this … It looks almost like a gunshot!"

The line goes dead while I'm inspecting the wound. I look down to see that Abuela has extended her non-wounded arm, holding her cane, and has laid it across the hang-up terminals on the old desk phone.

When she retracts the cane, there's no evidence of arthritis at all. She moves fluidly, like a dancer.

"Um …" I manage to say.

The cane drops, and she retrieves the item she must have been looking for in her bag: a tiny pearl-handled pistol I can only see for a few seconds before she puts it against my temple.

"Abuela?"

With no accent whatsoever — and without a hint of elderly warble — she says, "You can call me One."

I don't understand. Until I do.

There's a click as the tiny gun cocks. She has small wrinkled hands, but they seem to have lost no dexterity to arthritis — if in fact she has any, which I now seriously doubt. In half a second she's got my wrists bound behind my back. The time in which I could have overpowered her, though obvious in retrospect, quickly comes and goes. I'm all trussed up, my feet just so around a rolling chair, making it impossible to kick or run or even throw my weight around.

You know how supposedly the best judo masters are tiny, yet able to defeat giant opponents by using their own strength against them? This is that.

"That bounty was mine," she whispers into my ear, her voice still strange with its sudden lack of accent.

"What bounty?"

"On Bissct. Don't be stupid."

I struggle, realizing just how fucked this small old woman has managed to get me.

"That was you. In the cloak, at the bar. It was never Blackhawk." Then I look at her wounded shoulder. "I should have chased you down."

"I'm faster than you'd think." The voice is frozen steel. Without looking at her face, she could be Poison fucking Ivy. "You were lucky to hit me once."

The gun leaves my head as she moves. It's back every few seconds, each time in a different place to remind me it's still very much in play.

I regard her shoulder, considering the bullet wound. The one I put there, when I thought she was Blackhawk. In truth, the real Blackhawk was sitting in my getaway car. I should have known. Even if Abuela — *One* — is spry for an old gal when she stops faking, she's far past her prime. The "Blackhawk" I saw at the bar that night was too short and slightly stooped, as if humbled by age. Not a woman at her peak. Or, as I'd assumed, a man. If I'd been on my game instead of sloppy like Robert said — or *I* said — I'd have noticed, and taken it into consideration. Things might be different now if I had.

But they aren't. Legend says that One, as Zero's nemesis, was unfathomably intelligent. She's done her homework before finally revealing herself to me. It's taken her a few days to strike, and I'll bet anything she's used that time to learn all she can. She'll know that the other assassins are dead, that Heinzie is gone. She knows just how wily I can be, and all my moves. Taken as a whole — and especially if the twists in One's life moved her from social malcontent to killer — this situation is possibly the most dangerous I've faced. She can't *afford* to let me live. Whether I do what she says or not, I'm just as dead.

There's a knock on the door. She hisses at me to tell them to go away.

"Who is it?"

There's a lancing pain as she stabs me with something laser sharp. It hits me just above the kidney, where it hurts like hell but does no lasting damage. Yet.

"That's not what I said to do."

"Housekeeping." It sounds like Raymundo, the orderly: softer than overtly masculine, with a little lilt in his voice.

"Tell him to go away." And, to sharpen her words, Abuela presses the little dagger against my neck. I can't see it, but I can feel it fine. The way it throbs just above my carotid artery. If it's half as sharp as it feels, the wrong beat of my heart might be enough to open me up.

"Go away," I say.

"Housekeeping."

"Go away!"

"Too loud," she says. "Too suspicious."

"You told me what to say!"

"I wanted you to say it better." The knife moves, and I'm sure it's so she can cut me without killing me. I feel blood lick my collar. Whatever she bound my hands with is strong, and the position she's put me in is utterly useless for defense. She's good. As terrifying as any rumor I've heard about anyone.

"Say something kind," Abuela hisses in my ear, her breath rich with dinner mints. "Say, 'Thank you for offering.'"

"It's his job. That's why he's 'offering.'"

The knife presses and cuts.

"Thank you for offering, Raymundo!" Despite myself, my nerves are firing. In the past, I always had Robert to lean on. My brother saved me in the bar ... but that was only possible because I could save myself. Right now, delusion helps nothing. My hands are tied; his would be too.

I hear footsteps. Away.

She's behind me. I haven't truly seen her since she unmasked. Probably part of her strategy: Play to your strengths and cover your weaknesses.

"I know everything about you, Emil," says her disembodied voice. "I've been following you since the toss-up began."

"You weren't in the toss-up," I say.

"I was the failsafe. I was Heinzie's eighth."

"Bullshit. The failsafe is always the strongest."

"I'm not the strongest."

"Or the best."

"But I am the best."

"You're not the best ..." I trail off. I was going to end

my sentence with "... *Abuela*," but obviously that's not who she really is, or ever was.

"Who is?"

"Me."

"*You?*" She laughs an old woman's laugh — one that should come only with fond reminiscence about her grandchildren. "If you were the best, you'd know about the bug in your room."

Fuck. I guess I'm not done being sloppy after all. Good thing I'm retired.

"If you were the best, you wouldn't be out of your mind."

"They've always said that about me."

"Because you're ruthless? Or because you've thought for twenty years that your dead brother is alive?"

I thrash, but she's seen it coming. My backwards head-thrust connects with nothing. My hands, when I try to wrestle them apart, only work against the restraints, cutting into the meat of my wrists.

"Sensitive, aren't you?"

I feel her fingers lift my shirt. For an obscene moment, I think she might fondle me, but she sticks a bony finger into my new knife wound instead.

"Don't scream unless you want to die."

It's impossible not to, but I manage it anyway.

"Here's what you're going to do, Emil. Bisset was mine because Zero was mine. We have unfinished business. We have forever. I'm in this fight because Heinzie owes it to me. He was in hock for exactly one favor, and this was it. I got a head start; I was supposed to kill him."

"Nice job with that."

The finger reenters my wound. This time I yelp a little, but there's nothing more.

I exhale as the finger withdraws.

"I don't get a head start the same way as you. I'm not as young as I used to be. So I shadow someone else. Someone better. Someone stronger."

"Me," I say.

"You."

"I never saw you."

"I was outside when you took out those Florida meth dealers. I watched you, from another shuttle bus, when you killed that nice young bald man at the rental lot. I was in the room above you at your first L.A. hotel, then next door at each of the others. I may lack brute strength, but I'm excellent with technology. You didn't make a single move without me right behind you. There's no point at which, if I'd wanted, I couldn't have leapt ahead of you to take Bisset by the throat."

"Except when we actually caught him."

It earns me another jab with the knife, but this one is shallower. She's a cat with a mouse, playing before dinner. "You chose a wide-open place."

"Couldn't get your Rascal across the Big Boy lot in time, is that it?"

"No good assassin kills so publicly, unless they're far away themselves."

"I guess I'm not any good, then."

"And that's why, right now, you're going to move all that Pentz into my account."

"No thanks."

This time, I think it's her elbow that slugs me.

I can't die this way. I can't be killed by someone with tennis balls impaled on the bottom of her walker. It simply isn't dignified.

Please, God. If you're there, tell the world I died at the hands of The Punisher.

This right here is like a strongman throwing out his back picking up a napkin at a tea party.

"Let's try that again," she says.

"If you kill me, you won't get out of here clean."

"I got out of Shady Acres."

I throttle my shock at her being there. That she was that clearly under our noses, even before the toss-up. "Nobody died at Shady Acres."

"Nobody. Except the nice lady who had a heart attack and left a two-bedroom apartment open for me."

"You killed Rosmerta?"

"Pshaw. All I did was move up the timeline. It just took a push, that's how fragile she was. I thought the broken hip would do her in, but the second she hit the floor, her ticker took care of the rest."

Now I have two reasons for getting out of this. I talked to Rosmerta all the time before she passed on. She was sweet. A great-grandmother to six.

Except there's no getting out of this. It doesn't take much to best a man who doesn't see it coming — who's lowered his guard, and expects all the seniors around him to be exactly what they appear to be.

Another knock on the door. Raymundo is back, with his girlish voice. "Housekeeping."

"Not now," I say.

"Housekeeping!"

I try to look back, but One dodges out of sight in my rearview.

"He doesn't understand," I say. "He'll get someone with a key to that door."

"Tell him you want privacy. In Spanish."

"You tell him."

"I don't speak much Spanish. Only broken English."

She pushes me toward the door, keeping the rolling

chair just below my testicles. I shuffle. It's a great way to neuter my mobility — and, if I slip and fall on the seat, maybe me as well.

One reaches past me to unlock the door, then opens it a sliver.

In my ear she whispers, "Tell him '*No basura. Teniendo sexo.*' Then wink. You got it?"

"What's it mean?"

"'No trash. I'm having sex.'"

"I thought you didn't know Spanish."

"I know that one. This place is just a harem with wrinkles."

She opens the door a quarter inch, stops, then tells me, "Say one word different and I'll open your throat."

She's going to do that anyway. But okay.

One opens the door two inches for me to peek through, but immediately the orderly takes this as an invite and pushes inside. It's not Raymundo; it's a hobbling fellow around my height who's clearly got a developmental disability. I barely see his face as he shoves past, but that's fine. It means he doesn't see ours, either.

For a surreal moment, I freeze. A little old lady with a dagger has me by the throat with my hands tied, and the two of us are in a threesome with an office chair. If the orderly turns and sees us it's over ... unless, of course, he's too far gone to understand or care.

"Don't say anything," she hisses, backing us into a corner, trying to hide behind me.

I consider shouting, but what good will it do? I'll be dead in an instant, and One might take others with me.

No. I have to think. I can still maybe find a way out of this, if I can keep it going.

Or not. From all I've heard, One really was the best.

We fall still as the orderly moves to the trash can. But

even that happens agonizingly slow, and it's a dozen long, slow breaths while he attempts to shake out a fresh trash bag with one good hand. I don't want to offer help. He'll turn and see me if I do. Although we may come off as casual to a slow janitor who doesn't care enough to inspect us, I doubt this particular picture will withstand scrutiny.

The orderly shakes the trash bag but it won't come open. He grabs it between the thumb and ring finger of his bad hand and all the fingers of the other, and it's like watching garbage trucks attempting to mate.

Finally, after more than a minute, One takes a second restraint and seems to secure my bound wrists to a filing cabinet behind us. I know only because when I see her slip out from behind me and walk toward the orderly, I can't move. She turns before speaking, glaring into my eyes. Her look says, *Try anything funny, and it's lights-out for both of you.*

"*No basura.*" She doesn't add the part about having sex, probably because at this point it'd be confusing.

"*Si,*" says the orderly.

"Go."

"No go. *Si.*" And the orderly keeps shaking that same stubborn trash bag with one hand, slapping at it with a ruined hand that boasts only a thumb and two fingers. The index and middle are missing. Hell for this guy, if he wants to flip someone off.

A thumb and two fingers. Hell to flip someone off.

"Hey! *Stupido!* Listen to what I'm saying!"

While One has lost strength and speed over the years, the orderly has lost nothing. In assassin circles, the hacker-turned-killer is the one we're collectively most curious about. Still, the most fearsome remains the nightbird. *The black hawk.*

Blackhawk.

Renee.

The orderly spins faster than I can see. Her janitor's cap flies off, revealing a spill of long brown hair, and in the next moment the old woman's throat is wrapped with a garrote.

Renee looks up at me then, One thrashing uselessly in her grasp. The garrote has brushed aluminum poles at each end, one in each of Renee's hands. She has the thread between her two remaining fingers. She pulls, and my would-be killer gags.

Renee kicks something toward me, and I see that it's the woman's pearl-handled pistol. "I assume you'd like the honors."

I look down, still bound to both chair and filing cabinet. The pistol's right in front of me, but trussed-up like I am, it might as well be on the moon.

"No problem," I tell Renee. "How about I do some sleight of hand while I'm at it?"

She rolls her eyes. Then, with one wrenching motion, she kicks her arms and the garroted neck sideways. There's a crack like kindling in a fire.

One slouches to the floor.

"Eat more calcium," Renee tells the corpse.

THIRTY-TWO

On Vacation

IBIZA. Some rich guy's estate — a dude I don't even know.

It's surreal to be here, and even more so to feel safe, to have "enjoy yourself" as the only item on my agenda. None of it is familiar to me. I spent the first twelve years of my life hating growing up, then spent the last twenty murdering people for money. I'm new to being an only child; it's felt over the month since Las Palmas like I just lost my brother rather than it being old news by now. I'll admit I cried. It was a mess. I embarrass myself whenever it comes up, but Renee's been there each time to rub my back until it's over.

So yes. Ibiza. Some rich guy's estate. And the fact that I don't know our host isn't the strangest thing on my plate.

I'm pretty sure Renee won't kill me now. I can't be certain, but I'll take some time in paradise as a win even if it ends in my death. Besides, my internal compass tells me there'd be no real point in her ending me. For one thing, we're sharing the bounty. Now that we're in paradise, there'd be little reason for her to take it all. For another thing, she followed me to Cabo — and whether she did it to finish or save me, I found myself glad in the end. She kicked me a gun that I could have used to kill her. Helped to dispose of the body. Easy enough, since all we had to do was to cart it back to her room. Technically, the police could have looked at the old woman's neck and seen the mark from Renee's piano wire. But realistically, Mexican police can be bought — and retirement homes, where people die all the time of natural causes, aren't hot spots for murder.

We cleaned up the office. De-evidenced the murder scene. Renee stayed overnight, and we screwed so loudly, even the residents with hearing aids complained. Normal was back, as abnormal as it ever was.

In the morning, I asked her to come with me, then called for her ticket. Part of my offer was courtesy. The rest was need. I'm not used to being alone, and even as fucked up and codependent as it is to invite someone set to kill me on vacation (or retirement), I frankly don't care. There are typical people in this world who do typical things. I am nowhere near one of them.

"How was your appointment?"

She means with my therapist. Which I am absolutely not going to discuss because only assholes go to therapy. Assholes like me.

"I was just on a walk."

"You weren't lying down on a couch being asked about your mother?"

"Fuck you, Renee."

"How do you know Renee is even my real name?"

"It isn't?"

"I'm just saying. You don't know."

She pats the lounger beside her. I sit, then lie back when she won't stop staring.

"I know it's your name because we needed your ID to get your plane ticket."

"Maybe it's a fake ID."

"It's not."

"How do you know?"

"Because if it was, that'd be a simple answer. You don't want a simple answer. You want to fuck with me."

We fall silent. I consider the oddity of lying in the sun beside a person who so recently wanted to put a bullet in my head. But. Yeah. Who fucking cares.

"You can sunbathe topless here," I say.

"Knock yourself out."

"I was talking about you."

"No thanks."

"Come on. Just do it. For me."

"I'll do it if you take part in another thing you're allowed to do here," she tells me.

"Okay."

"Here, it's perfectly fine to sunbathe bent over with someone's fist up your ass."

"Whose fist?"

"Anyone's fist."

I tip my sunglasses from my forehead down to my nose. "Hard no."

More time passes.

"I know this pool from porn shoots," I say.

"You watch porn?"

"Never."

"Uh-huh."

A waiter brings a mai tai I didn't order. There's a pink umbrella in it. I reach for the drink after he's back inside the impressive home, but Renee takes my hand before I can grab it.

"Aww," I say, looking at our clasped hands. I squeeze, let go, then reach again for the drink. This time, Renee hits the drink instead of grabbing my hand. It hits the deck without breaking, sending ice cubes and mint leaves everywhere.

"Fine. I'll hold your fucking hand."

"You shouldn't drink," Renee says, readjusting her sunglasses.

"Why not?"

"Because that server was Nisha Swartha."

It takes me a minute, but once the words register, I hop up like a man atop a pile of coals. I stare at the house, at Renee, at everything.

"It's okay. She doesn't have a gun."

"How can you be sure?" I ask.

"There are metal detectors hidden in the front door jamb, and Nisha's not smart enough to think of ceramic."

"How do you know that?"

"I know the owner. See? You need me, Emil. Without me, you'd be wandering beaches, waiting for all the enemies you thought were dead but now, looking back, you can't be sure actually died."

She's right. I saw Nisha shot, but that was all.

"Who's the owner?"

"Melvis."

"Who?"

"Grampy. Hojo's grandfather."

Through the glass rear of the building, I see our enemy has been seized.

Returning my gaze to Renee, I realize she's just tapped something on her phone, likely to alert security. Only, security is rougher than I figured. They hold her hard, then go for long sticks that look like fireplace pokers from where I'm sitting.

Nisha must have healed well. I watch her best them,

break a pane of glass that must have cost ten grand at least, and sprint away across the front lawn.

"So that part was true," I say to Renee. "You do know Grampy."

"Grampy's the best."

"And they shoot porn in Grampy's pool."

"Of course they do. He wouldn't have it any other way."

She rises with a sigh.

"Where are you going?" I ask.

"If we don't find Nisha, she'll just come back."

Now I stand. "I'll do it. You're on vacation."

"You're retired," she counters.

"You're my guest. I invited you."

"We're both Grampy's guests," she says, indicating the house. Inside, servants are inspecting the broken window and loading automatic weapons.

"We let them do it, they'll get us all kicked out of the country."

Renee looks up at me. "You really want to kill a girl?"

"No," I say, "but Robert is dying to."

Revenge is served.

Twelve people bound by a secret arrive for an exclusive dinner only to find that the other guests are familiar in the most troubling of ways.

Pick up your copy of Pretty Killer Today.

A Quick Favor...

If you enjoyed this book, please take a moment to write a short review on your favorite online bookstore so other readers can enjoy it, too.

Thanks so much!

About the Authors

Nolon King writes fast-paced psychological thrillers set in the glitzy world of entertainment's power players with a bold, insightful voice. He's not afraid to explore the darker side of human nature through stories featuring families torn apart by secrets and lies.

Nolon loves to write about big questions and moral quandaries. How far would you go to cover up an honest mistake? Would you destroy your career to protect your family? How much of your soul would you sell to get the life of your dreams? Would you cheat on your husband to keep your children safe? Would you give in to a stalker's demands to save your marriage?

Johnny B. Truant is co-owner of the Sterling & Stone Story Studio, an IP powerhouse focusing on books and adaptations for film and television. It's the best job in the world, and he spends his days creating cool stuff with partners Sean Platt and David W. Wright, as well as more than 20 gifted storytellers.

Johnny is the bestselling author of over 100 books under various pen names, including the Fat Vampire and Invasion series. On the nonfiction side, he's also co-author of the indie publishing mainstay Write. Publish. Repeat. and co-host of the weekly Story Studio Podcast.

Originally from Ohio, Johnny and his family now live in Austin, Texas, where he's finally surrounded by creative types as weird as he is.

Also By Nolon King

Hidden Justice

Hidden Justice

Hidden Honor

Hidden Shame

Hidden Virtue

No Justice

No Justice

No Escape

No Hope

No Return

No Stopping

No Fear

Once Upon A Crime

Once Upon A Crime

Twice Upon A Lie

Three Times a Murder

Dead For Good

Dead For Good

Left For Dead

Dead Of Night

Wake The Dead

Dead For Life

Stand Alone Novels

Pretty Killer

12

Blown

Miserable Lies

The Target

Secrets We Keep

Close To Home

Heat To Obsession

A Simple Kill

Tell Me No Lies

Red Carpet Black

Fade To Black

Victim

Also By Johnny B. Truant

The Dead World Series

Dead Zero

Dead City

Dead Nation

Dead Planet

Empty Nest

The Fat Vampire Series

Fat Vampire

Fat Vampire 2: Tastes Like Chicken

Fat Vampire 3: All You Can Eat

Fat Vampire 4: Harder, Better, Fatter, Stronger

Fat Vampire 5: Fatpocaplypse

Fat Vampire 6: Survival of the Fattest

The Fat Vampire Chronicles

The Vampire Maurice

Anarchy and Blood

Vampires in the White City

The Beam Series

The Beam Season One

The Beam Season Two

The Beam Season Three

The Target